JESSICA SCHAUB

BOOK II: THE ELEMENTAL CHRONICLES

THE ELDER'S CIRCLE

KING BOOKS PUBLISHING

For information about permission to reproduce selections
from this book, write to Permissions,
KingBooksPublishing@gmail.com

Library of Congress Catalog Card Number
ISBN 978-0-9897039-1-8
Printed in the United States of America

You are an enclosed garden, my sister, my bride,
an enclosed garden, a fountain sealed.
You are a park that puts forth pomegranates,
with all choice fruits;
Nard and saffron, calamus and cinnamon,
with all kinds of incense;
Myrrh and alves,
with all the finest spices.
You are a garden fountain, a well of water
flowing fresh from Lebanon.
Arise, north wind! Come, south wind!
blow upon my garden
that its perfumes may spread abroad.

SONG OF SONGS 4:12-16

DEDICATION

I'm always curious about the people who read the dedication page, especially the dedications that list two dozen people and go on for more than a half page. Do you read it looking for your name? Are you trying to gain insight on the author? You are probably like me and view the dedication page like the 'bonus features' on a DVD.

A friend of mine checks the dedication page to make sure that she *isn't* listed. Apparently, she's afraid I will use her talent for finding trouble as a means to fuel my plot line. She needn't fear. All the names have been changed to protect her innocence.

Because you have made it to the third paragraph, I thank you for selecting this book. It's a commitment, I know. Books cost money and then take time to read. Time and money are our two most precious commodities and I thank you for investing both in this book. Yes, I do see it as an investment. Although this is a fantasy, there are lessons tucked between the lines for living an intentional life: taking chances, fighting for a greater cause, teamwork, and friendship.

My family deserves many thanks. I have improved my meal planning since my last book, so my children no longer complain about scrambled eggs for dinner. (If you are looking for meal planning ideas, I simply taught my children how to cook. They make many of our meals now and I have more time to write. It's a win-win.)

My husband, Bill, took one afternoon a week off to give me uninterrupted time to write. There's a lesson there for all married couples: if your spouse has a dream, no matter how crazy it may sound, support them. If nothing else, it will earn you a place on their dedication page.

A huge shout of thanks to Tiffany Cole. I asked her to give this manuscript a once over to see if it was ready and she went above and beyond. She gently pointed out that there were too many commas (I still do that, Mrs. Beck), directed me to think about where I hadn't written a scene clearly, and was kind enough to point out the strengths.

There are bonus features at the end of this book: the first chapters of Book III of this series, *Crimson Arrows*, and a few chapters of my soon-to-be-released book, *Lies in the Shadows*. So, off you go to another world with new friends for a grand adventure!

With Gratitude and Prayers of Peace,

Jessica Schaub

CHAPTERS

THE ELDER'S CIRCLE

JESSICA SCHAUB

The Birth

Victoria heard a woman's pain-filled cry. She stood in front of a squat cottage with a thatched roof that looked like it belonged in a painting of a peasant family from the Middle Ages. Bits of sunbeams struggled to pierce dark clouds, casting eerie beams toward the earth that faded quickly, filling Victoria with a foreboding anticipation. Victoria jumped when lightning shredded the sky. It wasn't her lightning. It didn't speak to her. It was wild and rabid. Rain and wind bit into the ground, pulling trees over, chewing on the branches, and spitting out the leaves.

Another scream drew Victoria's attention to a nearby glowing window. A young man ran toward the small house, crouching over a bundle in his arms.

"Do you need help?" Victoria called to him, but the roar of the storm carried her voice away unheard. She followed him, feeling surprised by her boldness at entering a stranger's home without invitation. Inside, two women huddled anxiously over a third woman who lay in bed swollen with pregnancy, which was quickly coming to an end. Victoria watched as the young man handed the older of the two mid-wives the bundle of material.

"These are all the blankets we have," he said, breathing heavily. Stealing a glance at the pregnant woman, he paled. She was covered in sweat. Her eyes were closed and she seemed peaceful for the moment. "Will she be alright?"

"A baby doesn't just walk into the world. They need some coaxing," the midwife said. "Tear this cloth in half."

The man turned toward the table to tear the cloth but Victoria was in his way. Instead of bumping into her, the man passed right through her.

Startled for a moment, Victoria dreaded experiencing a new kind of dreaming with such vivid details and about people she had never seen before. The women's dresses were homespun with earthen tones, their hair pulled into large buns at the base of their necks. The one-room cabin was outfitted with a few precious essentials: table and stools and a handful of cooking utensils. She looked at the dreamwalker. "Thanks to you, no doubt." She sighed. "Where else are you going to take me?"

The storm outside made its way in through tiny holes in the roof, leaving growing mud puddles on the dirt floor. Wind rushed outside and rattled the walls. Somewhere in the yard, a tree fell to its death in a rushing crash. Lightning flashed again, followed by an almost instant blast of thunder.

At the sound, the pregnant woman was instantly awake and gripping the thin mattress in pain. Her face was red with determination.

"One more time," the older midwife encouraged her.

Victoria looked away from the young mother's face. It was too personal to stare at the raw pain in her gritted expression.

"That's right," the younger midwife urged. "That's right. Once more."

Victoria watched the husband pull out his knife and tear the thick cloth. His hands shook terribly as his wife groaned in pain.

The baby slid into the world and the young midwife shouted for joy.

Everything stood still.

The women helping with the birth held their breath. The man stopped shredding the blankets. Even the dust particles in the air ceased swirling. Rain dripping through the roof fell slower. The air in Victoria's lungs burned as it stalled mid-breath.

The baby's cry broke the tension and the man gasped as the air resumed the stormy swirl. Spinning on his heel, the man rushed to his wife. Victoria followed and saw the mother holding a wet, pink baby on her chest.

"It's a boy," she sobbed, smiling. "You have a son."

The man laughed and gently touched his son's hand with the tip of his finger. "He's so tiny."

"Not for long," his wife said. "He'll be as tall as you. And just as strong."

"Have you chosen a name?" he asked his wife.

Tears streamed down her cheeks. "David."

"A healthier babe, I've never seen," the older midwife said. "Look, his eyes are already open."

"He wants to see the storm," the younger midwife said. "Such a fuss the sky is making."

The older woman looked out the window. "No longer. There isn't a cloud in the sky."

Victoria couldn't believe that the storm that had raged just a minute ago could have dissipated that quickly, but when she walked out of the little house, a vivid sky, with the sun settling into the horizon, greeted her. Rain dripped off the leaves, an old tree lay on the ground with its roots exposed, and the ground was pocked with deep puddles. Not a cloud remained.

She was about to turn back to the house to see the baby when she saw Bobby standing on the far side of the yard. He smiled at her and pointed to the darkness of the forest. She ran

3

toward him, but he faded when she came near. She looked to where he had pointed.

A small candle shone among the trees, casting much more light than it should have. In the glow, she watched her mother and her six-year-old-self dancing to the music on the radio. Victoria remembered that evening; there had been a tornado warning and her mother distracted her fears by cranking up the radio and dancing with her in the basement while the sirens screamed outside.

Her mother danced away from her toward a door, where she stopped dancing and leaned against the frame of the doorway to Victoria's bedroom.

Another storm stirred; Victoria could see it through the window of her room. She could see herself sleeping in her bed, completely unaware that the skies raged violently above.

Bobby and Tucker walked into the dream.

"You shouldn't have left us." Bobby shook his head in disapproval.

"I didn't mean to," she argued, but Bobby still looked angry.

Tucker's hands sparked to life with bright white flames. He looked at his hands curiously and offered Victoria the bouquet of flames. "It won't hurt. Here."

She shook her head and backed away.

Tucker laughed. "You summoned lightning and you're afraid of me?"

It scared her too, she realized. The moment in the garden when Ona's guards were attacking her, she felt the lightning as if she was the last barrier between it and its target. A gap in her efforts to keep the lightning back opened when the guard attacked. That's all it took; a moment of release and that man was thrown across the grass. Everything within her mind had slowed when the lightning struck. Her thoughts were as sharp and clear as the lightning itself. Victoria's mind understood the many layers of what surrounded her at that moment in the garden and again in the kiva. She knew where the guards were, understood their intent, could feel the electrical pulses of their heartbeats. Lightning had one desire: strike. The surging energy, sparking hot and quick, had forked in the air above the kiva, pushing against Victoria's elemental intent with fierce determination. Lightning wanted to dance across the floor in the kiva.

That's what frightened her–lightning was not a part of her elemental intent. Lightning wasn't a part of the Air, but it pierced the sky where Air lived. It didn't belong to the earth until the tips of the bolts connected with the ground. Although lightning burned like Fire, it wasn't flame. Lightning had waited for Victoria, but it was eager. Too eager, and she had a very difficult time holding it back.

The dream was not disturbing, for the most part, except for Bobby's distance from her. "I had to do it." She wanted him to understand. "We would have all died if I hadn't pulled the lightning down." As she spoke, thunder clapped again and lightning laced the sky, reflecting in Bobby's disapproving eyes.

"Just wake up," Tucker said as he juggled balls of molten heat.

And she did.

Just like that.

For the first time since the dream when Lucian gave her the dream walker, she could wake herself up from a dream.

The night was still deep and all her companions were sleeping around a dying campfire. Facing away from the group, keeping watch over the area, Tiw paced around the camp.

"Thank you," she said to Bobby, but he was still asleep. Well, she thought, at least dream-Bobby helped her wake up.

Her shoulders relaxed. Tiw's and Freya's sharp sphinx eyes were keeping watch. She was reunited with Bobby and Tucker and in the company of Collette and her Uncle Sebastian, a Green

Guard. Safe in the mountains away from Ona's dwelling, they were going to head home. All they needed was the talisman for the gateways. Easy. Yeah, easy would be good. As her mother always said, "Good is rarely easy."

She rubbed her eyes, stretched and decided to enjoy the night. The crescent moon did little to pierce the darkness. Years ago, even only a few months ago, the darkness would have frightened Victoria. Whereas before she wanted to see what was in the dark, she now felt safer wrapped in the blackness. If she couldn't see well, then neither could anyone else.

It was easier now, she reasoned, to live in the wild. There was no running water unless you camped near a river. Finding food was a full-time job, but her high school counselors always told her that she needed to work toward a career that was satisfying. Finding food was certainly satisfying. Even the view inspired her as she lay on the grass watching the stars slowly slide across the chalk-board black sky. The ground was fairly soft with thick grass, comfortable and sweet smelling. Up until recently, Victoria had never camped without a tent, sleeping bag and an air mattress, but after weeks of truly 'roughing it' she knew two things: a sleeping bag wasn't necessary and the stars were far more beautiful than she had dreamed.

She lay flat on her back with aching muscles and throbbing feet. While her body felt heavy with sleep, her mind replayed the events that brought her to this mountain. Her spring semester had started normally—new classes and the promise of a summer vacation. That all changed the day she slipped into her painting. It still sounded strange to her, to travel through a painting. Although she had managed it a few times, the disturbing sensation as she passed from one world to the next didn't ease with practice.

That first time was the worst: she had been standing in the school's art room one minute then in front of a tree she had just painted, which stood in a field of her own creation, the very next minute. The field wasn't made of paint. It was a real place with a real tree and grass. The scariest part was that there was no door back to her school. Luckily Mrs. Witherspoon had followed her into the painting and opened the way out. Victoria met Lucian in a painting too, but he wasn't just there by accident. His painting had been a prison—one he escaped by using Victoria.

That was so long ago, she thought, even though it had only been about a month ago. Maybe two. It hadn't occurred to her to keep track of the days. Since the moment she and Tucker stumbled into Lucian's prison painting, it just wasn't necessary to think about what day it was. Monday, Thursday, Saturday—they all meant nothing since there was no school, no time off, no alarm clock to sever the ties that dreams hold. There was also no homework, but Victoria would have traded three term papers with short deadlines over what she had been through. She had survived and supposed that ranked her as a National Honors Student, if only there were classes for living off the land, protecting relics, and fighting to live.

Just this morning, she had defied Ona, the leader of the Mage Council. Ona had taken them to an Earth Gateway and forced Victoria to open it by threatening Collette's life. As a Painter, Victoria could feel the gaps in paintings that led to other worlds. The Earth Gateway was different. A Painter, as well as three other mages, each with one of the elements - Earth, Air, Fire and Water—were needed. From what Lucian had told her, Ona had tried to open the Earth Gateway before, resulting in the death of Lucian's sister, Leora. No one died today when the gateway was opened, but Lucian had been killed as it closed and when the dust settled, Ona was nowhere to be found.

She didn't know how to feel about Lucian: his life or his death. She had only known him briefly, and most of that time she thought he was her enemy, an opinion based on the fact that he temporarily paralyzed her at their first meeting using a blend of herbs. He had been so violent at first, but just a few hours earlier, he had given his life to keep the last piece of the Grandfather's Key away from Ona. Lucian had either been trapped in one bad situation after another and did what he had to do to protect the Weapon, or he was insane. Bobby and Tucker were leaning toward the insane argument, but no one could deny his heroic act in the kiva.

Well, Bobby still blamed him for causing the trouble. After he had attacked Tucker and Victoria in his prison painting, he took Victoria in a dream. She went willingly enough when Lucian told her he knew where to find her father, but she never found him. All she had was his name–Alexander–and the terrible news that he had been cast away. She also learned 'cast away' meant being sent to the Seventh Terrace with beasts–dragons, specifically. A death sentence. Which was worse: the fact that mages had a death penalty, the fact that her father had suffered it, or the fact that dragons were real?

And now with Lucian dead, she didn't know what to do next. The dream of the baby's birth came to mind again. She needed to get rid of the dreamwalker before she ended up getting lost in a dream and spending the rest of her life sleeping. Anna told her that dreamwalkers could only be passed on in a dream. If Victoria wanted to get rid of the locket, she would need to give it to someone else and curse their world with dream-filled sleep and the danger of not waking up in the same place. There had to be a way to destroy the dreamwalker. She was going to figure that out.

Scarred Lessons

Pretending to be asleep was the only way Collette could find any quiet. Caladrius had rigorously questioned her about Ona, her treatment of Victoria in the Novaculum Saxum cell, and Lucian. Collette really didn't know how to respond to any of these questions, not because she didn't know the answers, but because the one person she had trusted to be a kind and just guide for the entire Mage Society had shown herself to be a cruel and deceitful enemy.

The Novaculum Saxum cells were deep in the cave system beneath Ona's dwelling. Years ago, Caladrius had taken Collette down to those cells to show her what happened to the most hardened criminals. When he told Collette to pick up one of the stones, it sliced open the skin on her palm near her thumb, but Caladrius healed it almost completely. "I've closed the wound so you won't bleed nor contract an infection," Caladrius had said, "but I'll allow it to heal on its own."

"I'll have a scar," Collette said when she noticed the

thickness of the cut.

"Let that scar serve as a reminder of this cell, of this place, and of what punishing evil costs."

"I don't understand. Should we not punish those who are evil?"

"Sometimes it is very easy to determine what is evil. But most of the time, it's not." Caladrius held her hand and ran a finger along the edge of her cut. "What seemed like a harmless stone left a terrible cut." He pressed his hand on hers and she bit back the urge to pull away from the pain. "And what will seem like a harmless act or thought or idea will destroy you, your loved ones," he hesitated, "and possibly the society."

At the time, that lesson felt extreme. Not only had she walked away with a scar, but she also knew that she didn't understand what Caladrius meant. An act of evil that could seem harmless, but might destroy the entire Mage Society? Impossible. Anything that might destroy a society of people had to be obvious. Why would anyone agree to something violent, or live by an evil ideal, or a dark action?

Did she understand that lesson any better now? Ona, a woman of high-rank and power in the Mage Society, a leader among mages, had threatened to kill Collette if Victoria didn't give her the key. Ona was obviously evil in her treatment of Victoria, but did Victoria deserve that punishment? What did Victoria have that Ona needed so badly? Ona was searching for the Grandfather's Weapon, a piece of a story, a legend. No one knew for certain if the Weapon even existed, and yet Ona was prepared to kill for it.

That's when Ona became the enemy.

It was so unfair, she thought. Her parents had been killed in action. She had no bodies to bury and only memories to mourn. Sebastian was the best uncle; she knew that when he resigned from the Green Guard to help raise her after her parents' death.

She wasn't the only one who was loved and cared for; the twins had demonstrated that they would do anything for Victoria. That fact prickled Collette's nerves. She had never had many close friends and certainly no one she knew would have done for her what the brothers had done for Victoria. But, she realized, she had gone as far as they had to protect Victoria.

Despite their bravery, Bobby and Tucker reminded Collette of children—still marveling at their gifts, still in awe of the beauty of the elements, still clumsy and unsure.

The Sphinx were amazingly strong and graceful. She had always looked forward to her first trip to the sphinx city; to meeting the creatures who were so intelligent, wise, and faithful; to witness the traditions of the society that even Council Mages sought for advice. Never did Collette expect the Sphinx to come to her! That alone was both a demonstration of their bravery and a complete lack of regard for the laws of the society, a very unexpected behavior for sphinx. Maybe they were not all she had believed them to be.

When Collette had taken care of Tiw, she had asked what compelled Tiw and Freya to leave their own terrace. "It wasn't exactly a choice," Tiw answered. "It was either follow the mages or die at the hands of the Ragnarok. Some would argue that I should have followed the laws to my death. I chose to live so that I might further protect the mages."

"Aren't laws meant to be followed?" Collette asked. "I mean, what's the purpose behind a law if it can be so easily broken."

Tiw's nostrils flared. Slowing her breath, she explained. "I would never break a law of the Creator. The laws of humans or the laws of the sphinx can be flawed. Breaking those laws is sometimes the only choice to be faithful to the Creator. Sometimes a soul must rebel."

And now Collette had committed the same crime, rebelled in the same way. She had tried to protect these mages. The consequences were harsh. While she knew she had done the right thing, she was afraid of what else might happen because of that choice. From being so certain that Ona was out of her mind, to doubting her own actions in the novaculum saxum cell by healing Victoria, Collette's mind whirled. At least she had her uncle and Caladrius. Her faith in her uncle was solid. He had given up everything to raise her after her parents were killed. Trust had been earned in her apprenticeship with Caladrius. She wanted to trust Victoria, Bobby, and Tucker. She knew what they were capable of; She knew the legends. Now she knew what Ona was striving toward.

Her parents had trusted Ona. Collette would not make that mistake.

Painting a Legend

Morning came swiftly on the back of a chill breeze. The group roused slowly, no one ready to wake up as all were obviously victims of poor sleep and hunger. The prospect of breakfast was bleak as there was very little food left; Sebastian had shared much of the food he'd brought the night before. Tucker offered to gather more fire wood so they could warm up, but Caladrius was eager to move on.

"I know what I must do," Caladrius announced.

"If it involves finding food," Tucker said, "I'm all for it."

"There will be food at Ona's dwelling."

"It's overrun with the Janus guards," Collette protested. "We'll be killed."

"Probably only arrested," Caladrius corrected. "It's worth the risk. Ona's mirror is the only way we can communicate with other Council Mages and the Sphinx Elders. We'll need help if we are to bring Tiw and Freya back to the sphinx city."

"We got this far without help," Bobby said. "We can return

13

the same way."

"Based on what you've told me," Caladrius said, "I don't think getting back to the sphinx city will be as easy."

Tucker scoffed. "You think getting here was *easy*?"

"Exactly," Caladrius pointed to Tucker. "You arrived here because you were chased. If you hadn't been forced to enter the gateway in Terrace Two, you never would have found Victoria. Tiw, you were injured."

Huffing in disgust at the reminder of her nearly fatal wound at the hands of a startled farmer with a pitch fork, Tiw glared at Caladrius. Collette had changed the bandage last night, but it was oozing again. For as little food as Sebastian packed, he brought even fewer first aid supplies.

If Caladrius noticed Tiw's anger, he acted as if it was of no consequence and continued. "To return safely and quickly to the sphinx city, you will need the assistance of the Council Mages and the Green Guards."

"Can we trust them?" Victoria asked.

"I fear it will be a dangerous road to make that discovery. But we do have help in the Green Guard. There are still Council Mages who can be trusted. I choose to believe that."

"You can believe whatever you want," Bobby said, "but that doesn't make it true."

Caladrius nodded. "Well said."

Sebastian paced. "Caladrius, those at Ona's dwelling would not know of your association with Victoria or the twins. It would be safer for just you to return to the dwelling to contact the sphinx and the other Council Mages."

"It would benefit my story greatly if Victoria were to accompany me," Caladrius said.

"No." Bobby stepped between Victoria and Caladrius. "She's not going."

"She must," Caladrius said. "Your story of the events in the

Kiva proves it." He looked to Sebastian and Collette for support. "I'm not wrong, am I?"

Sebastian rolled his eyes. "Again with your 'balance of creation' theory."

"Caladrius is right." Collette walked toward Victoria and lifted the chain around her neck. Sebastian gasped when they saw the locket.

"My dream walker?" Victoria asked.

"You don't know about the legend of the Painter?" Collette asked.

Victoria looked to Bobby and Tucker who both shook their heads. They had heard a little about the legend of the Painter from Anna, but she had been frustratingly quiet about the history of mages. "In our terrace," Victoria said, "legends are usually fabricated from a thin line of truth instead of gospel. Is the Painter legend the same?"

"That's the question generations of mages have been asking," Collette explained. "The Legend of the Painter is part fairy tale, part nightmare."

Sebastian cut in. "That's your father talking. Most mages believe that the Painter in the legend will save the society, not destroy it."

Victoria couldn't believe her ears. "Destroy the society?"

"Depends on which version of the story you listen to," Collette answered.

Victoria held up her hand, "Stop. I want nothing to do with this. Ona is dead. We can go back to the sphinx city and find my mom. I can go home. I'm supposed to graduate next year and go to college and eat pizza. Not jump from terrace to terrace pretending to be something I'm not."

"Ona is gone," Caladrius said. "I don't think she's dead."

"What other explanation is there?" Bobby asked.

"I don't know," Caladrius said. "I intend to find out."

15

"How?"

"By returning to Kivavallis and using the mirrors to communicate with the sphinx elders. They can provide us with the means to return safely, although admittedly not easily, to the Third Terrace. Legend or not, that is the safest place."

"Tell me the version of this legend you believe," Bobby asked Collette.

Collette looked to her uncle.

"Go ahead," he sighed, making it clear to all with his frown and crossed arms that whatever Collette was about to say was not what he believed.

Turning to Victoria, Bobby and Tucker, Collette began. "The legend of the Painter, some believe," she added for her uncle's benefit, "is best told to children at bedtime. Once you hear the story, you can decide for yourself.

"The Creator gave us the world and everything in it. The Grandfather, the first mage, divided the world into seven terraces, protecting the species that were sure to perish and setting the mages as protectors over each terrace. It has always been foretold that despite the goodness of the Creator and the wisdom of the Grandfather, the society would someday come to fail. For years, mages ruled each terrace peacefully."

Tucker interrupted. "You mean that the mages have never had an uprising?"

"Hundreds," Collette said. "But some mages are still waiting for *the* Legend. My father used to say that war brings out the heroes. It's during times of supposed peace, when the seeds of dissension are sown. That's when it takes great courage to be a hero. First to recognize the evil, and second, to know how to respond.

"The Painter would come during this unrest to set all things right with mastery over all four elements. She would not be bound by anything, time or space." Collette looked at Victoria.

"Me?" Victoria laughed.

"You're a Painter," Collette said. "You told me you were an Air mage but I saw what you did with Ona's fire. Do you have all four elements?"

Victoria felt the color from her face draining. "I'm no legend."

"And the lightning?" Tucker interrupted. "How does that figure into the legend of the Painter?"

"That's where the story divides," Sebastian said. "Some people, Collette's father was one of them, believe that the Painter in this legend will destroy the Mage Society. Others believe that the lightning the Painter commands could be what destroys the evil that is damaging the society."

"And the Grandfather's Weapon?" Victoria asked. "Is that a part of the Painter legend?"

"It's said that the Painter in the legend is the only one who can wield the Weapon," Collette explained.

"What do you believe?" Bobby asked Sebastian.

Sebastian shrugged. "That the society might be slipping into a time of darkness, especially after yesterday's events. I believe that Ona had blood on her hands; my sister's and brother-in-law's blood among others. But I don't believe that having one rogue Council Mage constitutes an evil time. I do think we should make our way to the sphinx." He turned to Caladrius. "With Ona's death or disappearance or whatever happened, they will need your testimony. A new Council Mage will need to be selected."

Caladrius turned to Victoria. "I know that your time with Ona was terrifying. We must use the mirrors to speak with the sphinx. We must have help if we are to return all of you safely."

"Ona had help," Victoria said. "Her guards."

"My rank in the society is still respected," Caladrius said. "If you are with me, you will be safe."

"And this legend? Do you think that I'm that Painter?"

17

Caladrius hesitated. His eyes looked pained as he tried to find the right words. "I think we will find out. I don't know if these events fit the definition of 'evil times', but they certainly do require a brave response."

"And this?" Victoria held out the dream walker. "Can you help me destroy it?"

"Destroy it?" Caladrius frowned. "Why?"

"Because! It's bad. It robs me of me. I can't stay in one place. Sleep is dangerous."

Caladrius was quiet. He studied Victoria's face. Finally, he nodded. "Yes. I think I can help you find a way. The best place to start is back at Kivavallis."

Victoria turned to Bobby and Tucker. "What do you think?"

The twins exchanged looks. Victoria knew they were communicating in that strange way of theirs, the slightest expression telling entire stories. Finally, they nodded. Bobby spoke for them both. "Caladrius is right about our needing help. We don't know what happened to Anna and Worthmere. If they need help, maybe we can alert the Green Guard to search for them. But we must stay together. If we can do that, we will be strong enough."

"Strong enough for what?" Victoria asked.

"To survive," Tucker answered.

GUILTY BY ASSOCIATION

The sphinx city had, up until now, been Anna's sanctuary. After the Great Scourge, those horrible years when mages were chased out of their homes or killed, she had come to the sphinx for protection. She had shown up as a child with three other mage children, tiny and afraid, the only remnants from the Second Terrace.

Her childhood had been spent in a place much like the sphinx city; pristine country, silent women and arrogant men. Her mother had been sweet and full of joy despite the idiosyncrasies of the politics of the time. A Water mage who kept the growing seasons particularly fruitful, her mother flourished in green places and cared for each bloom of spring and summer as one would expect a mother to care for infants.

Many nights, Anna was kept awake by her parent's laughter at the antics of men who thought they knew everything. Her father was supposedly one of those men, but thinking back to those years, Anna recognized his colleague's arrogance for what it truly was: fear.

It was difficult to imagine the sphinx's arrogance as a result of fear. Anna had seen the annual competition to be selected as a sphinx soldier; and she had fought side-by-side with the sphinx against Ragnarok. They had little to fear in a fight. It was the battle within the soul of the city that was causing the greatest of all terrors.

Despite the Sphinx Elders beliefs that the female gender was not capable of higher thinking or soldiering, she truly loved them all. Maybe it was the recollection of home, but she was accustomed to that mentality and appreciated the beauty of the city and its perfection in arrangement and architecture.

Until now.

She stood on the porch of the guest house and stared out over the remains of a devastated city. Only a few weeks before, she had given Victoria a lesson here. That day had been peaceful and sunny. Today's weather was similar, but a shadow of unrest clouded the future.

Across the lawn, the Hall of Art lay wounded. The entire west wing had collapsed on blackene grass. Dozens of gateways had completely burned away, leaving melted gold and silver frames twisted among the broken slabs of fallen marble. The attack on the Hall of Art had come from the Ragnarok, an attack in full presence of the entire sphinx community at a time when Anna and Worthmere were a terrace away, but somehow Anna and Worthmere were being blamed.

Interesting was the word Worthmere used to describe the Elders logic. His terminology normally had no limit, but it had been particularly colorful since they returned. Anna knew that his mind was consumed with worry over Victoria and the twins. It had been his call to divide up to search two different terraces for Victoria. None of them had been heard from and, according to Parnassus, no one had been sent to search for them.

The lack of trust among the Elders resulted in Anna and Worthmere's confinement in the dwelling set aside for humans.

As if the Elders lack of action hadn't been enough, a fence of thorn branches stood in a close circle around the house. The dwelling where Anna had spent so many happy days was now her prison. Her paints and canvas had been taken away from her, as punishment.

She sniffed and wiped her nose. Again. The ride down the frigid river had given her a terrible cold. When they finally crawled out of the water, Frigg left them on the bank to go in search of help. Hours later, two very unhelpful and seriously egotistical sphinx wandered toward them. Anna smiled, remembering Worthmere's disgust at the young sphinx's behavior and lack of concern.

"Didn't Frigg ask you to help us? Didn't she tell you what we've been through?" Worthmere had asked them.

"Frigg told the Circle of Elders quite a story. They sent us here to bring you back."

"Well, thank you. If you would help me with Anna, I can hold onto her while you carry us there."

The brown Sphinx scoffed at the idea. "I am no mule."

Worthmere stood to his full height normally impressive for the average man, but to the Sphinx, he was only shoulder high. "You refuse to do the duty of a mule with honor, yet you act like an ass."

The other Sphinx leaned down and looked at Anna. "She does look very pale, Hauk. Perhaps we should."

"I'll not carry *anything*," Hauk replied.

Anna remembered the other's name. Finn. Two overly righteous Sphinx with a reputation for petty haughtiness.

"Do you know who this is?" Worthmere asked Hauk. "Anna Witherspoon, a very well-respected mage among the Sphinx."

Hauk laughed. "Well-respected? Since when is a fugitive considered to be the cream of society?"

"Fugitive?" Anna was shocked.

21

"Since you left," Finn explained, "the Hall of Art has been attacked and a mage has been killed. All suspicion points to you."

"Sophia." Worthmere sighed. "They're accusing Anna?"

"Of course," Hauk said.

"Anna didn't kill Sophia," Worthmere said. "Sophia was dead before we even arrived in Woodland Hills."

"So says a fugitive."

"And how do I suddenly become a criminal?"

Hauk smirked at Finn and turned his back. "By association."

Anna and Worthmere took their time walking to the sphinx city, stepping cautiously and slowly. As the sphinx grew more impatient, Anna and Worthmere slowed their pace. They heard the whispers between the two Junior Sphinx about whether or not they should leave the two mages behind to come to the city in their own good time or if they should split up and return with a horse and wagon. Which one should be left to walk at a snail's pace while the other was given the privilege of returning to civilization? And where would they find a horse and cart? Sphinx, by nature, preferred to not use animals as beasts of burden. To admit the necessity of one meant a weakness. The argument was never settled as their pride allowed no compromise. Finally, just when Worthmere was about to tell the two sphinx to go on and he and Anna would follow, they crested a hill and looked over the blemished landscape of the sphinx city. Waiting for them was Abner, Elder Parnassus' nephew.

"It's about time," Abner said as he stood and faced Anna and Worthmere with a stern face.

Hawk lifted his nose higher, almost looking at the sky instead of Abner. "You could have helped us."

"And leave my post?" Abner was appalled at the idea. "I've heard that your delay to help Anna and Worthmere may threaten your ability to be a witness at their trial."

"They were uncooperative." Finn said.

"The Elders sent you to find them and return them quickly," Abner reminded them. "I believe their exact words were, 'by whatever means necessary'. It seems as if your delay has cost Anna her health." Abner looked at Anna's red nose and droopy eyes.

"Then we leave you to supervise their return," Hauk said, clinging to his authority.

Abner watched the two sphinx walk away, then turned to Anna and Worthmere. "You two look terrible."

"Not as bad as that." Worthmere pointed down the hill toward the city.

Never had Anna seen so much as a blade of grass out of place among the Hall, the Library and the Elder's Circle.

"How were the Ragnarok able to get close enough to the city?" Worthmere asked. "Where were the guards?"

Abner looked toward the Elder's Circle across the lake. "The patrols were cut back shortly before you arrived with Victoria. Uncle Parnassus was against it and debated fervently to keep the patrols, but he was out-voted. Terrible part of a majority rule—if the majority is trying to line their pockets—figuratively speaking, of course, when concerning sphinx—the decision is usually not in the best interest of the populace. Come on. There are a few things you must know before we get to the Circle. Things that I don't want you to learn on your own."

"Sounds serious," Worthmere said.

"Nothing seems harmful until the consequences are studied." Abner knelt on the grass. "Climb up Anna."

"Oh, thank you," Anna sighed in relief.

"Who is studying these events?" Worthmere asked.

"No one, of course." Abner stood and led the way to the city. "That's where the greatest mistakes occur. I can see it so clearly when I read the histories. I often think that if those in decades and centuries past had pieced together what was going on, they would have chosen differently. Now I see it firsthand. I see the pride that blinds and the ignorance that numbs. No one sees what is happening."

"Except you," Anna smiled. "You are much like your family."

Abner blushed. "I am proud of my family. Pride seems to be the driving force behind the changes, so I'm trying to be cautious. The Elders want you brought right to the Circle, but you are clearly in no condition." He looked at Anna. "I'll take you to the dwelling. Ambrosia made creamy kale soup yesterday. I'll see if she has any left."

"Won't the Elders be put out if we don't go there straight away?" Anna asked.

Abner smiled. "They certainly will."

୨୦୯୫

Two days later, when Anna's fever was gone and her nose was no longer bright red, Abner escorted Anna and Worthmere toward the circle. He gave Anna a few tips on Elder's Circle etiquette. "When you enter the Elder's Circle, you will be taken to the platform."

"That's for trials," Worthmere was surprised. "Is that was this is?"

"They are calling it an *Inquiry*, thus the platform."

Worthmere rubbed the back of his neck. Anna could see the tension pulsing in the veins of his temples. The platform lay at the base of the Elder's podiums and is usually the place the condemned stand while the Elders determine what the punishment will be for mages who are found guilty of a crime against the Society.

"I don't understand," Anna said. "Why the platform?"

Abner shook his head in frustration. "Although you have not been found guilty of anything and the evidence against you has more holes than a cloud has rain drops," Abner began, "the placement of where you will stand still carries that guilty appearance." He added, "This is another format of inquiries that has been altered recently."

"I noticed that when I went with Elder Parnassus to ask permission to enter another gateway when we were tracking Lucian," Worthmere remembered. "Sphinx who were not Elders were allowed to question me."

Anna frowned. "I thought only Elders were allowed to speak at the Circle."

"That was tradition, but that's been deemed 'a potential detriment to the educational benefits of the Circle', and has been 'altered to allow a more progressive education'," Abner spoke nasally. Worthmere snorted with laughter as Abner continued with his own voice. "Now, the Junior Elders may speak, sharpening their egos on the reputations of others."

Worthmere stopped walking and stared at Abner. "*Junior* Elders? That's the worst oxymoron I've ever heard."

"You have the moron part right," Abner said. "An effort has been made to treat everyone fairly by giving them all authority within the Elder's Circle and so we now have Junior Elders, the sons of the Elders. If an Elder has no son, he may select a younger sphinx to serve as a Junior."

"Elder Parnassus has no son," Anna said. "Who did he choose?"

Worthmere laughed. "Ambrosia."

"She's the best in the bunch. Her tongue is sharper than all the other's intellect combined." Abner smiled proudly.

"I would have thought the Elders would have been more careful in their wording after Frigg's stunt with the soldier trials last year," Worthmere said. "This doesn't say much about their learning curve."

"Then there is some hope," Anna said. "In Ambrosia, at

least."

Abner sighed. "I don't mean to sleet on your party, but one intelligent Junior Elder will not have much impact."

"The phrase is 'rain on my parade'." Anna smiled.

Abner looked over his shoulder at her in surprise. "But rain is such lovely weather."

"You're right," Anna said. "About both. Ambrosia might not be strong enough to keep the Elder's from making further changes, but I wouldn't put it past her to really muck up the works."

Ancestry

Elder's Circle, which was set apart from the city just as the Elders set themselves apart from the lesser races, was a great monument to sacred traditions. Sphinx are nothing if not traditional beings, almost to the point of simple-mindedness, Anna thought, although she would never use 'simple-minded' to describe Elder Parnassus, Ambrosia, or Abner. The Elder's Circle was both a building and the name of its members. Of course, there is a formal name for both, but those names have been kept safe and hidden in the hearts of its members for so long, hardly a soul remembers that the names had ever been uttered.

Crafted from gray granite, the Elder's Circle was the only large building in the city not gleaming with white marble. The granite was beautiful in its own right, peppered with black and glinting quartz. From a distance, the perfectly round building was the pride of the Elders. The walls stood twenty feet tall, enclosing an area within that would house the entire Library of Ages.

From a distance, the building reminded Anna of a green-frosted cupcake. Like other buildings in the city, the Elder's Circle had no roof. Instead, two massive trees, viewed as the connection between earth and sky, had grown for hundreds of years in the center of the building and provided a leafy roof. Among the branches, scores of birds made their homes and raised their young.

To the sphinx, the building was a symbol of Creation; the roundness of the earth reflected in the shape of the building. The true beauty of the Elders Circle was only seen from the interior, and today, for the first time, Anna witnessed what few mages had ever seen. She tried not to think about the fate of some of those mages. Many who had been asked to stand on the platform had been found guilty of their accused crime and cast away to the Seventh Terrace, a land reportedly ruled by dragons. While she loved to travel and see new places, she didn't want her last experience to be a tour of a dragon's belly.

Her first impression of the Circle was one of respect for the artistry of the entrance's archway. Carved into the stone wall on either side of the arched doorway, two trees stretched their branches to the apex with intricately plaited tree roots reaching to the ground on either side of the entrance. Bulging out from either side of the roots, two pillars stood like frozen eddies of water. Separate pillars stood on either side of the swirling stone, holding bright lanterns that burned day and night.

A draft tunneled through the entrance from the long hallway that curved along the inside of the building, lifting Anna's hair and beckoning her forward. The Elder's Circle was not just a meeting place for dignitaries, but was a potent gathering of all the elements: built of stone from the earth, welcoming the air of the sky, housing a stream of water within and kept bright by flames of fire on lantern posts.

The hall was etched with images of great mages, sphinx, and places from around the world and throughout the terraces. Anna recognized many of the stories and figures on the wall: the creation of the world before the fall, a depiction of the horrors that entered after, a massive tower collapsing, and a dozen more stories her mother told her. Sphinx and Council members who served during times of war were forever commemorated. As they walked toward the far end of the tunnel, they passed the history of the Seven Terraces.

The hall ended at a bright opening in the top and center of an amphitheater. Wrapping around the building on their left and right, long curved stones provided seating. Each of the seven stone levels was wide enough to allow a sphinx to sit comfortably and long enough to hold almost one hundred sphinx or people. The Elder's Circle was normally filled with the occasional onlooker or visiting dignitary, but today it held nearly the entire city's population. The air hummed with the sound of over a hundred sphinx voices.

As if on cue, the audience stopped their buzzing conversation when Anna and Worthmere stepped into the open and walked down the broad, stone steps toward a grassy lawn that filled the eastern half of the interior. Linking the rising platforms of the stadium seating for onlookers and an earthen gateway was an arched stone bridge that spanned a small creek, which ran through the structure. Sentinel trees, the same trees whose leaves capped the roof, grew from either side of the bridge on the side closest to where the Elders stood; on seven tall stone platforms rose from the ground like granite tree trunks, each backed with a tall post holding an open flame.

A creek, burning lanterns, grassy earth supporting massive trees, and a constant breeze—all the elements were present and accounted for. Embedded in the grass lay a perfectly round and flat granite stone, an elaborate stone mosaic of a mountainside illustrating a few sparse trees clinging to the sides with ice and snow topping the peaks. In the heart of the mountain, not far from the apex, a dark cavern swallowed the light. Made from ebony, the stones were eerie. Anna knew what must live in that cave. This was a gateway to the Seventh Terrace—the only gateway that could skip terraces. It required a great deal of skill to open, but the Sphinx Elders, despite their current short-comings, were not short on elemental skill. One false word and she, Worthmere, and Parnassus would find themselves at the base of that mountain. The remainder of their days would be few and would be spent dodging dragons.

Anna had heard descriptions of this earth gateway, but seeing it with all four elements so carefully placed and maintained, and Parnassus standing alone on its surface, caused her steps to falter. Worthmere put his hand on her back and whispered, "Steady."

For a mage standing before the Earth gateway, it was like standing on the edge of all existence looking down at the eternal pit.

Abner led the way to the earth gateway nestled in the grass right in front of the Elders. Wings denoting their status were perched on their backs and held in place by leather straps with silver buckles around their thick necks. The looks of superiority were well-practiced. Only two Elders held an expression of sympathy; one was Elder Parnassus. He was not among his peers, but standing next to Anna and Worthmere on the platform. The other was Elder Amberson, an elderly sphinx who wore an expression of pain at seeing his dear friend on trial.

"We will begin," stated a sphinx with gold wings and a large chest plate inlaid with emeralds. This was Elder Aurum, now the highest ranking with Parnassus having been the first). "The accused, Parnassus, is hereby charged with dispensing the Map of Art to an apprentice mage without the consent of the Elders Circle and without the consultation of the Council Mages. Anna Witherspoon and Worthmere of the Green Guard stand as witnesses of this crime." He turned to a young man who sat at a desk at the base of Elder Aurum's podium and said, "Make note that Miss Witherspoon and Worthmere of the Green Guard are also scheduled for their own inquiry at a later date. Their testimony into this situation is tainted by their own crimes."

Worthmere tensed and Anna slipped her hand into his. "Steady," she whispered.

"Do you deny these charges?" Elder Aurum asked.

"Yes," Parnassus said. "I gave the Map of Art to a Green Guard, not an apprentice mage."

The onlookers broke their silence and a low hum of disapproval disrupted the reverent proceedings.

"Silence!" Elder Aurum called out. He waited to proceed, breathing deeply before continuing. "And by giving the Green Guard the Map of Art do you understand what will become of you?"

"Friend, do you understand what would have happened if I hadn't given him the Map? You are not asking the correct questions."

"This is an inquiry to decide your fate."

"No. A inquiry, by definition, is a meeting to hear the witnesses, discover the purposes for their actions, and determine if a trial is necessary. But that is not your agenda today. You have already determined my guilt before I even stepped through the door. Now hear my reasons."

"This is not the time!" a stout sphinx with pale fur and black wings bellowed as he tried to regain control of the arena with the fury of his voice.

"That is true, Rufus," Parnassus agreed. "You should have listened to me months ago when I first told you of the threat." Parnassus raised his voice, facing the Elders but addressing the entire room. "As mages, our entire history has been a series of maintaining peace and balance between our neighbors and the terraces. As sphinx, our history has been to serve as guardians of the gateways and the keepers of the Library. You have forgotten what that indicates. Instead of humble guardians, sphinx have gained the reputation of arrogant, power-hungry hopefuls. The members of our society are the most highly educated among the mage culture, yet they cannot see what is before them."

A Junior Elder spoke from the seating behind them. "What exactly are we not realizing?"

Elder Parnassus tightened his jaw at the obvious lack of formality and respect. "That the balance of the Mage Society is *already* broken. The Grandfather's Weapon is being hunted."

"We are not here to listen to fairy tales," an Elder with silver wings said.

"Then let me share a true story with you," Parnassus said. "The Grandfather of the Mage Culture created a device that divided the Creator's world into seven terraces. We know that and accept that as truth. Over hundreds of generations of sharing the story, the other purposes of the Grandfather's Weapon have been either forgotten, altered, or cast aside as fiction."

"The balance is not broken." Silverwings tried to regain the floor, but Elder Parnassus ignored him.

"Victoria Nike grew up not knowing what she is. She lived near twins. Twin mages. You know the power of the number three. You've heard of the difference in elemental intent in identical twins. They knew nothing of the Mage Society, and yet a rogue Council Guard found and attacked them in the Fourth Terrace."

"The Council Mages have denied any such guard," Silverwings argued.

"They have either lied or did not know the truth," Parnassus said.

Ambrosia stood, taking advantage of her new role as Junior Elder to help her father. "To say the Council is misleading us is to say that the entire Mage Society is no longer functioning within the laws of the Creator."

"Exactly. The very fact that they have deceived us, that three mages were hidden for over sixteen years, and that a new Council Guard has been formed is the proof that the balance is broken."

"And how does this explain their actions?" Silverwings pointed to Anna and Worthmere. "Destroying gateways and murdering a valued member of our society?"

"*If* they destroyed the gateway, I would want to know why. During times of tribulation, extreme deeds are necessary. If they didn't destroy it, someone else is responsible—someone you can't look for until you know the truth. And Sophia *was* murdered, but not by Anna and Worthmere. There are witnesses in Woodland Hills who can prove their innocence. You need only to summon them here."

A collective murmur ran through the onlookers. Many agreed with Elder Parnassus.

"If the Grandfather's Weapon is real," Parnassus continued, "you must ask yourself what protection is in place to keep the weapon from being found? The elements? The balance? The terraces were constructed out of one man's fear of losing power to a deity. We are living the result of a sin. One man took matters into his own hands and forever changed the course of the divine plan."

"The Creator granted us all free will," Brasswings said.

"Yes, free will," Parnassus said, "but also the laws. The laws are being ignored, forgotten." He looked out at the crowd of Junior Elders. "The Weapon can restore the divine laws and our relationship with the Creator, or it can destroy everything."

"And you believe that Victoria Nike is the mage to find the Weapon and make the right choice?" Silverwings asked.

"I do."

"Such confidence in a human!" Elder Aurum scoffed. "Why? You know very little about this young girl."

"And the twins," added Elder Rufus. "They may make the

number, but what more do they have?"

Parnassus paused and looked up the steps at his daughter. They had discussed this possibility, but prayed that it wouldn't happen. Now that they were there and Parnassus stood in front of his peers, stripped of his wings, the moment they had feared was upon them. It wasn't just a career that was lost or a reputation; they stood alone on the brink of war, for no other sphinx had grasped the significance of the events leading up to this moment.

Parnassus smiled sadly.

Ambrosia nodded.

"Victoria Nike is not just another mage. She is the daughter of Alexander Veracitous. The twins have been raised by Adam Caius."

The room exploded with disbelief. Words of shock and stronger statements against Parnassus bounced off the stone walls and reverberated through the air like knives. But Parnassus didn't flinch.

Elder Rufus scoffed at Parnassus. "My friend, you are truly lost among these lies. Alexander Veracitous is dead. Dead because he was killed by Adam Caius."

NURI

The Elder's Circle had never ended in a riot before and Worthmere was glad he and Anna survived. Once Parnassus had announced who Victoria and the twins really were and who their fathers were, chaos ruled. The Junior Elders couldn't help but erupt in a torrent of shock. Even Anna had been stunned by the news.

Because the Elders had no control over the Circle, they dismissed the inquiry. Abner and Ambrosia escorted Anna and Worthmere to their fenced prison where they waited for Parnassus. There had never been a reason to imprison a sphinx before, and in their haste to separate Parnassus from everything, he was now required to live in the house with Anna and Worthmere.

As the thorn fence was lifted by two guards, Abner and Ambrosia followed Anna and Worthmere into the small yard.

"Frigg!" Anna smiled and jogged forward, throwing her arms around the sphinx's neck. "I've been worried."

Frigg smiled. "I'm fine. I need nothing but a good night of sleep."

"They questioned her for forty-eight hours," Abner told Worthmere. "She never changed her story."

"The truth cannot be changed," Frigg said.

"Speaking of truth, is what Parnassus said possible?" Worthmere asked.

"It is," Ambrosia confirmed. "My father will tell you more when he returns." She looked at Frigg. "I had food delivered while we were gone. Real food. Let's eat and you can tell Abner and I about your questioning. I have a feeling that protocol was not followed."

The sphinx went into the little house, leaving Anna and Worthmere on the porch that overlooked the city.

"How could it be true?" Anna whispered to Worthmere as they stood at the door, watching the sphinx bolt around the city, spreading the rumors.

"Does Parnassus lie about anything?"

Anna sighed. "Why didn't he tell us?"

Worthmere turned to face Anna. "What would you have done if you knew that Adam was the boys' father?"

She didn't answer.

"You know the reputation Adam had."

Anna wiped a tear from her eye. "Better than anyone."

Worthmere gently put his hand on Anna's cheek and lifted her chin to face him. He wiped a second tear off her cheek with his thumb. "I'm sorry."

"It wasn't your fault."

"The hell it wasn't." A voice came from the house, startling them both. Worthmere recognized the bald head at once. It wasn't an easy face to forget, with the wrinkled and pale scars from a burn that had forever eaten away the skin from his right eyebrow back into his hairline and down his cheek bone. Although the healer who had helped him was highly skilled, the skin was still lighter than the rest of his face.

"Nuri," Worthmere said and shook Nuri's hand. "Good to see you."

Laughing, Nuri pulled Worthmere into a brotherly hug and patted his shoulder. "You look good—for a prisoner."

"Yeah, well," Worthmere shrugged it off. "Just a little misunderstanding. It will be cleared up."

"Ever the optimist," Nuri said, looking past Worthmere to Anna. "We met long ago."

"I remember," Anna said, holding her hand out to greet him. "Trina introduced us."

Smiling, Nuri nodded. "Speaking of Trina, she's on her way here. Seems that the trouble you've stepped into might not be that easy to clear up."

Worthmere moved toward the table on the porch and invited Nuri to join them. "Sounds like we need to hear what you know."

Nuri sat down. "I caught the tail end of that fiasco of a hearing—I mean, inquiry." He raised his eyebrow indicating that he knew what the Elders had been planning. "The sphinx are shaken to the core. With that Map of Art missing, a tool we will need to protect our kind, we are weakened."

"Protect us from what?" Anna asked.

Nuri pointed toward the damaged Hall of Art. "The Ragnarok have teamed up with Minotaur and have attacked the sphinx. Do you know why?" Nuri didn't wait for them to answer. "The rumors you've heard of a group of rebellious Green Guards is true. They call themselves Janus Guards. They seek the Grandfather's Weapon."

"We know the Janus Guards exist," Worthmere said, "just not their purpose."

Anna leaned forward. "What do they hope to do with the Grandfather's Weapon?"

Nuri shrugged. "Depends on which bedtime story they believe. Perhaps they have a different belief of what it can do. All

I know for certain is their attempts to gain it are destroying our prized treasures."

"You're here to tell the sphinx what you know?" Worthmere asked. "I didn't hear mention of you on the list of witnesses."

"No, I was on my way to Delphi. I stopped here to deliver a request to use the Map of Art. Ona has asked that it be in the possession of the Green Guards. Now that it's missing—" His voice trailed off. "Seems Ona's fears of it being misused were correct. I'm just surprised that Parnassus is to blame."

Under the table, Worthmere pressed his foot lightly over Anna's, a warning to not allow any reaction give away their concern about the Council Mages.

"You said Trina was on her way here?" Anna asked.

"As the Council Mage of the Third Terrace, her presence is necessary," Nuri said.

"Did Ona send for her?" Anna asked.

"I don't know." Nuri looked at Worthmere, then Anna. His eyes narrowed. "You two know more than you're telling."

"We do," Worthmere said.

"Well?" Nuri held his arms out, waiting to be let in on the story.

Worthmere laughed. "This isn't a card game. I'm not going to show my hand just yet."

"Bluffing again?" Nuri asked, leaning forward and winking.

Keeping his face straight, Worthmere gave no indication of what he knew. "When all the chips are down, then you'll see what I'm holding. Until then," he shrugged, "we play."

A tense silence lingered.

"You might not win this game," Nuri stood and picked up his rucksack.

Worthmere walked with him to the fence. "Where to now?"

Sighing, Nuri pointed west. "Delphi. Ona wants me to check on a few mages."

"Ophidia?" Anna asked.

"Perhaps." He extended his hand to Worthmere, who shook it. "I'll check in on you on my way back."

Nuri called out and the two sphinx guards lifted a section of the fence. He waved one last time, then headed toward a horse near the tree line. Worthmere kept his eye on him.

Anna came up behind him. "You have strange friends."

"He's no friend."

"What do you mean? He's a Green Guard."

Shaking himself of a thought, Worthmere turned and smiled but no joy shown in his eyes. "That he is."

The Second Strike

Returning to the First Terrace Council Mage dwelling was not a pleasant little hike through the wilderness. The mountain where they had camped the night before wasn't really mountainous, like the Rocky Mountains, but exhaustingly hilly. That was little consolation to Victoria, who had basically been starved for days.

Victoria promised she would never paint the landscape that lay between the oasis and Kivavallis. Or maybe she would if she ever painted a prison. Cinder stones scattered the gritty and hard-packed earth like cast-away marbles. It was nearly impossible not to step on them, but when she did, the roundness of the cinders bore painfully into her skin. She was still without shoes and Freya offered to carry her. Victoria accepted at once and promptly fell asleep on Freya's back. The swaying motion rocked her into a dreamless slumber.

The sun cast down blazing rays of moisture-sucking heat, scalding the earth and sapping their strength. Sebastian and Caladrius were the only two with canteens of water, which lasted until late morning. Collette used her elemental intent to draw water to the surface when she sensed it was close, but it was cloudy and tasted strongly of iron.

Bobby and Tucker used what they had learned from their father to find edible yucca roots for her, but they did little to satisfy. She graciously accepted a strip of pickled prickly pear Sebastian had hastily packed. The taste was far from appealing and she would think of her pickled prickly pear meal each time she smelled stinky feet.

When the city of Kivavallis finally came into view, the entire group hesitated. Within the limits of this city, within the walls of Ona's home, were Janus Guards. Not Green Guards, men and women who had taken the oath to protect the Mage Society at the cost of their own lives if necessary, but traitors to the Creator.

Caladrius' face shown with righteous anger as he told the young mages what he had heard from other healers who traveled the terraces.

"It seems the loyalty of Janus Guards knows only the highest bidder."

"Thugs for hire," Tucker said. "Great."

Caladrius tried the new phrase out for himself. "Thugs for hire. Thugs. A cruel or vicious thief or robber. To the highest bidder. Yes. I like that. Very accurate."

Tucker sighed and glanced at Bobby. "Excellent. Two of you have photographic memories. I can hear the dinner conversation now, quoting dictionaries and famous men. I bet the girls just line up to meet you."

"That will have to wait," Caladrius said. "For now we part ways for a short time." Turning to Tiw and Freya he comforted the warriors. "Sebastian will protect you. Stay near him." The two sphinx simply nodded. Caladrius turned to Bobby and Tucker. "You must be careful. Being twins."

Tucker held up his hand, stopping Caladrius' explanation. "We know. Looking alike makes our elemental intent doubly strong. Thing is, it really doesn't."

"Let's leave that to curiosity," Caladrius warned. "If things do not go as planned, the only weapon we have might be the expected danger of twins."

Caladrius took the lead. He walked as though nothing in the world was wrong. As they passed through the dusty streets of Kivavallis, Victoria noticed that most of the residents paid them little heed. Others watched the procession carefully and shared muttered concern over Bobby and Tucker.

Victoria whispered to Collette, "Are all of these people mages?"

"They are."

"What are their roles in the society?"

Collette frowned in confusion.

"Green Guards? Healers? Painters? What other roles are there?"

Collette was surprised. "You really know nothing of the mage culture."

"You know that I don't. Do you really have to remind me of everything I *don't* know?"

Collette cleared her throat, ignoring Victoria's obvious irritation, and explained. "Not everyone is as gifted as you are. The Green Guards are exceptionally talented with their elemental intent, as are Painters. Healers are something different as some of our healers have so little elemental intent that it's difficult to believe they are mages at all. Healing is more empathy and knowledge of anatomy than anything. These people," Collette looked around the street, "make their living in trades. Most are farmers, using their earth and water elements to entice plants to grow in the desert. Others are Air Mages who calm the heat to help the farmers." Collette shrugged at the simplicity of her city. "It all runs on a very elaborate exchange of bartering. Once, my mother needed our sheep shorn. A neighbor down the way needed his roof patched, but couldn't because he had a broken leg. My mother arranged for two boys to do both jobs in exchange for setting up a water reservoir for their garden, which had been stupidly planted where there wasn't a drop of water in sight. Because the roof was patched so well, the neighbor gave my mother," Collette stopped talking when she saw Victoria's exasperated expression. "Well, it all worked out."

As they walked through the squared threshold leading to Ona's living quarters, three Guards stepped in front of them. Two wore the traditional green clothing, a uniform of solidarity within the Mage Society. Victoria wondered if they were true to their oaths or if they were Janus Guards. The third guard was young and wearing black. Victoria didn't know if this boy was just a rebellious Goth-mage or was being punished for impunity and forced to wear heat-absorbing black in a desert.

"Caladrius," the blonde guard welcomed them. "We've been hoping you would return soon with news."

Victoria glanced nervously at Bobby and Tucker.

"I'm afraid my search isn't yet complete," Caladrius continued, undaunted. "These young mages will need a meal as quickly as possible."

The blonde guard nodded to a younger boy in black. "Gerald, have Samantha send up a tray of food." He glanced at the dark circles under Victoria's eyes. "Make that two trays."

Gerald bowed and dashed from the room.

"Thank you, Reggie," Caladrius said to the blonde guard. "It's been a difficult journey."

"Did you find Ona?" Reggie asked as he led them to the meeting room where Victoria had met with Ona every morning before her imprisonment.

"I did not." Caladrius patted Reggie on the shoulder as they walked. "But hope must not be abandoned. The Janus Guards are crafty. If they have taken Ona as we suspect, then they will reveal themselves and their demands soon."

"Poor Lady Ona." Reggie's face was pained. "I hope they don't—" He didn't finish his thought.

"She's strong," Caladrius reminded him. "I think if she has been taken, her abductors will find more fight than frill."

Laughing, Reggie agreed. "I hope the other guards find her, or at least a hint of what may have happened. From what I hear, it's been quite a week here."

"Other guards?"

The other Green Guard spoke. "I took it upon my standing as Nuri's second in command to do everything possible to find our Council Mage." He glared at Caladrius, challenging his authority.

"Well done, Milo." Caladrius didn't hesitate for a second, but Victoria felt her stomach flop and her head spin with exhaustion and hunger when she realized the 'other guards' Milo spoke of were likely Janus guards.

Caladrius caught her arm, steadying her and leading her to a chair. "Gentlemen, this poor thing has been through quite an ordeal. If you all wouldn't mind helping Gerald with the food."

Reggie nodded and eagerly urged Milo to help him.

After they left, Bobby and Tucker rushed to Victoria. "Are you okay?"

"Nothing a little food won't cure." Victoria managed a weak smile. "Just when I heard that other guards were searching—if they find the bodies at the kiva—"

"It's more of a question of *when* they find the bodies," Caladrius said, watching Victoria closely. "When Gerald brings food, drink as much as you can. Eat a little. Then we'll go to the mirror and contact the sphinx."

Gerald returned, bent under the weight of a huge platter of food. Reggie followed with three pitchers of beverages. Milo carried nothing but a sour face.

Caladrius clapped in delight. "Ah, Samantha never fails to amaze!" He leaned over and sniffed one of the pitchers. "Don't drink this one." He looked at the young mages. "It's meant to aid in sleep. We'll save this one for later." He set it on the far side of the table. "This one, however," he smelled a second pitcher, "is just what you all need. A boost of energy." He poured five tall glasses of the red, thick liquid.

Tucker leaned toward Collette and whispered, "What is this?"

"Cactus fig juice."

Bobby cautiously sniffed the juice while both Victoria and Tucker drained their glasses. When neither of them gagged, Bobby sipped.

Tucker smacked his lips together. "Tastes like strawberries."

Pouring Victoria another glass, Caladrius glanced at Reggie and Milo. "Try some of these." He handed Victoria some square pieces of hard bread. "Dipped in the bean sauce, it's quite good. Alone," he scrunched up his face, "well, it's called stone bread for a reason."

Doing as she was told, Victoria drank two more servings of fig juice and ate while Caladrius spoke with the guards. "How many were sent to search for Lady Ona?"

"Three," Milo said. "They should be back before nightfall with a report."

"Hopefully they will return with Lady Ona," Reggie said.

Victoria reached for more food. She liked stone bread. It could have been actual stones she was dipping in the bean sauce, but she didn't care. The food was helping. The fig juice was sweet and thick. As she drank, she felt her muscles awaken.

Reggie noticed Victoria's bare feet. "Don't tell me you walked in this heat barefoot!"

"Oh," Victoria tucked her filthy and swollen feet under the hem of her dress. "Well, I—"

Reggie's eyes narrowed and for the first time, he took in

45

Victoria's dress, her hair, her eyes. Looking at Bobby and Tucker, he straightened his stance and raised his hands. They all felt him pull his elemental intent toward him. The room shivered in anticipation as Reggie, an earth mage, stood ready in a building made of clay bricks.

"I told you," Milo said. "She's the one Lady Ona imprisoned."

"Stand down," Caladrius commanded.

"She almost killed one of us," Milo said.

Standing, stretching to his fullest height, Caladrius spoke. His voice oozed comfort and his words dripped with serenity. "There has been a grievous misunderstanding. Until we understand what really has been going on, you have no reason to fear. All will be put right." Reggie and Milo's shoulders relaxed and the determined glare on their faces eased.

Even Victoria relaxed. The tension in her back that had been pinching her shoulders together for days enjoyed the ease of peace. It *would* all be put right. They would talk to the Sphinx Elders and find a way back. Her mom would arrive at the sphinx city, unharmed. Tears moistened Victoria's eyes as she imagined hugging her mom and telling her all about what has happened. If she could just have her mom back, she would be okay—everything would be okay.

Reggie's hands dropped to his side as he stared open-mouthed at Caladrius. "Yeah," he muttered.

From the doorway, another voice broke the peace. "You!"

Everyone turned and saw Bernadette glowering at Victoria.

"Thank goodness, Bernadette." Collette stepped into action. "We need your help. Come in."

Victoria felt a tranquil tone in Collette's voice as she had in Caladrius'. The soothing effect it had on Bernadette was strong, but Victoria didn't feel the same stillness in her soul as with Caladrius' reassurances. Bernadette willingly accepted Collette's invitation to join them, as if tea would be served and they would all sit down and enjoy the food together like old friends.

Staring at Victoria, Bernadette took a seat and waited patiently for the next set of directions from Collette. "Bernadette, we need your boots."

Bernadette lifted the hem of her dress and began untying the laces. She handed the boots to Collette who passed them off to Victoria, whispering, "Put these on quickly."

Nodding his approval, Caladrius winked at Collette. "Now, gentlemen," he turned his attention to Reggie and Milo, "I need to use Ona's mirror to contact the sphinx elders."

Milo blinked slowly, trying to wake from Caladrius' drugging voice. "Only Lady Ona can grant permission—"

"And in her absence, I am in command."

His face reddened by the reprimand, Milo apologized. "Of course."

With the boots firmly tied around her feet and up to her knees, Victoria stood.

Bernadette blinked and opened her mouth to speak, but Collette was quick. "Thank you, Bernadette." She handed the dazed girl the empty pitcher. "Tell Samantha thank you for the food."

Shaking her head, Bernadette was struggling to break free of Collette's voice.

"Bernadette, take the pitcher to Samantha." Collette tried again.

"No!" Bernadette yelled, leaping up from her chair and running toward the door. "Collette, you're a traitor!" she called as she ran down the hall shouting for help.

Reggie watched Bernadette go with mild curiosity. "She's upset about something."

"Girls," Milo shook his head, confounded by Bernadette's sudden dash from the room.

"The mirror," Caladrius reminded Reggie. "We must get there now."

"Of course. This way." He started walking out the door. As Caladrius followed, he beckoned to Victoria to join him.

Before they had taken two steps into the hall, Milo reached his arm out and woke from Caladrius' efforts to keep him stupefied. "Why do you need the mirror?"

"Why are you questioning your superior?" Caladrius' voice was rank with authority.

Milo's shoulders drooped again and he turned and walked down the hall. Victoria heard several people running up behind them. Caladrius kept his face calm, but she could see beads of sweat on his forehead. Several guards, led by Bernadette, swarmed around them.

"What is the meaning of this?" Caladrius said.

"That's her!" Bernadette pointed at Victoria. "She's the one that Ona had in the prison."

Milo held up his hands to the other guards, indicating that everything was sunshine and roses. "Caladrius has asked to use the mirror."

"Why?" one of the guards asked.

"It is not our place to question authority," Milo answered, repeating Caladrius' words.

The guard kept his eyes on Caladrius and lowered his head like a wolf about to attack. "Why don't you explain it to me."

Caladrius, undaunted, proceeded. "James, this is Victoria. She is indeed the one Ona had imprisoned. We need to communicate with the Sphinx Elders to determine what should be done with her."

"You mean a new prison?" James asked.

"If that is what they determine, yes," Caladrius looked at Victoria.

"I'll ask again, Caladrius. What is going on? I've been to the kiva. We found four dead guards. Ona was not there."

"I don't know where Ona is," Caladrius admitted. "I don't know what happened in the kiva. Victoria does. We need to bring her to the Elders so they can determine what is to be done next."

James took a step toward Victoria. "No. I saw what this girl did. She has lightning."

Caladrius nodded. "I know."

"Then why would you take her from here? Ona needs her."

Victoria shook her head. "Ona is dead."

James frowned at her. "Was that the grave we found at the kiva?"

"That wasn't Ona," Bobby said.

James sighed in relief. "Then where is she?"

"You don't think she's dead?" Victoria eyed him carefully. "You know something."

He held up his hand to stop her and she felt the heat in the room focus around James. "Not another word from you."

"Or what?" Tucker stepped between Victoria and James and the heat intensified. Small flames danced on Tucker's hands.

James face paled, but his words did not betray his fear. "You are outnumbered. Until we find Ona, you all will be kept in the cells."

"No." Victoria felt the wounds on her hands and knees twinge at the memory of the Novacula Saxum prison's floor covered in razor-sharp rocks that had cut her hands and feet, keeping her in constant pain.

Smiling at her fear, James nodded at the other guards with him and they grabbed Bobby's and Tucker's arms.

"No!" Victoria yelled. Raising her hands, she drew the Air to her and welcomed its eagerness to help. In the back of her mind, where her mediation garden had been stripped, she saw dark storm clouds rolling in and felt the twisting surge of lightning's willingness to enter her world with burning fingers.

James backed up, but his guards kept their grip on the brothers.

"Let them go," Victoria said.

"Or you'll call lightning?" James said.

"I don't have to call it," Victoria said. "It's already here." A white-hot bolt struck outside and all the guards jumped. The one holding Tucker let go, but Bobby's capturer was too stubborn. Victoria tipped her head and looked at him. "Really?" she taunted him. "You think your element is a match for lighting?"

James laughed, but signaled to the guard holding Bobby to let him go.

Bobby straightened his shirt and walked over to Victoria.

Tucker shook his head at Bobby. "Dude. We were just rescued by a girl."

"Now what?" James asked. "You think you can take us all on?"

"I don't want to fight," Victoria kept her hands up and encouraged a strong breeze to sweep through the windows. "But, yeah, I think I can take you all on."

She felt Bobby tense at the idea, but she could see Tucker smiling at her courage.

James believed her. He had seen it. Milo had not. Without warning, Milo charged forward, his earth element shaking the floor. Victoria encapsulated him in a bubble of Air where he remained suspended inches off the floor with a look of embarrassed anger on his face. Reggie loosened the ground under Victoria's feet, obviously hoping to knock her over and weaken her hold on Milo. Keeping one hand toward Milo, she reached her right hand out and halted the cracking ground.

Reggie gasped. "Two elements."

"You *are* the one." James smiled. "Ona was right."

"Ona was NOT right! She used me and threatened my friends." Dark, foggy anger slipped into her mind. Light flashed in

50

her mind and she winced at the stinging heat of it. Everyone took a step back, even Bobby and Tucker. That's when she saw it. The lightning in her mind wasn't just a weapon. When it ripped across the sky in her meditation garden, she caught a glimpse of a different place.

"Victoria." Caladrius' voice was sappy with his controlling tones.

"No." Gritting her teeth, she focused on keeping the lightning in her mind. Caladrius was trying to help, but it was weakening her hold. The wind outside charged through the windows, lifting curtains and haunting the hall as unseen windy fingers tore at hair and clothing. Dark clouds blocked out the desert sun and the smell of rain and the spicy scent of electricity tickled their senses.

"Send it back," Bobby shouted over the sound of wind.

Thunder rolled. James, knowing that Victoria was responsible, pulled a knife from his belt and swiftly pulled Collette into a headlock. "This should even things a bit."

Wiping her left arm, Victoria tightened the Air around Milo and sent him crashing into James. All three—Milo, James and Collette, crashed landing heavily on the floor. Tucker quickly pulled Collette out of the way. A small eddy of air spun through the hall, dust pelting faces and eyes.

Caladrius tried again. "Victoria, you must stop this."

Victoria screamed in frustration. With her arms stretched out, she held Air and Earth in her mind. Both waited for her to call on them. The lightning was just waiting for a chance to slip through her grip and strike. "To me!" she shouted, trying to keep the white-hot light in place. She was talking to the lightning, but Bobby, Tucker and Collette ran toward her, ducking to avoid flying debris.

Lightning illuminated the hall. She saw it again. The space between the lightning looked the same as the way out of a gateway felt. That first time when she and Bobby had brought Tucker out of the prison gateway, she couldn't see the way out, but she'd felt it. It was small and invisible. This way between terraces was small, but it was clearly visible.

Another bolt cracked, ripping instantly from sky to earth and tearing the delicate wall of the terraces. Victoria saw her friends slip into the space between. White bolts burned into her vision. She could sense Caladrius' voice, with its deep baritone influence, trying to stop her. But she couldn't be stopped. The lightning raced toward her as if she were a magnet and the flashes of light were hot bits of metal. A second flash opened the way out again and she took it, following her friends and praying that Caladrius would somehow get Tiw and Freya home.

THE SPACE BETWEEN

Bobby felt the Air push him off his feet. He landed on his back and all the air in his lungs rushed out of his mouth. It was completely unexpected, falling backwards. He had been trying to reach Victoria in the crowded hallway in Ona's dwelling, but here he was, laying on his back, gasping for air like a fish on land. He recognized the sun in the sky, which was weird, because they were inside with the guards. Had he fallen out a window? They were up a few levels in Ona's dwelling; a fall from even two stories up would break bones. Pain seared his lungs, but he wasn't sure yet if he had broken anything.

Another breath escaped him. He just couldn't fill his lungs. He could hear Tucker talking to him through a long tunnel. The light was starting to fade to a pin prick. But a moment later, precious air rushed into his lungs and he gasped again and again, feeling warm breath returning, his ears no longer down a tunnel, but out in the open.

"Can you hear me?" Tucker was asking.

Yes, Bobby answered. He wasn't quite recovered enough to use his voice.

Tucker sat back and sighed in relief. "He'll be fine."

Bobby noticed Collette kneeling beside Tucker. Her face was red and pinched with fear. "Let's help him sit. He doesn't have any broken bones."

Bobby frowned at her. *How does she know? I fell out a window.*

No, man. Tucker helped him up. *Worse.*

Bobby looked up to see which window he had fallen from, but the dwelling was gone. He saw only sky. Along the ground were low shrubs, a few cacti, and miles and miles of hard-packed sand. "Where are we?"

"Million-dollar question." Tucker looked intently at his brother. "You don't have any broken bones. Just had the wind knocked out of you."

All around him, he saw only desert. "Where's Victoria?"

Collette and Tucker exchanged nervous glances.

"Where?" Bobby shouted.

Relax. We don't know.

What do you mean? Bobby asked.

Tucker looked distressed. "I think we were pushed into a different terrace." From horizon to horizon, there was flat expanse with nothing but sun and heat and ugly bushes.

"She didn't follow?" Bobby asked in complete despair. Then anger flashed. "She did it again." He stood and searched the area for Victoria.

"We don't know what happened," Tucker said, although he didn't sound convinced either.

"I want to know how we came to be here," Collette said. "It's impossible to just—be in a different terrace without a gateway."

"You didn't see it?" Tucker asked. "The, you know, the space between."

Collette's forehead wrinkled in utter confusion. "Space

between what?"

Tucker pinched the bridge of his nose with his finger and thumb. "It was in the storm. I could see glimpses of it between the flashes. It was," he gestured toward the land, "this."

Bobby shook his head, "Impossible."

"Yeah," Tucker laughed bitterly, "Impossible holds little meaning when faced with reality. She did it. She opened a way here."

"Why?" Bobby asked. "Why would she send us off and stay behind?"

"I don't know. Maybe it was the only way she could help us. Maybe we were too close to it."

Bobby's head clouded in a swirl and his knees were suddenly jelly-like and wouldn't support him.

"Whoa!" Tucker grabbed his arm and held him up. "What's wrong?"

Bobby felt a hot pain in his side. When he pulled his hand away, his palm was bloody. "What happened?"

Collette lifted his shirt and pressed her hand against a deep cut on his side. "Get him down." Bobby sat painfully and Tucker eased him to lay down. "This," Collette took the silver triangle from Bobby's punctured shirt pocket, the last piece of the key for which Ona had nearly killed them all. "You must have landed on it."

"You can heal that," Tucker said, examining the wound on Bobby's side. "It's not too deep."

Bobby winced and pressed the back of his head into the dirt, trying to get away from Collette's healing. "Feels deep. Feels like fire."

"Shush," Collette scolded him gently. "It won't hurt for long. Tucker's right, it's not very deep. Nothing important has been punctured."

"Except me," Bobby said from between gritted teeth. "Ah!

Stop!"

Collette didn't stop and even had the nerve to smile at Bobby's discomfort.

You might want to keep it down, Tucker teased him. *She's going to think you're a wimp.*

I don't care what she thinks, Bobby answered, but he didn't make another sound while Collette worked.

Tucker glanced at his brother's side when Collette removed her hands. *She's good.*

Bobby held his breath a moment longer, then slowly released the air when he felt that the pain was gone.

When will this be over? When can we go home? Bobby spoke the words privately. There was only one person he trusted with this weakness.

We can do this, Tucker checked his brother's pulse and then patted him on the shoulder. "You're exhausted. It's been, well, it's been a long time since we've been able to take a deep breath."

"Sorry I yelled at you," Bobby apologized to Collette as he sat up slowly.

"Tucker's right," Collette said, ignoring his apology and making him feel worse. "You're exhausted. We should try to find some shelter."

"How?" Tucker looked around.

"You're an Earth mage," she spoke to Bobby. "Listen or feel, whatever it is you do, for the vibrations."

Tucker raised his eyebrows in surprise. "Does that make sense to you?" he asked his brother.

"Yeah," Bobby blushed. *I just can't seem to think straight. Such a fool!*

Don't be too hard on yourself, Tucker encouraged him. *This is some seriously strange stuff.*

Bobby ignored Tucker. Kneeling, he placed his hands on the hot earth and allowed his element to wander out. For several minutes he explored the surface terrain. A dim quiver of footsteps reverberated in the west.

"That way," he pointed.

Tucker tossed the silver triangle into the air and caught it. "I'll hold onto this. Although, I think we should bury it out here in the middle of nowhere."

"Let's find out where we are first." Collette started walking in the direction Bobby indicated. "This might not be 'nowhere'."

⏴⏵

The sun shone relentlessly on the three mages as they walked through foreign lands in the direction Bobby said they should go. As the Earth mage, his directional skills were best—or so he hoped. The landscape was harsh. Not Sahara-harsh with its great dunes and no vegetation, but dry and hot. Tumbleweeds skipped along the hardened sand, chasing just ahead of the wind in an endless game of tag. The sun beat down on them without remorse. Bobby felt his face and neck tighten with sunburn.

"How far do you think we have to go?" Collette asked.

"I have no idea," Bobby said. "I just know that somewhere in this direction, we'll find people."

"But how far?" she repeated.

"I've never been here before," Bobby snapped at her. "And I don't have the map anymore. I'm not a guide."

Collette stopped walking. "I'm not entirely sure how it's done, but we might be able to work it out."

"Fine," Bobby said, tossing his hands in the air. "What do I do?"

"Alright," Collette cleared her throat and looked around. "Are you good with maps?"

Tucker laughed. "Is he? Before any hikes or road trips, he memorizes the maps. We never need one because he has them

57

crammed in his head."

"Then you'll make a map in your head based on what you sense."

"And how do I do that?" Bobby asked.

"I really have no idea," Collette answered. "Both of my parents were Water mages. Let's keep walking. You can practice reaching out with your elemental intent and mapping it. Reach out and select a landmark. Maybe a particular shrub or a land formation. Then when we reach that spot, you'll be able to measure that distance."

Bobby nodded. "If I can determine how far a small distance is, then I can just amplify that to reach out to something. Hopefully something helpful."

"Yes, exactly," Collette said.

Bobby placed his hands on the ground and looked toward the horizon. There wasn't much on the surface that stood out, just a dry sea of scraggly plants and cacti. It was what lay under the surface that was interesting. For a landscape that seemed so barren, it was teeming with life just beneath the surface: a burrow of coyotes, several desert mouse dens, insects galore, snakes and scorpions—all were comfortable in the shade of their dugouts. Bobby smiled as his elemental 'stroll' through the earth disturbed the creatures from their sleep. He felt the insects flutter into a frenzy, the mother coyote wake and check her little ones, the snakes freeze as they waited for the sensation to pass. Closing his eyes, Bobby practiced transferring images of the layout into a map in his head. Having the layout of the underground network of dens and burrows wouldn't help him much. It was like Collette suggested, a small shrub or a large boulder that he used as markers.

A short while later, Bobby was fairly certain he knew the distance to the village. "This is amazing!" he said. "Worthmere never told me that mapping it out was possible."

Tucker wiped his forehead. "You know Worthmere. He preferred that we learn things on our own."

"Well," Bobby said, "I think he should have made an exception. This is very helpful."

"How far?" Collette asked.

"About eight miles."

No one liked that news. Tired feet and parched throats grew more extreme at the thought of walking eight more miles in the barren land.

Silan the Original

Bobby knew they were close, but he feared the village wouldn't be close enough. His mental map of the earth revealed that the village was quite still—the people were either resting in the heat of the high sun or there just weren't that many people. He hoped there was water—water by the bucket.

Thirst was an angry beast within him. Even his eyes were thirsty, dry and scratchy as he blinked and squinted. Collette stopped asking "How much farther?" and settled into a glazed-over walk.

Bobby glanced at Tucker. *Can you make it?* he asked.

Do we have a choice?

I'm thinking we should stop and wait for night. It will be cooler. It would be easier to walk if I didn't feel like an advertisement for human leather.

Probably, Tucker answered. *But we've already come this far. And I'd rather come to this village in the daylight. Seems safer.*

Bobby nodded. *I'm not sure how much we'll find there. It feels very still.*

Abandoned?

Something or someone is there. Just not many.

Trouble?

Bobby shrugged. *We'll know soon.*

Sometime later, Bobby stopped his forward stumble. Tucker almost didn't notice. His eyes were nearly closed as they made their way through the arid land. "What?" Tucker's throat was so parched it hurt to talk.

He kneeled and placed his hands on the earth. *Someone's coming,* Bobby answered.

Dangerous?

Could be if we don't respond right. Bobby said. *He feels angry. Anxious.*

"What's going on?" Collette asked, unaware of the silent conversation.

"Someone is coming straight toward us," Bobby said. "Be on your guard."

"I feel useless. I'm a water mage and I don't even have enough spit to wet my tongue."

Standing, Bobby wiped the dust off his hands. "There," he looked at the horizon where the silhouette of a man was just visible.

As the man came nearer, Bobby saw that he wasn't much older than they. He was slender and dark, young with sinewy muscles. His clothing was simple but well made. His pants were made of animal skin and his loose shirt looked odd with the pants, reminding Bobby and Tucker of pictures of children in Africa wearing an assortment of donated clothing. His long, black hair was braided in four braids from his forehead, over the top of his head and down his back. Although Bobby and Tucker were bigger they both knew that this man could beat them both in a fight.

Fierce. It was always just a word to Bobby, like Tucker's

fierce appetite, but now he saw it illustrated in every aspect of this being's posture and glare. The young man held a long staff in one hand and walked as if he was ready to pounce, should anyone give him reason. It wasn't the twins for which this native was challenging with his stance; it was Collette.

Tucker stepped in front of Collette and stared back, keeping his hands at his sides. If this person was a mage, raised hands meant an attack, unlike back home where it meant 'I mean no harm.' The man lowered his staff and straightened his body.

"Do you understand me?" Tucker asked.

The man nodded. "I do." He studied them, their clothing, their skin color and Collette. "Your faces." He looked at Bobby, then Tucker, then back to Bobby. "You share the same face," he spoke slowly, trying to pronounce each word correctly. It was obvious that English was not his native language.

"We're brothers," Bobby and Tucker said at the same time.

"Where are your foods?"

"We, um," Tucker looked to Bobby for help in explaining how they came to be in a desert without anything.

"We were abandoned here," Bobby said.

"Abandoned?" he repeated, frowning.

"Left behind. The people we were with are gone."

"Dead?" he asked.

"No," Bobby said. "Just gone. We don't know where."

"Can you tell us where we are?" Collette asked him.

The man turned his attention back to her and gripped the staff tighter. "Keep your place!" he spoke through gritted teeth.

Tucker held his hand out. "Calm down, she's just—"

"No woman may speak out of proper turn. You must know this."

"Where we come from, women are equal with men," Tucker said.

"That is for your people," the man said, eyeing the brothers with scorn. "But here among the sands, men stand tall. Women wash our feet."

Collette's jaw dropped open. "How dare you!"

"Silence!" The man thrust his staff toward her, but Tucker grabbed the end. Both Bobby and Collette felt the heat from Tucker's elemental intent gather as he released scalding flames up the staff. The man dropped the staff like a poisonous snake and staggered back. "You are Originals."

Bobby and Tucker looked to Collette for an explanation.

"He means mages. There are several tribes in the Second Terrace who call mages Originals."

"You mean not all mages are in the Society?" Bobby asked.

"No. It has to do with religious practices." She turned to the man. "We are Originals. All of us. In my terrace I am a healer. You will speak to me with respect."

"I will honor my brothers and sisters of the earth," he acknowledged, but he said 'sisters' like it tasted bad. "My name is Silan."

"I'm Collette; this is Bobby and Tucker. Silan, we are in need of nourishment."

Silan took an animal skin sack off his shoulder and handed it to Tucker, who accepted it but handed it to Collette first. "It's common to allow the women to drink first," Tucker said.

Frowning, Silan scoffed. "Why?"

"Because it shows the woman respect. It shows that you put her before yourself."

Looking at Collette, Silan seemed to almost laugh at the idea. "A woman, better than a man?" He shook his head. "Perhaps you do not understand because you are not whole."

Bobby and Tucker looked to Collette again for a translation.

"He means that because you are twins," she said. "Some of the more simp...ah, secluded cultures believe that twins are really one person divided into two beings."

63

"You *teach* these Originals?" Silan asked Collette.

"Teaching them isn't easy. I am traveling with them."

"Ah," Silan seemed satisfied. "Slave."

Tucker opened his mouth to argue, but Collette stopped him. "Save your breath. I appreciate the attempt to teach him something worthwhile, but you can't undo years of traditions with one little conversation." She took a drink from the animal skin and made a face. Tucker understood why when he took a drink; the water was not the crystal clean, bottled goodness they had at home, or even the crisp refreshment from a river. It tasted like dirt. Bobby didn't seem to notice the earthy taste.

"I'll take you to my grandfather." Silan started to walk back in the direction from which he had come, but he turned his head to talk to the brothers. "He will want to meet the Legends."

"What Legends?" Bobby asked.

Silan frowned. "I am just a young Original. My grandfather has much wisdom. He will tell you." He turned again and led them to his village.

"Any memory of Legends?" Bobby asked Collette.

"It's probably about your being twins," Collette said. "The idea of two people having identical features is the source of many legends in mythology. Of course, it's all nonsense," Collette said. "The idea of dual powers and the sanguis myth."

"Anna never told us anything about myths of twins in the Mage Society," Tucker said.

"That's because they are *myths*," Bobby said. "Nothing true, just stories."

"Stories to explain that which is unexplainable," Collette said. "That's what Caladrius always said. He said that behind every story there was a sliver of truth."

"So, I'll ask again," Tucker said. "Do you know what stories this terrace might have about twins?"

"Not specifically," Collette said.

"What about un-specifically?" Tucker asked.

"Myths of twins usually deal with duality," Collette said. "The concept of opposites. Sometimes the twins are stronger than others because they can share thoughts or abilities. I think Silan believes that you are one person in two bodies. A birth which gave you more than one element, making you more powerful, but also limits your abilities because you can never be complete, can never be one. There are some terraces that destroy twins at birth for fear of the wrath they might bring."

"You're joking!" Tucker said. "I thought stuff like that stopped way back with the Spartans."

"Some Terraces and cultures within each terrace are probably very Spartan-like," Bobby explained.

"Right." Tucker sighed. "Let's hope that this Terrace and this culture isn't like that."

"I think we are in the Second Terrace," Collette said quietly. "If we are, I would welcome a Spartan mentality."

"Why?" Bobby asked.

"The Great Scourge happened about thirty years ago in the Second Terrace. Thousands of mages were killed. Even today mages don't travel to certain regions of the Second Terrace. Tensions are still high."

Bobby looked around. "Where in the Second Terrace did the Scourge happen?"

Collette shook her head. "Everywhere."

Fence of Bone

They walked toward a river, then followed the slow, muddy waters upstream to Silan's village, which was surrounded by a mud-packed wall with thorny sticks and cactus spines coating the exterior in spiky armor. Within the walls, a collection of tiny homes built of mud bricks and mud mortar were succumbing to the natural elements the way mud does.

Unlike the neat rows and stacks of square adobe homes that lined the streets in Terrace One, these homes looked like giant piles of dung hollowed out for living space. Remembering the slums outside Delphi which were constructed of manure bricks, Tucker instinctively held his breath, but he eventually grew light-headed and cautiously tested the air. If the homes were made of dung, they had apparently lost any stench under the bleaching power of the sun. It was the smell of unwashed bodies and heat that filled his nose.

"I don't like this place," Collette whispered.

Silan glared at her.

"He's already furious when you speak," Bobby said quietly. "Maybe you shouldn't say anything bad about his village."

"Well," she whispered, blushing at having been reprimanded, "don't you agree? Something is wrong here."

The doors of the homes were low to keep the hot air outside. Women sat on the thresholds of their abodes and watched their children play dusty games while weaving or grinding or cooking over tiny stoves contained in hollowed-out stones. All the villagers stopped their activities and watched as Silan led Bobby, Tucker, and Collette to his home. Collette nervously tucked her hair behind her ear and played with the ends. The women here were shaved bald. Even little girls were bald. Tucker walked close to Collette, staring sharply at the people who glared at her long tresses.

Maybe we should have just kept walking, Tucker said to Bobby.

To where? Bobby asked. *It was follow him or die of thirst. Let's just respect their culture and move on as quickly as we can.*

A small hut on the far end of the village stood apart from the others, divided by a low fence constructed of stones and bones. The hut was different from all the others and could have been a cozy get-a-way with the tiny flowers growing as close to the little hut as possible. Built from stones instead of mud bricks and having a cloth door instead of no door, Silan's home appeared to be a refuge in a sea of scorched earth.

A young girl sat under the shade of a thin tarp, pounding a meager handful of grain into flour. Like the other women, her head was clean shaven and she watched them carefully as they entered the small, stone house.

Look at her eyes, Bobby said.

One dark brown and one blue eye.

A Painter? Tucker asked. *Out here?*

"Who is that?" Bobby asked Silan.

"A disgrace."

"What?" Collette asked. "Why?"

Silan's nostril's flared. "To speak to a girl about a girl." He shook with frustration. "Her gift is useless. Her eyes do not match. Disgrace."

Their hostile host led them through the cloth door and into the surprisingly cool shade within the tiny home. All the furniture was low to the ground; a flattened rock table sat nestled into the earth holding two cups and plates. Along the far wall were two thick mats with woven blankets folded in the center. On one mat sat a tiny wrinkle of a man, mostly hidden in the cool darkness.

"Grandfather," Silan said to the dark figure. "They are here."

A flint stone sparked and a small lantern was expertly lit, revealing a face marked with countless decades in the sun. The old man smiled a wide toothless grin when he saw Bobby and Tucker. Silan introduced his grandfather. "Nunco. Gatekeeper."

That's one of the Red Men, Bobby said to Tucker.

Collette nudged Tucker's arm. "Bow your heads. Acknowledge his greeting." They did as they were told.

"Three. Not right number," Nunco said, his voice as wrinkled as his skin.

Bobby looked at Silan for an explanation. Silan frowned, "You know number?"

Bobby exchanged looks with Tucker. "Of course I know the number three. But it obviously has a greater significance to you."

"Four is count of Mother," Silan explained. "Four children, four faces, four offerings."

Tucker stared blankly at Silan, "The Mother?"

Nunco spoke eagerly. "The Mother. All we need."

Tucker looked at Bobby. "Any clue?"

"Nope."

"Your mentors have taught you nothing," Collette said.

"You know 'The Mother'?" Bobby asked.

"Of course," Collette said, scowling at the insult. "The Mother is the natural world. The four children are the seasons, four faces—"

"The directions," Bobby interrupted. "North, south, east, west."

"And the offerings must be the elements," Tucker concluded.

"Where is the white one?" Nunco asked. "The one who pulled the light from the sky?"

Bobby shifted his weight uncomfortably. "We don't know."

Nunco stared at them, searching their eyes for more. "You have key?"

Lie, Bobby said.

"It was taken," Tucker said, feeling the weight of a fourth of the key against his chest.

Nunco leaned forward, his eyes darkening, fearful or maybe angry, it was difficult to read his expression, but it was clear this was very bad news.

"No key. No good." Nunco closed his eyes and shook his head.

"There's more," Bobby continued. "the white one, sent us here by accident. We need to find her."

Silan looked at Bobby and stood. "Sent you here? Through a gateway?"

"I'm not sure."

"Storm." Nunco looked up, his cataracts glossing his vision. "She called the storm. Very dangerous."

"Victoria's not dangerous," Bobby said, "just—"

Just what? Tucker asked. *The girl can pull lightning from the sky. I love her too, but that does sound dangerous.*

"Victoria," Nunco repeated. He said nothing else as he seemed to have fallen asleep with his eyes open.

"Victoria," Bobby said again. "We need to find her. Is there a gateway nearby?"

"You chase heart. That help only one." Nunco leaned forward. "You very strong. Strength in heart, but there is weakness too. The balance shifts around and inside. Mind lead.

Heart guide. Decide what you follow. One lead to life, other end life." Nunco sat back, breathing deeply. "Nunco's knowledge of Originals is not same as yours."

"What now?" Bobby asked, feeling every bit of hope dry up like the land outside.

"Best wait," Nunco said. "Eat. Drink. Sleep. Tomorrow, answer will come."

As long as the answer isn't armed and dangerous, Tucker thought.

Bobby agreed. *Food and sleep sounds good.*

Silan stomped to the far end of the room and tossed a few scraps of cloth onto the floor. "You stay here. She will give you food later," he nodded toward his sister who was peeking through the door.

"What are these for?" Collette asked.

"Sleep."

They all looked past Silan at the thread-bare cloth on the dirt floor. "Well," Collette cleared her throat, "I'm sure we'll sleep very well tonight."

Silan grunted an acknowledgment of Collette's gratitude and left the little house.

"Where is he going?" Tucker asked Nunco.

"Silan offers his gift to the waters. He tries to bring rain." Nunco spat on the ground. "He is not strong. Weak like father. People die."

"How long since the last rain?" Bobby asked.

"Seven moons."

"Why don't you leave? Find better water?"

"Ancestors are here." Nunco pointed outside. All three mages looked through the little window to the fence that surrounded Nunco's house. The bones.

೮つC೪

70

They remained inside, grateful for the shade and wishing Silan would suddenly become the most powerful mage of all time and bring enough water to fill every cup in the village. Instead of dwelling on their thirst and hunger, they made small talk. They moved to the farthest corner of the hut. Nunco seemed to be sleeping, so they kept their voices low.

"Have you been outside your terrace before?" Tucker asked.

"No." Collette said softly. "I'm still training with Caladrius. I was supposed to travel with him next year to the sphinx city."

"How are we going to find Victoria?" Tucker whispered.

"She could be anywhere," Bobby said. "She might still be with Caladrius. She might have gone farther than we did. If that happened, she's alone and will need help. We can't just wait here."

"But that *is* what we will do." Collette said. She turned and faced the brothers. "You are from Terrace Four, aren't you?"

"Why?"

"Caladrius told me that mages from Terrace Four are impatient."

"Victoria needs us," Bobby said.

"What she needs is for you to follow what is in front of you. We are here with Nunco. Perhaps we will learn something valuable."

"Or it could be a huge waste of time."

"What would you do right now to find Victoria? Which direction would you go? Where is the nearest gateway? How do we learn where Victoria went? Go ahead and rush off. Or, you can wait and see if there is something here we can learn."

Bobby remained restless. "We should ask the old man what the silver triangle is."

Tucker put his hand to his shirt where the cold metal pressed against his skin. "Do you think that's a good idea? I mean, he was pretty angry that we were the wrong number. If he finds out we don't even know what this thing is, we might become another addition to that bone fence out there."

Collette shivered. "We keep that to ourselves. There is so much more going on here than we know. It doesn't help that you two are like infants." Collette scolded them like Anna did when they trained at the sphinx city. "It's like you just walked through your first gateway yesterday."

"It *was* only about a month ago when Lucian attacked Victoria and Tucker," Bobby said.

"And thanks to that terrifying experience," Tucker added, "we've been enrolled in the elemental crash course."

"Well, you're still alive," Collette said. "You are either quick learners or lucky."

"I'm Lucky," Tucker said. "He's Quick Learner."

Collette sighed. "I guess that makes me Still Alive."

A Lie of Honor

Hours later, Parnassus returned from the Elder's Circle and Anna and Worthmere cornered him immediately. "Why didn't you tell us?"

Looking at Anna with compassion, he sighed. "I assume you are questioning my silence in regards to the parentage of your young apprentices."

Not amused by Parnassus' calmness, she crossed her arms and waited for an explanation.

"It's not what you think," he started, but Anna interrupted him.

"I certainly hope not. Xander Veracitous was a good man. Adam Caius was a thief. I've never believed that Adam could kill anyone, but to think that he is the boys' father?"

"You're right that he never killed anyone, let alone Xander. And he was a great thief, but he didn't work alone."

"You're telling us Xander and Adam were in on it together?" Worthmere asked.

"They were two of the three responsible," Parnassus

admitted.

"Whoa," Worthmere held up his hands. "You? You were a part of that?"

"What are you talking about?" Anna asked.

"The scrolls that Adam stole from the library. No one ever figured out how he did it and there still isn't any solid proof that it was him. But when Xander was sent after him to bring him to be questioned by the Elders and the Council, Adam retaliated and Xander was critically wounded, but not before he sent a mortal blow to Adam. They both died—wait." Worthmere looked up, doing the calculations in his head. "They can't be the fathers. Victoria and the twins are too young."

"Exactly," Parnassus said. "That story of both of them fighting to the death was the story I fed to the Council and the Elders. In truth, Adam and I stole the scrolls and he left with them for safe keeping. He knew that if he were believed to be dead, the scrolls would be safer. No one would look for him. Xander was here when on a mission for the Council, shortly before Lucian's sister was killed. When he and Diana returned here afterwards, we came up with that story to protect them both. Xander and Diana went to the Fourth Terrace to help Adam keep the scrolls safe. The children were born a few years after they went into hiding."

"Lucian," Anna repeated.

Parnassus looked sadly at Anna. "Yes. He was found accidentally. To protect the scrolls from being found, he took the full blame so that I could continue to protect the Library and the Map of Art."

Anna's face reddened. She had been the one to paint Lucian's prison. "He was innocent the entire time."

"He didn't want you involved," Parnassus told her. "He knew that Ona was seeking the Grandfather's Weapon. His own sister was killed in the attempt to open the gateway just outside of

Kivavallis. Lucian was afraid you would get hurt if he told you any of this."

Anna stared at Parnassus for a long moment. As tears welled in her eyes, she turned and slowly walked into the house.

Parnassus shook his head and looked down. "I never wanted to lie to her, but I made a promise to Lucian."

"You probably saved her life by keeping that promise," Worthmere said. "Where are the scrolls now?"

"I sent two Guards after them shortly after you arrived here with the children. I had hoped they would return by now."

RIVER OF BLOOD

Silan returned late in the evening, sweating profusely from his failed efforts to pull even a drop of rain from the sky. He sulked about, ordering his useless sister to prepare a meal. No one dared to complain about the bits of dried meat, pasty beans and silty water. It was a feast for famished travelers. The sister cleaned the dishes and tidied the house, refusing to allow Collette to help. They slept surprisingly well on the hard ground thanks to the meager dinner and exhaustion.

As the sun awoke the earth and began yet another stampede of heat across the landscape, the air was thick, as if they had cotton stuffed in their ears. It was different from the quiet in the early hours before dawn. This was not a peaceful silence. Silan stood at the door, tense and silent.

"Did something happen?" Tucker asked Silan.

"Yes." Silan scanned the village with sharp eyes.

"What?"

He shook his head, frowning.

If Tucker had learned anything about Silan, it was that he was a man of few words. Whereas Bobby spouted information to anyone with ears, Silan willingly shared only the air they breathed. Nunco, with a long stick in hand, walked past Silan and toward the river. The four mages followed, Silan's sister behind them.

If yesterday's walk through the slums seemed depressing, then today was sinister. Just as Bobby opened his mouth to ask Silan a question, a scream tore through the village, rousing everyone into action. Silan ran toward the river with the other mages close behind.

The cringing smell of panic was more intense as they approached the river. Another odor, deeper than dead fish or river muck lingered in the air. Iron—sharp and cold and reeking of death.

Several women held clay pitchers and stared at the river, tears streaming down their cheeks. A river of blood oozed by the bank, edged with a wall of dead fish. As they approached, one of the older women turned to Nunco and yelled.

Silan looked sadly at the shore, the dark red stains still clinging to the sludge along the bank.

"Blood." Bobby said.

Nunco walked to the river, touched the surface of the water, and examined his fingers. Bobby had read about Moses and the Nile turning to blood, but he had always imagined just red water, like food coloring in a glass of water. This was nothing like that. The river flowed slowly by, a deeper red than the color of blood when it drips off a paper cut. Nunco's fingers, the sand, the rocks, the dead fish, and the birds were all coated in blood. The source of life, that precious liquid flowing through all veins, had choked everything in and near the river, bringing death.

"What does this mean?" Collette asked.

Nunco pulled himself to standing with Silan's help and turned to the mages. "You brought death." Nunco shook off Silan's hand and glared at him. "Go! You brought this evil upon us. Do not return until you rid our land of these devils."

Silan stared open-mouthed at Nunco. The villagers who had gathered around the river had stood silently at the bloody waters until Nunco yelled. Then they awoke from their shock with a violent anger and started throwing rocks at the mages. The first stone hit Collette in the leg. Tucker reached for Collette and pulled her away from the river, covering her with his own body best he could as they ran.

The villagers did not follow, but the stones they cast found their mark even after the mages ran through the gate of the cactus and mud wall. Slowing only after the sounds of the screaming villagers died away, the mages assessed their injuries. Collette had a few bruises and one cut below her cheek. The bruises needed a compress, but as there were no supplies for healing treatment, they suffered without.

"Go!" Silan shouted and pointed in a general direction.

"Aren't you coming with us?" Collette asked.

Silan's mouth twitched. "No! I will redeem my honor. Go!"

"We should stay together."

Silan deflated. "My gift." He looked back to where the river lay. "My gift is dead."

"Just here," Tucker said. "Once you are away from here it will come back."

"There is no water for me outside my people's land," Silan said, taking a step back. "You caused this. Remember the screams of my people. Our blood is upon your souls." Silan continued to walk backwards. "Go!" He pointed. "Find another place. Maybe *they* will kill you. Maybe they will not know what you are." Silan backed away from the mages until he reached a different path leading away from the village. He turned and ran, not going home and not coming with them.

"Now what do we do?" Collette asked, her voice precariously balanced between control and tears.

"We go in that direction," Tucker said.

"Alone?" she asked.

"No. Together."

Collette looked at Tucker, a glimmer of trust growing in her eyes.

"Where?" Bobby looked around. "Do we trust Silan that the people in that direction won't kill us? Or that there even are people out there?"

"We should be able to manage," Tucker said.

"How?" Bobby asked.

"Like we always do," Tucker said. "On the backs of prayers."

DROWNING IN RAINDROPS

Ambrosia took her time in the garden. She had been unable to focus her thoughts long enough to remain in her meditation garden. Like a plague of unruly cats, her thoughts went whichever way they wished. She had instructed countless mages on the skills necessary for focus and peace of mind, yet here she was, incapable of allowing her mind to slip into prayerful concentration. Instead of fretting, she left her dwelling and wandered among her garden. The aromas from the roses, violets, and chrysanthemums calmed her as she walked under the apple tree branches that bent toward the ground. The fall crop would be abundant.

The flowers seemed dull today, and not just from the lack of sunshine. Even the harvest of eggplant and okra didn't bring a sense of joy to her heart. The kale was wilting and a fresh swarm of tiny beetles had descended on the vegetables.

She wondered if anything would ever make her smile again. It was peak blooming season and many vegetables hung heavily on vines or lay near to rotting on the ground.

So wasteful to allow the food to go for so long unattended,

she scolded herself.

Despite her regret for the waste, she couldn't bring herself to do anything about it. What good would it do to harvest green beans now? Would the watermelons restore her father's name? With her father excommunicated from the Elder's Circle and with Anna and Worthmere imprisoned, why would anyone care about a tomato?

No sphinx had even been dismissed from the Circle or fully excommunicated. There had been a few threats to previous Elders, and their lives had been utterly destroyed because of it. But to have been convicted of treason—there was no comparison for the height of that shame.

Shame. Ambrosia thought about that. She didn't feel ashamed.

She knew her father had been right to give Worthmere and Victoria the Map of Art. A chuckle escaped her as she remembered Tucker's teasing about the sphinx's way of naming things.

"Seriously? Sphinx City. Circle Lake. Hall of Art," he had laughed. "Not much for naming things."

Ambrosia frowned. "What else would you call a round lake?"

Tucker thought for a moment. "Who founded this city?"

"The sphinx."

"Yes, but which one? Why not name the city after a sphinx who established it? Or the Hall of Art could be named after the Sphinx who designed the building."

"Well," Ambrosia had thought back to the history of the city. "There was one sphinx who first had the idea that we build our dwellings in a circle. That was Elder Wrungbuttle."

Tucker laughed. "Wrungbuttle-ville."

Ambrosia smiled, catching on. "Or Wrungbuttle-ton."

"Given the option, Sphinx City *is* the better choice," Tucker said.

"But that is not the name of this city," Ambrosia told him. "That's just what we call it, what everyone calls our city. *The* sphinx city, not Sphinx City, a proper noun. The true name is protected."

The memory brightened her mood for a moment.

That is the problem with the Sphinx Elders, Ambrosia thought. Everything is right or wrong, yes or no. And yet they don't see the details within the culture of mages that are leading to a fallout. Hidden mages and terraces where they can hide among the electrical fields. Who could ever guess how many mages are still alive that the Council believe to be dead? What the Elders need is a bright, shiny, can't-ignore-this kind of event. No, Ambrosia shook her head. Be careful what you wish for. Her father had always said, "A wish may seem to bring an answer, but it comes with many friends—mostly unwanted."

"It will happen regardless," she said aloud.

"And what would that be?" a familiar voice asked from across the hedgerow.

"Elder Amberson," Ambrosia blushed. "I'm afraid you've caught me talking to myself."

"I find those conversations to be the most invigorating," he smiled. "How are you managing?"

Elder Amberson had been her mentor. He still was, in a manner of speaking, the way a teacher will always be a teacher to a student. "Not very well. It appears that this is my first true test for focusing on my prayer time. I'm finding it increasingly frustrating."

"I understand." He walked closer and Ambrosia met him at the hedgerow. "If I may offer a sprinkle of advice?"

Ambrosia nodded.

"It is during these times that we must not worry about the outcome of our meditation. Our prayer may not be demonstrated in a manipulation of the elements, but that doesn't mean that our time in prayer is wasted."

"You are talking of the guidance of the Creator."

"I am. There is value in the time spent in prayer, the quietness it brings to your heart, the value of this effort in doing nothing else, except listening to God." Elder Amberson allowed her the time to think about what he had said.

"I know what you are saying is right," Ambrosia finally responded. "But the more powerful desire in my heart is for action, not silent prayer."

"Ah," Elder Amberson winked. "Who said it had to be silent?"

Ambrosia eyed him suspiciously. "You have a plan."

"I do. But I cannot help you with it at all. If you succeed, you might save your father's life and reputation, which the other Elders so stupidly lump together as the same thing. It is not."

"And Anna and Worthmere?" she asked.

"Well, I don't know if it's that good of a plan." He looked across the wide lawn at the Library of Ages. "How brave do you feel?"

"Like a thousand spears would never pierce me," she hesitated, "and like a raindrop would drown me."

"Excellent. Let's get started."

End of an Era

Nuri paced in his room. Delphi, in the Third Terrace, was quaint in its furnishings: simple architecture, simple travel, simple people. Even the sphinx in all their wisdom remained simple. They held fast to the old laws, the old ways. Up until now, the simplicity of the sphinx had frustrated him. Why didn't they advance in their ways? Why did they insist on keeping their noses pressed to the pages of the books they held so dear?

It used to bother him—all their traditions and adherence to the law. That had changed when Ona converted one of the Elders to her way of thinking. Her plan, at its core, was to seek freedom from the laws. Selling that idea to key figures throughout the Mage Society had taken years of careful selection and conversation. Slowly, the Elders opened the Circle to younger sphinx, allowing them to ask questions about proceedings and then encouraging them to question the proceedings. Apprenticeship was the backbone of the Mage Society, but Junior Elders were not apprentices. They were given the right to question authority without even having been given the information of what authority's role was and why it should be respected.

Nuri had earned his authority and under the shift toward freedom from the laws, he prided his ability to keep his status at all costs.

The installation of the Junior Elders was a great boon to Ona's cause but it was the Junior Elders who decided to forestall the soldiers' training on the ideal that knowledge was the superior power.

Nuri had been stunned when he learned that the sphinx trials were called off. For the first time the training for competition of soldier rankings and promotions would not take place.

Everyone was so overwhelmed with the changes among the sphinx that no one paid attention to the Janus Guard. While the sphinx lessened their army and spread the power of their government thinly over Elders and Juniors, Ona increased her army of Janus Guards by several species.

Well, at least, that was the plan. It had been almost a week since he had heard from Ona. He knew the first key lay hidden in four pieces in an Earth Gateway. He also knew what was needed to open that gateway. So many things could have gone wrong. He knew she wasn't dead. A woman with that amount of strength and that kind of determination would not be killed by three inexperienced mages. Lucian was there too, he reminded himself. He was a very strong mage. Ona had greater plans than to die at the hands of a traitor like Lucian.

If anyone was stubborn enough to hold off death, it was Ona. He smiled at that idea, an image of her crossing her arms across her chest, throwing her weight onto one hip and staring down Death like a disobedient child.

No, she's not dead, he told himself, but something did go wrong. Terribly wrong. There was no other reason why she hadn't contacted him.

He still felt her blood pumping through his veins, the power of her element still very much alive within him. It felt good, that constant connection, assurance of her life. Not to mention the heightened elemental intent of his own gift. Unfortunately, being a Sanguis mage didn't help him to find her. Both he and Ona were Fire mages, which made them formidable in a battle but did little to track each other across terraces. That, in Nuri's opinion, was the only useful talent of Earth mages.

He still remembered the burning fury of the flame the first time he called his element after the Sanguis ceremony. They stood outside, far from Kivavallis with a small, lit candle. With only a thought, the flame burst outward. It consumed the air, ate through the walls, exploded like gun powder. He and Ona were thrown back by the force. As the air cleared, he slowly sat up, testing his arms and legs for broken bones. Crawling to Ona, he was afraid that her still form was all that was left of her. He quickly snuffed the small flames that ate at her clothing and checked her pulse. At his touch, her eyes fluttered open. He embraced her gently, but she didn't linger in the moment.

"You're hurt!" she winced in horror at his face.

"I know." He straightened his face of concern, knowing that any injury he had was nothing in comparison to the burns of his youth. He ached and was singed here and there, but that was a small price to pay for the enhanced gift of Fire. His badge of pride were the burn marks on his face from that first fire.

Their sacrifice to each other was not made out of love, she reminded him, but for duty. That was the only reason he was here in Delphi: duty. There were no mages here he cared to check on. The lie to Worthmere about his visit here was just another pebble on a mountain of lies. There was a Painter, just as there always was in larger cities, but he would not trouble her. The greater duty was to find Ona and learn anything he could from Ophidia. He had been to see her several times throughout the years and it still gave him chills. If Ophidia could help him find Ona and gain the

Grandfather's Weapon, it would be worth every slithering chill.

Nuri knew that Worthmere didn't trust him. Worthmere was old school, tied down by the laws of the society and green to the core.

But he also saw that tender moment between Worthmere and Anna. Interesting. Anna was a formidable opponent to finding and using the Grandfather's Weapon. Ona knew that Anna had researched the Weapon after Lucian's imprisonment. If she pieced together the other events, then they did have a problem on their hands. Ona had used Anna's curiosity to seek out Victoria. As much as he hoped Ona was okay, he knew Victoria was more important in finding the Weapon. To gain Victoria's allegiance would practically seal their success.

Success was a prize to be won; a prize frustratingly difficult to win.

There was nothing he could do until he received a message through Ophidia. For some reason, he was denied entrance into the amphitheater. He returned the second day, walking the narrow paths to Apollo's Garden, washed in the first fountain, drank from the second and then waited. He knew Ophidia's assistants saw him; he made eye contact with each of them, using expression alone to show the urgency of his mission. But his agenda was of no concern to Ophidia. She was at the mercy of her visions. And so, he waited.

Waiting in Apollo's Garden was torture for Nuri. The flowers were just passed their peak bloom; the grass was thick and warm under the sun, which blazed brightly. The lush peace in the garden allowed Nuri's mind to wander to his youth, the days when he could sit among the tall rushes and hide from his parents. His mother had grown hollyhocks along the south wall of the cottage, much like the tall blossoms along the wall in Apollo's garden. Painful memories of being ripped from his parents during a revolt against a community of mages in the

Second Terrace haunted his thoughts.

It had happened in other places in every century. Nuri knew that now, but that knowledge granted no consolation. Pulled from their beds, their houses were burned, they were told to leave and the mages could do nothing to protect themselves or their belongings. It was against the laws. All night he had listened to his mother try to comfort his sister over the loss of their dog, a Labrador who had tried to protect his family.

The sky that night was bright with the flames that cut and burned through every shred of wood, paper, and cloth, leaving only a black mark on the earth. At seven, Nuri suspected he was a fire mage and felt sick for weeks at the destruction his elemental gift could cause. He never wanted to use it.

The mage community banded together to travel to the next city to a friend of his father's, a mage who had a mirror and a painting. They would find refuge elsewhere. But the vengeful villagers had other plans. Burning their houses was just the beginning. Ridding their village of the mages was not enough. As the sun set on that first day of travel, the sound of horses bearing down on them sent the mages running for shelter among the low bushes of the prairie.

It was too much for his father. He stood tall on the land that day and pulled to him every drop of blood and tears the villagers had spilled. As they approached, he sent out an earthquake that shook for miles. The men were knocked off their horses; beasts without broken legs scattered, leaving the men and their long weapons. Nuri's mother called for her husband to stop, to not hurt them because they didn't understand what they were doing. She later explained that his father did what he thought was necessary to save his family.

Among the confusion, the mages escaped and found safety in the Third Terrace among a city of mages. They became refugees, welcomed but receiving little help. Life was hard for mages in every terrace. To start from scratch was difficult and his mother never fully recovered. They had a home. It was small and built quickly along with several other structures to accommodate such a large number of people at once. It still confused Nuri why no one thought to build the refugees sturdier homes.

It had been years since he thought of those early days in the refugee camp. Shame made his heart thump. The same emotions he felt as a child—the helpless weakness he had endured—sickened him. Never again.

He stood, leaving the memory behind, and walked back to the fountain to wash his face. Maybe it was the water, he thought, that made the memories so vivid. It was necessary for the visions. His mentor had told him that long ago and he had forgotten until this moment.

Another memory lingered around him, teasing him with its clarity. His first vision from Ophidia was as clear in his mind today as it was the moment she placed her hand on his arm. Ona was a Council Mage in the vision and she was performing the Sanguis ceremony with him. Nuri was never one to believe any kind of prophetess, but two years later, he found himself realizing that vision as he and Ona slit their lifelines and connected their elements. It was an ancient ceremony, forgotten by most mages and discouraged by the Council, but Ona insisted upon it. They had a plan to find the Grandfather's Weapon. Being Sanguis Mages gave them an edge.

The first visit to Ophidia was mostly curiosity with a dash of a friendly wager. So many men he knew quaked at the knees at the mention of Ophidia. Absurd—to be afraid of a woman! That belief lasted until Ophidia touched his hand and was renewed when he understood the passion Ona felt for finding the Grandfather's Weapon.

He had wanted to stay in Kivavallis with Ona when she found Victoria in her garden, but she had insisted that he needed to come to Delphi. They needed a hint of what was coming. That's all Ophidia gave: hints. Her prophecies were vague and useless when they were misinterpreted, but they were always accurate. He knew from experience that it was unlikely he would understand the visions she would give him, but as the course of their mission continued, he needed to have the ability to recognize their path.

Later that afternoon, Ophidia's priestess finally summoned Nuri. With a sigh of relief, he followed. The dark hall to the temple was still dark. The snakes surrounding Ophidia lay contentedly around and over one another.

Ophidia was as stunning as ever. Even the sulfuric vapors didn't distract from her olive complexion. A small lump in his stomach twisted when they made eye contact. He knew what was coming. Her voice was so abrasive it sent debilitating shivers down the backs of his legs. She watched him approach. The last time Nuri came to Ophidia, she never looked at him, but this time she watched him carefully.

He bowed to her. She pulled a leaf off the branch in her hand and chewed it thoughtfully for a moment before reaching a trembling hand out and taking his hand. Waiting for the message, the vision from Ophidia, Nuri watched her mouth open wide in shock. A scream ripped through the air and Nuri nearly stumbled backwards from the fury of the vision.

A woman dressed in white stood in the middle of a circle of stones. No. Not one circle. Many circles. The outer circle, the fourth circle, was built with tall doorways, some made of stone, others of wood; a few were simply gaps in the earth or rips in the air. Through each door, a different land could be seen.

The woman in the center held a book. She read aloud. Nuri could see her lips moving, but he couldn't hear her voice. Around the circles, wind, fire, earth and water spun madly until she raised her hand to calm them. The elements settled into points on the edges of the circle, like the four points of a compass.

Nuri could see dead bodies sprawled on the ground, men and women, their faces hidden. The woman stood alone and continued to read from the book. She closed the book and planted a seed at her feet. A tree grew, stretching its branches to the sky like a giant waking from a nap.

Luscious fruit grew heavily on the branches, round and red and growing in clumps like grapes, but much larger.

Ophidia let go. Her scream still echoed through the cavernous room.

Nuri stared at her for a long moment. The vision meant nothing to him. Instead of answering his questions, it created more. Was the young woman in the vision Victoria? What were the stone circles? Where were they? Were they real or symbols for something else? He would report it to Ona; maybe she would understand the significance.

He bowed to Ophidia and turned to leave. He had nothing to fear from this place, but her eyes were as dark as hell itself. He hoped he would not be asked to return.

He stepped out of the temple. The sun was behind a thick cloud, the rays shooting out from behind like petals on a flower. Nuri closed his eyes and raised his face to the sky. The sun, the source of his power, warmed his body. How he loved to stand in its glow. Although the clouds hid some of the heat, it was enough to evaporate the damp darkness of Ophidia's temple until only a clammy memory remained.

A woman's scream pulled him back into the temple. Nuri was running toward the sound before he realized what he was doing. One of Ophidia's attendants ran down the dark hallway and right into him.

"What happened?" he asked.

"Dead! She's dead!" She pulled herself from Nuri's grip and ran out of the temple, her cries echoing off the stone walls. Nuri continued forward, passing the writhing snakes that twisted spastically over, under, and around each other.

Ophidia lay still, her skin and eyes gray except for two bloody puncture marks on her upper arm. The fissure in the ground, which had for thousands of years spewed toxic fumes, was still.

Nuri stood over her form, staring at the last descendant of Apollo's line of priestesses. He smiled. Things were shifting in their favor. Mages seeking any kind of knowledge about he and Ona and their true mission within the Mage Society had one less place to look.

A Delphinian priest stood across from Nuri, staring at him, apparently unmoved by the death of his priestess. Nuri watched him carefully as the priest left the temple. Following him to the courtyard, Nuri watched curiously as the priest walked toward a pale man wearing all black. They spoke in hushed tones, the other man looking surprised at the news the priest shared. Nuri recognized his uniform; the short black tunic and loose pants were common in the Second Terrace, but the emblem of the seven-tiered pyramid was only worn by the stooges who worked for Martina. If she was looking for the Weapon, then Nuri did have something to worry about. Martina was known for her persuasion. If money didn't buy what she wanted, then those who stood in her way mysteriously disappeared. Although Nuri was a formidable mage who oversaw the growing band of Janus Guards, Martina had her own followers.

After Martina's man left, the priest walked to a large wooden statue of a great snake that twisted around a dead tree. With a great effort, the priest pushed the snake statue over. The ground shook under the weight of the impact and dust rose into the air in thick clouds.

Nuri looked for the priest among the dust. He was gone. A low hum filled the courtyard, steadily growing as the dust didn't settle, but continued to rise, twist, and fill the air. Nuri backed away from the cloud as he saw gnats and fleas fly from the dust and speed away to descend on Delphi, raising a scream of alarm from the people.

Nuri didn't hesitate. He didn't run for the Painter's gallery but straight back to the sphinx city. It was a long run, made easier by the horse he stole from a young boy delivering vegetables to Delphi for market. The crimes of stealing a horse and injuring a boy haunted Nuri for a moment, then were replaced by the pride of his greater mission: finding Ona and the Grandfather's Weapon.

Rockheart

It only took a few hours of walking in the scalding heat for Bobby to know that he could go no further. Collette used her elemental intent to search for water. Her first try was still too close to the river; only blood bubbled to the surface. Later on the second day she tried again but was only able to moisten the sand.

Traveling in darkness cooled their skin. Bobby was glad to be walking; it kept the chill from consuming his body. He read somewhere in a book that deserts could be cold during the night. Cold wasn't the right word. It wasn't just a feeling on his skin, like an ice cube set against his neck. The desert's cold was dark, a cold fear of not knowing what lay ahead and knowing what was left behind. It was a cold that shook him to the core with chills that reverberated off his mind and nerves.

The heat of day was worse, biting at his skin and stealing his sweat. Exhaustion, stinging eyes, and headaches were just the minor effects of the heat. It was the heaviness in his thinking—the belief that blood really could boil–that endangered his motivation to keep moving forward. The scientific explanation for mirages evaporated from his memory when the suggestion of water quickened his step, only to transition to maddening disappointment as reality devoured his target.

When they found a little shade, they each crawled under small shrubs and waited for nightfall.

The time alone was a blessing. Bobby thought of Victoria and how he might find her. He assumed that Tucker would be thinking something similar.

Collette had hardly said anything since leaving Silan. The river turning to blood had badly frightened her. She was a terrace away from home with strangers, witnessing a plague of Egypt.

Bobby didn't realize he had fallen asleep until Tucker woke him.

"Dark. Time to go."

No one was eager to start walking, but the sooner they found a shred of civilization, the better.

Bobby, with his hands on the earth, checked for signs of life. He frowned when he felt something.

"What is it?" Tucker asked.

"I'm not sure." Bobby lay flat on his stomach and put one ear to the ground. "I can hear people talking. It's weird."

"Not as weird as your hearing voices in the dirt," Tucker said.

"I usually don't." Bobby dusted off his clothes as he stood. "I usually hear vibrations from the activity of people or animals. It's almost like there are people in the ground."

Neither Collette nor Tucker said anything.

"Well, it's not far," Bobby said, ignoring their obvious lack of confidence. "We can be there before dawn." He led the way toward the voices he heard. Every now and then he stopped to make sure they were still walking in the right direction. With only a crescent moon, the night sky was dark, making it impossible to see more than a few feet ahead. As if teasing the parched mages, a high bank of clouds slipped across the sky, blocking the already meager light of the moon.

"Oh right!" Tucker yelled at the clouds. "Shade us from the only light we have so we walk in complete darkness, but don't block out the sun!"

Bobby smiled in agreement. "It shouldn't be far—" with his next step, he felt nothing but air beneath his foot and fell forward, rolling down a long hill, smashing his back, his side, his face, down the rocky surface. The fall didn't end before his head bounced heavily on the ground.

∞∞∞

"Bobby," Collette said, touching his head.

His eyes focused on her. "I fell."

Collette giggled. "I know. You're okay. Just a little scrambled."

"That's normal," Tucker said.

"Next time you lead," Bobby said as Tucker helped him stand.

"I'm not the Earth mage. Next time use your element. It probably would have given you a heads up before you went cart wheeling into a crater."

"Crater?" Bobby looked around. The clouds had passed, selfishly keeping all the water. The sun was rising in the east, the sky arched above, cast in pink with the first hints of another scorching day.

They were in a vast depression in the earth. Bobby examined the edges. A crater hole, with a narrow, winding path zigzagging down the side. There was some green foliage in the crater; trees and shade and hopefully water. All around the edge of the crater, paths led out to every direction. Several people hauling carts could be seen coming and going. Bobby squinted his eyes at the animals that pulled the carts. Camels.

"I've heard of this place," Collette remembered. "It's a

96

trader's market. I think it's called Rock Center or Rockheart or something like that."

"I don't see any buildings," Tucker said. "Are you sure this is a city?"

"As long as there's water," Bobby started walking toward the closest structure.

"But without currency, it doesn't matter what we find there," Collette said. "We can't pay for anything."

"They can't charge for water," Tucker said.

"Yes, they can," Bobby said. "In the middle of the desert, water is more valuable than gold."

Tucker started walking toward a path that lead to the center of the crater. "Then let's get there and see what our options are. We can stand here all day guessing what needs to be done and die of thirst."

The options were slim. The heat in the center of the crater intensified. To find relief, the Traders dug their stores into the ground. There were no buildings here. A few rough structures provided shade for camels and horses, but everything else was under the earth. Little signs stuck out of the ground like wooden flowers next to wooden ramps that disappeared into the earthy cool. Pottery, beadwork, cloth, small farm animals, lizards, and water. They went down the door marked 'Water' first.

Once out of the sun, Bobby stood staring at the underground city that lay before him. From all the little doors, he assumed that each Trader had his own hole, but he now saw they were all connected. Each row was a wide tunnel. Each store was either a dug-out alcove within the cave or a wooden storefront built along the wall. People walked up and down the tunnel with their baskets and handcarts, trading and arguing over prices.

Wooden beams, stone pillars and ceilings lined the maze of tunnels lit by smoky—and stinky—oil lanterns.

"I expected a mine," Bobby said. "You know, with simple

rafters and dirt walls. This—this is amazing."

Thick wooden beams carved with swirls and intricate floral patterns covered every inch of wood. Between the beams, the walls had been carved as well. Sometimes the stone between the beams was etched in fresco reliefs of local legends, none of which they recognized. Other sections were painted in vast landscapes, providing a hint of life beyond the desert and bringing a slice of lush green to the people who inhabited the dark spaces of the cave.

It must have taken decades to dig all this out," Bobby said. "The craftsmanship is amazing."

"More like 300 years," Collette corrected him. "If I remember correctly, these tunnels go on for miles. Some were hand-dug and some are natural caves."

"Where did all these people come from?" Tucker asked.

"There is a residential area within these caves," Collette said. "It started small, this city, and people have continued to dig. Sometimes they dig into undiscovered caverns and the space opens up entire new branches."

"You mean they live and work underground?" Bobby asked, his tone one of awe.

"Not completely," Collette leaned closer, "but if you look, some of these people haven't seen the sun in months. Maybe years."

She was right. Many people manning the markets were pale and pinch-faced. Their lack-luster hair was the closest thing to a non-color Bobby had ever seen. Their eyes bulged, seeking light. As one particularly pale man walked past a lamppost, he squinted despite the fact that the lamplight was encased in greasy glass, giving off dim illumination.

Collette pulled both brothers back as they started to wander toward the water sign. "It also means that this is the Second Terrace. Mages are still murdered by those who don't understand our gifts. Be careful."

Tucker looked around at the people. "Right. No fancy tricks. Let's just get something to drink, find some food and figure out what to do next."

They followed the signs toward a water merchant, enjoying the strange architecture. Stalagmites had been sawed off like trees, leaving the trunks to serve as tables or counter tops where merchandise was sold. One area had a collection of fifteen to twenty stalagmite trunks for a restaurant. Tucker glanced at a plate of food as he passed. Nothing looked familiar. With a restaurant named Salamanders, he was afraid their specialty was not steak and potatoes.

Beyond Salamanders, an impressive set of columns–stalactites which had joined with the stalagmites–stood grandly on either side of a massive door. A man with black robes and greasy blonde hair sat at a stalagmite table, which held a thick book. Bobby half-expected him to write with quill and ink, and he laughed when the man clicked a Bic pen and wrote down the name of the next person to be admitted through the door, as if he were Saint Peter himself.

"I guess mages from our terrace know how to make money on the side," Bobby said.

"It's against the law," Collette muttered.

Tucker pointed to the door. "What do you think that place is?"

Just then, the door opened, manned by two men armed with spiked clubs. A raised platform with a dark wooden desk was poised at the far side of the room. Another man in black robes sat mightily and watched as the next person was admitted.

"Looks like a courtroom," Bobby said. "With no jury."

"Let's stay out of trouble," Collette nodded toward the direction of the water vendor. "Tucker is right. Water is all we need. Maybe a gateway, if there's a Painter down here."

99

They walked to the spring of water which sprouted from a line of spigots on the stone wall and collected in a basin. To Bobby, it looked like a child's wading pool—a built-in, shallow pool lined with tiles. No child dared go near it. This pool held precious water. Expensive water. Three large men guarded the little pool with spiked clubs. It was obvious who owned the spring. He was tall, well dressed, and clean. A heavy purse hung across his chest and he absently jingled the coins. Along the rim of the pool were small buckets, large enough to hold a quart of water. Hanging on the rims were small tin cups.

"How much?" Tucker asked the tall man.

"Cup or bucket?"

"Bucket."

The man eyed the filthy mages carefully. Bobby had the sinking feeling that this man didn't have set prices. He determined what his customers could afford and set the price a little differently each time. With blood stains on Bobby's shirt and Collette's black eye from the villagers' stones, it was anyone's guess if he would charge them more because their need was clearly great. "What do you have?"

Tucker reached into his pouch and pulled out several pieces of irregular shaped metals, unpolished and rough. Bobby recognized the pieces as the bits of silver Worthmere had given Tucker long ago.

The tall man took a piece of the metal from Tucker's hands an examined it closely. "Three."

Tucker handed over three small chunks of silver and the man pocketed the metal in his purse and motioned for one of the men guarding the pool to fill a bucket.

The man set the bucket on the rim of the pool and handed Bobby, Tucker, and Collette a cup.

The water was cool and sweet. With the first sip, Bobby felt the water put out the fire that burned his mouth and throat. It hit his stomach and awoke a hunger.

Collette drank all of the water in her cup, watching the guard from the corner of her eye. Bobby watched her.

She looks nervous, Bobby said.

Why?

As they stood watching the constant stream of customers, the owner of the well did indeed have different rates for different situations. Those who brought their own containers for water were charged less. Those who simply needed a drink were charged more. As another couple stood on the far side of the well, Collette nodded with her head ever so slightly, indicating that Bobby should look. He followed her gaze as she looked at the couple's bucket of water. It was set on the edge of the well, just like theirs, but unlike their bucket, the other was leaking.

Bobby and Tucker smiled. Of course! Collette was a water mage. Her elemental intent prevented them from being robbed.

To give them all time to have their fill of water, Collette talked with one of the well guards about the different traders in the crater. "There's a butcher down the tunnel. Sixth on the right, I believe. One of the best lizard meats in Rockheart."

"Any Painters?" Collette asked.

The man laughed. "What on earth would ragged travelers want with art?"

"An artist, then," she clarified.

"To line the walls of your home with masterpieces?" he laughed harder.

She stared at him, not indicating any purpose. He gave her directions and continued to laugh.

Tucker was still drinking when the well owner turned. "How much water did you give them?" he asked the guard. Without waiting for an answer, the owner peered into the bucket to find it still half-full. "Thieves!" he yelled. "You've robbed me!"

A few people walking by stopped to watch the argument.

Tucker took advantage of the audience. "You are the thief, water-keeper." He held the bucket high so the on-lookers could see the small stream of water escaping back into the spring. The holes drilled in the bottom of the bucket pointed guilt to the spring owner.

In a split second, dusty traders swarmed, demanding their money back. Others dipped buckets into the water and drank their fill before the guards could stop them.

Tucker smiled. "What a crime. Let's go find this Painter and hope she isn't a thief as well."

The sound of the fighting and yelling around the water spring died down as they walked away. Following the directions the man at the spring gave them, they turned left down a tiled corridor. The twins had seen shopping malls and vast markets in their own terrace, but never underground. Collette, judging by the awed look on her face, had never seen anything like it, either. Her head turned to the left then to the right as they passed vendors with wool, silk, odd-looking fruits, boots, leather goods, and farming implements. Mouth-watering smells from food vendors made their stomachs ache: baked roots of some sort drizzled with a gravy, fresh bread, and unfamiliar fruit; it was almost too much for them. Tucker bought some bread and apples from one small storefront and they sat on stone-carved stools with other customers and ate. Under normal circumstances, the bread was nothing special. The roughly ground flour made it very chewy and without butter it was dry, but the baked apple made the whole meal superb. Dripping with a sweet dark syrup, they dipped chunks of bread into the juices and savored every bite.

"If we find a Painter, what do we do?" Collette asked.

"Yeah," Tucker licked his fingers clean. "How will we know which one we need to enter?"

"I think I can figure it out," Bobby said.

True Colors

Caladrius worked diligently to maintain his position as leader in Ona's absence. Collette, Victoria and the twins had disappeared in a strange lightning storm four days ago. He had read through everything he knew about storms, lightning, and terraces to discover how they had slipped away from him. Information was scant. It all referred to the Grandfather of the Mage Society, a story remembered with such a combination of fear and skepticism that people either devoted their entire lives to it or cast it aside as legend-twaddle.

Since their disappearance, Caladrius could easily discern which of the guards were trustworthy and which couldn't be trusted to deliver food without tainting it. His daily activities consisted of directing the guards to maintain the security of Kivavallis. To maintain appearances, he had sent Green Guards to neighboring cities to search for the young mages and Ona. It was a wasted search, for Caladrius knew that if they had all traveled by lightning, they would not be found soon, if at all. The burned bodies found at the kiva were proof that lightning didn't always strike the same way twice.

"Excuse me." Milo entered the room and bowed slightly toward Caladrius. "The enclosures for the sphinx are complete."

"It's a shame to keep such majestic creatures in a crude prison," Caladrius lamented. "If only they would behave in the guest rooms. Transfer them, but do so cautiously and with three times the number of guards you think you need. If I've learned anything about these two sphinx, they are craftier than their leaders."

Milo bowed again and left the room.

"Oh, Milo," Caladrius called him back, "any news from Sebastian and Reggie?"

At this Milo smiled. "Not a peep. I don't expect they will come back anytime soon or with any good news."

"Thank you." Caladrius excused Milo.

He knew that if Sebastian were to be imprisoned, the Green Guards still loyal to the old ways would question his authority. To send him off with several Green Guards into the war-torn area of the Third Terrace to search for Ona was just the answer. While he would have preferred to have Sebastian locked up deep in the cellars of Kivavallis, it really did bother him to see the sphinx imprisoned. He knew how the sphinx culture adored their gardens and the woods surrounding the city. Up until now, the sphinx had been kept chained to posts in the center of Ona's garden. The new prison was much more worthy of traitors: underground and dark.

A movement off to the side caught his attention. Standing in Ona's mirror was Nuri, looking more bruised and filthy than usual. His white scar looked all the more pale next to the rash of red spots covering his face and neck.

"Fleas?" Caladrius questioned.

"Yes. A swarm." Nuri rubbed his neck, winced, then clenched his fist in frustration.

Caladrius tried to hide a smirk. "I have a salve that would

ease the itching."

"The sphinx have an ointment too."

Nodding in appreciation for the sphinx medicinal care, Caladrius knew that Nuri's refusal for medicine had nothing to do with easing the itch and everything to do with trust. "Another plague?"

"I was in Delphi when Ophidia died. A swarm of biting fleas swarmed the city."

"We knew this would be a possibility," Caladrius reminded him.

"I remember. Any news from Ona?" Nuri's face reddened.

This time Caladrius didn't try to hide his smile of satisfaction. It always invigorated him to see men of such power try to protect themselves from the soothing lull of his speech. Nuri was good, he knew, but his efforts to fight Caladrius' effect on his will power would drain him. "We've found nothing."

"And the girl?" Nuri asked.

"Missing along with the twins."

"You don't seem worried. Or did you drug yourself with your own words?"

Caladrius laughed. "Hardly. Guards have been sent to the other three terraces and she was not found there. Reports of the twins and Victoria were brought back. They slid to the second terrace. We have guards tracking them."

"I know you spoke with Trina. What did you tell her?"

"Nothing that would help her find them any sooner." Caladrius turned and picked up his drink. He nonchalantly sipped, irritating Nuri with his casual manners, as if they were discussing nothing more than the weather.

Nuri shifted his weight. "Trina is onto us."

"No," Caladrius swirled his drink slowly, "she knows a plot to undermine the old ways exists, but she has no clue who is behind it."

"And what will you do when you have them all back again?"

"According to Victoria, Ona has the key. She will return and we can continue with our plans."

"How can you be certain she's will return?" Nuri asked.

"I'm not certain. Time will tell."

The Bic Man

What concerned Bobby was how he would find the Painting that would take him closer to Victoria. It didn't matter if they ended up in China and Victoria was in British Columbia. He would find a way to make that journey. A horse, a car, a plane, a boat—whatever it took. The gateway was their greatest obstacle.

The problem was more practical.

It was obvious that he had no money to buy a painting with Tucker's little bits of precious metal, and he needed to hide the fact that he wanted to enter one—if he could find the right one. It didn't help his nerves that last time the Council had warned all the Painters to only allow mages with a talisman to enter paintings. He had no such thing and didn't even know what the talisman looked like. The odds of entering a painting were slim.

Tucker and Collette stayed in the main hall where they could see the Painter's shop. If this Painter was a member of the Mage Society, she would immediately recognize the significance of twins. After a quick game of rock-paper-scissors, Bobby won—or lost, depending on how he looked at it—and headed toward the gallery alone.

The Painter's small gallery was right where the tall man said.

The carved-out space was a little larger than most and it definitely had a back room, most likely for storing paint. A woman with long brown hair sat with her back to the tunnel, painting. Her features were hidden, but Bobby knew that when she turned around her eyes would speak to her true profession. Bobby looked at Tucker, who nodded encouragement.

He stepped up to the Painter's alcove and did his best to look like a window shopper.

"Birthday or decorating?" the woman asked, looking up from her canvas at Bobby with a brown and blue eye.

"Birthday," Bobby lied. "My mother."

"Have a look." She went back to her painting.

Wasting no time, Bobby filled his mind with Victoria, setting every nerve on finding her. The first painting he checked was of a prairie of tall brown grass growing on low-riding hills. Large boulders dotted the scene, filling the hills with stony obstructions. Bobby pulled his search back. This was just a painting. He skipped over the paintings of fruit and flowers, of a boat filled with oppressed fisherman. Gateways held no people in the paint. On to the next painting of a mountain valley, a bowl of trees divided by a wide river. Just another painting.

"Don't fall in," the woman said. She was standing right next to him, her head almost to his shoulder.

"What?" he jumped, trying his best to be casual.

"You are very focused on the paintings," the Painter stared into his eyes, "almost like you are looking for something."

"Um, the hidden meaning behind the painting." Bobby's mind raced as he tried to sound convincing and not give away his real purpose. "I'm fascinated with what the artist felt and what message is being shared."

"And what do you see here?" the Painter asked, pointing to a lush scene of swamp land skewered with thick, straight trees all hung with green moss that dangled like dull tinsel.

Bobby studied the painting for a few moments before speaking. He remembered talking to Victoria about what she painted and why. She told him that the emotions of that moment were reflected in the scene, that a painting is not just of a place or a person, but a feeling or a message.

"I see a forest drowning. These trees are forced to survive with their roots submersed in the water. The life around them is thick and slow. It doesn't change much, no seasons, always summer. I think the artist felt trapped by her place in life and the expectations placed upon her." He looked at the Painter.

"Very good." She smiled.

Bobby was suddenly uncomfortable, like he had peeked into this woman's personal thoughts. "I'm sorry. I probably said too much."

"Not at all. I'm glad the painting spoke to you."

Me too, Bobby thought. He knew he didn't need to go there. None of these paintings would bring him closer to Victoria. None were gateways.

"Do you see one your mother would like?" she asked.

"Not yet."

She watched him carefully as he looked at several more paintings. Bobby was acutely aware of her stare and tried to reach out to Victoria without looking like anything but a potential customer. "You are not here to buy a painting are you?" she asked.

He remembered his father's words: *Honesty will win many a friend.* It was a great risk, but necessary. He would never find Victoria unless he could find an actual gateway. "I'm here to find a friend. I'm hoping that if I can track her in a gateway, that you will let me enter."

"Just you?" she asked.

"Well," Bobby hesitated, but didn't take his eyes off the woman. "No."

"And how many people do you hope to enter?"

"Three."

The Painter glanced back at the front of her shop and rubbed her arms nervously. "Are you one of the twins I've heard about?"

Bobby sighed and resigned to tell her the truth. "Yes."

"And the third one with you?" she asked. "Who is that?"

"An apprentice healer."

"The Council told us you were with an escaped prisoner."

"He's dead."

The Painter stared at him. Her hand went to her pocket, and Bobby had the sinking feeling that in her hand was a red stone, ready to be cast into the mirror next to her, telling the Council where they were. He didn't know what to do. Should he try to explain that he and his twin brother were absolutely no threat to the Mage Society? Was that true? Lucian was dead and a river had turned to blood. Even he was starting to believe they were guilty of something. But what could he say? He didn't know Lucian at all. He could only stand there and try to appear as non-threatening as possible. He didn't look away from her stare but didn't glare back at her either. He simply stood there and prayed. *Please help us. I need to find Victoria.*

"There!" the angry voice of the spring owner called from the hallway. "There are the thieves!"

Three men with the spiked clubs rushed into the art gallery and surrounded Bobby, dragging Tucker and Collette forward. The Painter backed away.

"You," one of the men said, "follow me."

He turned as if no one had ever dared deny his request. When Bobby hesitated, the man behind him pressed the club into his back. The spikes pierced his shirt. Any more resistance from Bobby and the spikes would have also pierced his skin.

Everyone felt the ground vibrate.

"No!" Collette yelled at Bobby. "You can't! We're

underground!"

Bobby shook his head and looked around nervously. "I'm not."

Run!

Bobby and Tucker heard the voice and knew the other had not spoken. It had always just been the two of them who could communicate so fully without speaking. Now, there was another.

The ground rumbled stronger. Three pots of paint fell from the shelf, splattering all over the guards and several paintings.

I said run!

Tucker grabbed Collette's hand and made for the door. Bobby was just a few steps behind.

"What are you doing?" Collette pulled her hand out of Tucker's and stopped running.

Tucker stopped, took her hand again, looked her straight in the eyes and spoke. "You must trust me."

"I don't." Collette's jaw was set.

"We're going anyway."

"Come on!" Bobby came up behind them.

Straight.

The hall was narrow and the few shoppers in the way slowed them down.

Left.

Pulling Collette behind him, Tucker ducked down a smaller hallway. It stretched for about thirty feet then dumped them into the restaurant district. Bobby bumped into a server with a tray of drinks and steamed salamanders. The noise startled the patrons and drew the attention of two of the guards carrying the spiked clubs.

Faster. Straight.

Tucker pulled Collette faster, and she willingly sped up. Mistake or no, running from the spear-clubbed guards seemed like a good idea.

Left again. Now!

This corridor was wide and surprisingly filled with small donkey's pulling carts. The first donkey spooked and backed up, ramming the cart into a doorway. Dashing between carts, people, and animals, they could hear the guards in pursuit behind them, shouting orders for people to move out of the way.

Right.

Another wide corridor with less traffic gave them the open space they needed to put more distance between themselves and the guards. Behind them, they could feel the earth awaken. Several barrels tipped over and one of the guards tripped. He fell lightly, rolling and continuing his run, barely missing a step. The earth responded to the unseen mage again, this time becoming soft. The guards feet sank ankle deep in red soil, this time slowing them for good when the earth stiffened, trapping both guards.

"Ha!" Bobby shouted, slowing for a moment. "I never thought of that!"

"This isn't you?" Collette asked.

Keep going.

"Let's go," Bobby said, continuing their run. "This way."

"How do you know?" Collette asked, following them without Tucker pulling her along.

"Someone's guiding us," Tucker said breathlessly. "I can hear a voice."

"Any idea who's talking to you?" Collette asked, huffing as she ran. "I mean, I'm sure it's occurred to you that we might be following directions to—to trouble."

"Whoever it is doesn't sound dangerous," Tucker said.

"Oh, really?" Collette spoke between panting breaths. "Because if someone—was talking to me—in my mind, I would think that—kind of invasion—would be dangerous."

Straight. Quickly.

The passageway led them toward the large black doors where

they had seen a courtroom within. The guards still stood outside with the clubs. Worse, the man from the spring was there, smiling greedily as the three of them came into view. They quickly turned to run, but found themselves surrounded by guards.

Bobby and Tucker waited for the Earth to soften and swallow these guards, but there were no tremors. Bobby considered using his elemental intent, but Collette shook her head. "Don't do it."

She's right. Be still.

One of the guards stepped forward and pointed toward the black doors and the man with the Bic pen. "Go."

The man from the spring jeered at the mages. "These are mages and they used their gift to rob me of water."

"What say you?" the Bic man asked Tucker.

"I say that all we did was keep the water in the bucket. There were holes in the bottom."

"Again, Leon?" the Bic man asked.

"Of course not!" Leon scoffed at the accusation. "My buckets are as sound as solid rock."

Tucker couldn't believe his ears. "There were witnesses. At least a dozen people saw the water leaking out."

"Where are those witnesses?" Leon asked. He turned to the Bic man. "Send investigators to my spring. You'll find that every bucket is in perfect order. But these—mages," he said the word with disgust, "are misusing their gift to rob me."

The Bic man, with his hand poised over the book, hesitated. "Mages? Have you seen the boys? They are twins. Everyone knows there are no twin mages."

Leon studied their faces. "Well, maybe they aren't. But she is," he pointed to Collette. "It was her doing the stealing."

"Are you a Water mage?" the Bic man asked Collette.

"I am."

"And did you use your elemental intent to rob this man?"

Collette hesitated. "He over-charged us for water. He had

holes in the bucket. I just kept the water in."

The Bic man clicked his pen but didn't write anything. "And your name?"

"Collette Springtide."

He looked to the twins.

"What's going to happen?" Bobby asked.

The Bic man hesitated this time, casting a glance at Leon. "You must know the history. It tends to go particularly harsh for mages."

Collette nodded and blushed fiercely.

"Leon," the Bic man said, "I will send a messenger to you when her trial is set."

"Trial?" Leon sputtered. "The girl just admitted she's guilty of being a mage!"

Bic man held up his hand. "Just as there are rules to protect you, a vendor, there are rules to protect the accused. Even though she admitted her guilt, there still stands the matter of finding witnesses to attest to her story. It will take time. A messenger will be sent. I am also submitting a request for a full-time guard to monitor your business, at your expense of course."

"What?" Leon shouted. "I'm robbed by this girl and now I have to pay the wages for protection?"

"This is the third accusation in two months against you, Leon. You know the laws. Good day."

Leon bowed a curt farewell, spun on his heel and left.

The Bic man shook his head. "That man brings more trouble than he's worth."

"Any chance the trouble he brought you today is worth glancing over?" Tucker asked, feeling brave.

"No." He wrote in the book again, called for a guard and instructed him to take the three youths to the Minister of Foreign Affairs.

They followed the guard through the black doors, but he

didn't lead them toward the tall bench where the judge sat staring at them as they skirted the room and walked through a hall leading away from the courtroom.

Unwelcomed Guests

Worthmere woke early, but once again, Anna was already awake. A fresh pot of tea sat on the table. The sky was still dark, but far to the east, the horizon was pink. Anna stood at the window, watching the sunrise.

"Still not sleeping?" Worthmere asked quietly.

"No." Anna didn't turn around. Worthmere assumed she didn't want to be seen crying.

He brought the tea pot to her and refilled her mug when she held it out for him. "They'll be okay," he assured her.

She looked at him with tired and red eyes. "How do you know? It's been so long."

"They're strong. You saw what they could do."

Anna sniffled. "They are strong. But they are also so inexperienced. And separated."

"I'm sure the boys found her," Worthmere said.

"I hope you're right."

"Me too."

Anna studied Worthmere's face for a moment. "You look tired too."

"Parnassus snores." He yawned. "Ambrosia hasn't brought us any pastries."

"Her father is imprisoned." Anna sighed. "I imagine she's a bit too busy to bake sweets for us. One of the Junior Sphinx brought this." She walked to the small table in the kitchen and lifted a towel off a bowl, revealing what looked to be a serving of cold stew fit for a pig.

"What is that?" Worthmere wrinkled his nose.

"I have no idea." Anna covered it up again.

Just then, Parnassus walked into the room and stretched his back. "I miss my own bed. Is this breakfast?" Parnassus peered under the towel and scowled. "The final insult," Parnassus said. "The leftovers of the city."

"I suppose as prisoners, we can't really complain. I mean, the accommodations could be worse," Worthmere said in his sickeningly cheerful tone.

Anna groaned and flashed a dirty look his direction. "I would throw something at you to smash that ever-cheerful expression," Anna said, then smiled. "But allies are so few, I won't risk it.

"Here's a cheerful thought," Parnassus looked around the room. "For a prison, this isn't terrible. In the past we would have been chained in the center circle of the sphinx city until the Elders made a decision. At least here there is a roof and food."

"You call this food?" Anna asked, pointing at the bowl of slop.

"If we look at this offering of food as a kindness, it actually makes it taste better," Parnassus said. "They don't have to feed us. The prisoners long ago were not fed at all. A few actually died of starvation before the Elders reached a decision."

"How is that justice?" Anna asked.

"And how is that supposed to make us feel better?" Worthmere wondered.

"This is not justice, but stupidity. And it won't make you feel

117

better." He looked out the window at the city. "This place is blackened with fire and pride. Our government has been undermined. I've seen this coming for some time now. I feel confident, unfortunately, that this is only the beginning."

Worthmere took a sip of tea, smacked his lips and sighed. "Thank you for painting that rosy picture. Shoots holes in my hope."

"Holes in hope are expected." Parnassus sniffed the bowl of slop and crinkled his nose. "We must not allow it to disappear completely."

The day continued just like every other day—staring out the window and wondering where Victoria, Bobby and Tucker were. Ambrosia had come for her daily visit, sneaking in contraband in the form of fresh fruits and vegetables and a few books from her father's library.

Now, as the sun began its decent across the afternoon sky, Anna waited. She craved news about her young apprentices, about Tiw and Freya who had so selflessly given their reputations and possibly their lives to keep Victoria safe. She waited for news of any sort that would dictate when the trial would resume. She watched the Library of Ages, the coming and going of the sphinx and Elders. She watched the ridiculous marching of the Junior Elders in the exercises meant to enliven the mind through brisk walking, knowing that if a band of half-trained soldiers attacked the sphinx city, the Junior Elders would run in confused panic to protect their newly acquired status, leaving the Library and the remaining wings of the Hall of Art exposed.

"Nuri's back," Worthmere told Anna, joining her at the window. Across the lawn, standing between the Hall of Art and the Library of Ages, Nuri stood in close conversation with Elder Aurum and Elder Amberson who listened intently with stern faces. "That doesn't look like good news." Worthmere squinted his eyes and leaned forward. "Does it look like Nuri has the chicken pox?"

Anna shielded her eyes from the sun with her hand. "You're right. He doesn't look well."

They watched as the conversation between Nuri and the two Elders continued, body language detailing a new and stressful event. Their heads shook in disbelief, eyebrows furrowed deeply.

As Anna watched, she noticed Worthmere had turned toward Circle Lake, watching with growing interest as he tipped his head, as if he was trying to hear a conversation in the distance.

"What is it?" she asked.

"I'm not sure." He listened for another long moment.

Parnassus joined them. "I feel it, too."

Anna reached out with her elemental intent, scanning the skies for a disturbance. "I don't sense anything."

"Not in the air," Parnassus said. "Look." He pointed with a nod of his head.

The water of Circle Lake was stirring. Anna knew the wind was not strong enough to cause this much turbulence. They watched in fascinated horror as the water turned green, boiling not with hot, splashy bubbles, but with frogs. Bursting from the water, thousands upon thousands of frogs leapt onto the grass, hopping toward the city like slow, slimy waves.

No one else noticed at first. The Junior Elders continued with their senseless marching, unaware that the amphibian invasion was well underway.

"I can't believe it," Anna said as the first frogs hopped heavily on the ground. "Where did they all come from?"

Parnassus groaned. "Oh no."

"You know what this means?" Worthmere asked.

"The protection surrounding the Grandfather's Weapon has been breached."

The Junior Elders finally noticed the advancing frog march. For a long moment, the group of sphinx stood in disbelief, trying to make sense of the scene before them. Slowly, they backed away from the small creatures.

Nuri was the first to take action, his commanding voice carrying over the scene. "Gather your mages. We need to push them back!"

Elders Aurum and Amberson shouted orders to the Junior Elders and were met with a weak response.

"We aren't soldiers," Finn retorted. "What can we do?"

"Use your element!" Elder Amberson said as he stomped his front paw into the earth. A fissure broke forward and snaked toward the frogs, swallowing them up as they leapt clumsily over one another.

Nuri's fire was far more impressive. Frogs surged away from his flames, but their numbers were too many. For every frog his crisped, ten more jumped out of the lake.

"Where is Ambrosia?" Parnassus worried.

"The Library," Anna said. "She told me she was going to do some research."

"She'll be safe." Parnassus sighed. "The Library is well built and the windows are high off the ground."

"Safe from frogs?" Worthmere said. "Are these dangerous?"

"They'll ruin anything they trample. There won't be many plants left after our gardens are drowned under a sea of frogs. The greatest danger is the reaction."

"You mean what the Elders will do when they figure out that the Weapon's defenses have been breached?" Anna asked.

"No." Parnassus pointed to a group of Junior Elders who stumbled over one another trying to get away from the frogs. A sphinx with dark yellow fur tripped over another sphinx who slipped when he stepped on a frog. Judging from the looks of pain on the third sphinx that fumbled over the pile of Junior Elders, his leg was badly injured, if not broken.

"Oh," Anna said.

They all backed up into the dwelling as the frogs made their way toward them. The thorny fence that prevented them from leaving the prison also kept the frogs out. Several green and brown creatures limped away with blood trailing behind from the impact against the thorns.

"Well," Worthmere sighed. "Our prison keeps plagues out."

"This plague." Parnassus said. "There will be more and a prickly fence will not protect us."

"What do we do?" Anna asked.

"For now? Nothing. Let the Elders figure this one out. They'll come to us. Until then, I'm going to watch this and enjoy it. Whoever said 'vengeance is sweet' knew what he was talking about."

One More Crime

"So, this Minister of Foreign Affairs," Tucker spoke to one of the guards. "Is he a nice guy?"

"No." The guard raised his eyebrow at the other guard who smiled. He stopped at the end of the hall and knocked with a thick black knocker on a towering blue door. Almost immediately, the door opened and a slight woman stepped aside, indicating that they should enter. All three walked warily through the door. Inside, the room was much like a furnished cavern. The ceiling was the roof of the cave, complete with stalactites. They all dripped calcium deposits onto stalagmites on the floor. Between some stalagmites, walls had been built. Others were surrounded by pieces of furniture. Soft red and yellow floral carpets were cast here and there, giving the entire area a feminine touch. Along the wall to their left, a massive table with stalagmites for legs stood surrounded by a dozen finely crafted wooden chairs. The ceiling above the table was white stone, illuminated by a crystal chandelier with only half of the candles lit.

Sitting at the head of the table, a woman in a well-fitted black dress sat staring at her guests. It was clear by her features and healthy coloring that she didn't spend great amounts of time in Rockheart. The people here were pale and small, but this woman was tall with dark hair and skin. When she stood and beckoned them forward, they all saw that she was just as tall as the twins.

"Welcome." She bowed, and Collette bowed in return.

She nudged Tucker. "Bow."

The woman laughed. "It's quite alright. I know they have been raised in a different Terrace with social customs much different than our own." She smiled at the twins. "It goes beyond my wildest dreams."

"You are the Minister of Foreign Affairs?" Bobby asked.

"I am."

"How did you lead us here?" Bobby asked.

The woman turned toward the table and motioned for them to sit down. "Geraldine," she called to the woman who had opened the door, "please bring some food and drinks."

Geraldine bowed and left.

The Minister of Foreign Affairs sat down at the head of the table. "To answer your question, I wasn't sure it would work. However, the skill of telepathic communication is strong in my family."

A long, awkward moment of silence rested between them.

Collette broke it. "How are you related to Bobby and Tucker?"

"Ah," she laughed, delighted about something Collette had said. "I should have known. My brother always was a nostalgic fool."

Bobby leaned forward. "Wait. What? Your brother?"

"Yes, my dear delusional brother. Adam Caius."

Tucker shrugged. "Who is that?"

The woman leaned back. "You don't know?"

"Never heard of him," Tucker said.

Geraldine walked in with a heavy tray of drinks, poured water for everyone, and set a tray of sliced fruit and what looked like roasted frog legs on the table. Collette drank, but couldn't even look at the frog legs. When Geraldine left, the woman continued.

"Adam Caius, my brother, was a Green Guard to Ona Beltane. He, according to the reports—if you believe such things—was killed nineteen years ago. His body was never recovered." She took a sip of the water.

"I'm sorry to hear that." Bobby said, wondering where this story was heading.

"Adam was married. Isabella was a beauty and an accomplished Fire mage. She died shortly after my brother, oddly."

Collette and the twins remained silent.

"The circumstances surrounding her death raised questions for me. She had been sent to the Third Terrace to manage a forest fire. Her task was to discretely use her gift to calm the fire enough so the people of that area could gain control. She died in that fire, conveniently, with no remains for identification." She gestured with a flick of her hand, as if she were rolling a set of dice. Bobby felt that their entire visit there was far more dangerous than a rogue toss of the dice. This felt like the greatest gamble of their lives.

"Just before his disappearance," she continued, "my brother confided in me that he believed that the Council was corrupt. As Minister of Foreign Affairs, I have a unique position to manage the coming and going of mages between the terraces. By telling me his doubts, he hoped I would use my position to affirm his accusations."

"And?" Bobby asked.

"And I found nothing." She looked at Tucker, then Bobby. "Until now."

"Us?" Tucker asked.

The woman's demeanor softened. "Yes."

"Look," Bobby leaned forward, "I see that you think our father was this Adam Caius. But our father's name is Rhys Martin."

Laughing, the woman shook her head. "My father's name was Tukaius. Isabella's brother was Robert. My name is Martina."

"No way," Tucker stared dumbly at the Minister of Foreign Affairs. "You're our—Auntie Martina?"

"I prefer Madame Minister."

No one moved. Collette sat there watching the painfully defunct family reunion as Bobby, Tucker, and Martina stared at each other.

"Um, should we hug or something?" Bobby asked.

"Not necessary," Martina held up her hand. "Because what I must do next will spoil all future family events."

"Oh, boy." Tucker sighed. "That does not sound good."

"Do you know why your father left? Why he took his wife and hid from the Society?"

Bobby and Tucker remained silent. They had no idea why their parents were hiding in the Fourth Terrace. They assumed it had something to do with the Grandfather's Weapon and Ona's search for it, but because of what Ona had shared with them, they now knew that neither their father nor their mother were in the kiva almost twenty years ago.

Martina smiled, but there was no joy behind it. It was a knowing smile, one that covers shame. "My brother was, or is, I suppose—if he's still alive—one of the strongest earth mages known. He could track a cricket without it knowing, or he could cause an earthquake that caused damage in several terraces." She paused for a moment, remembering something. Her eyes darkened in a deep frown. "Instead of joining our parents in a political career and a respectful life of rule and power, he used his element to become a world-class thief."

"What?" Bobby interrupted. "Our dad's a thief?"

"*World-class* thief," Tucker added, smiling. "What did he take?"

"Nothing has been proven, no reliable witnesses. With his apparent death, his guilt or innocence was a moot point. But I know my brother. I know he took a series of scrolls from the Library of Ages in the Third Terrace."

Tucker whistled. "I bet that wasn't easy."

Martina shook her head in amusement. "No. I'm sure it wasn't. Even more difficult was to overcome being his sister."

"Sure," Tucker understood. "Having a brother who steals from the Sphinx and then disappears? Can't have been easy to convince others that the sticky-finger ability didn't extend to you."

"Indeed." Martina took a sip of her drink. "Do you know where the scrolls are?"

"Not anymore," Tucker looked at Bobby. "I'm assuming that's what dad handed us in that leather bag."

"Lucian took it," Bobby remembered. "Man, it could be anywhere."

"Lucian," Martina repeated the name. "He escaped?"

"We were following him when we ended up here." Tucker said, thankful that Collette was keeping her mouth shut.

"He should be easy enough to find," Martina said casually. "That idiot never could stay out of trouble for very long. I've also been told that you have the Map of Art."

"What do you want with the Map?" Tucker asked.

"Rumors are that twin mages have surfaced and are traveling with a Painter," she looked at Collette, "and are seeking the Grandfather's Weapon."

"You want the Weapon?" Bobby asked.

"There are many things I want," Martina stood and rang a bell. "But because the girl you travel with is not a Painter, I'll just take the Map."

"And what will you do with us?" Tucker asked.

126

"Prison. Your father can wonder what happened to you, just as I wondered all these years about him." She held out her hand. "Please."

Bobby shook his head. "We don't have it."

"Who does?"

"It was destroyed," Bobby said.

Martina's face reddened and her nostrils flared, but her voice didn't betray her fury. "To purposefully destroy a vital archive of the Mage Society is a crime punishable by death."

"It wasn't intentional," Bobby argued, but Martina held up her hand for him to stop.

"On these matters, I'm a judge and jury."

Tucker held out his hands to stop his Aunt. "Wait. Why punish us? Why not work together?"

Martina chuckled. "What could you possibly do to help me?"

Tucker's face shown with confidence. "What do you think our dad has been doing the last two decades? Sitting and waiting?" He laughed at the absurd idea.

Martina narrowed her eyes at the boys. "He's been training you."

Tucker nodded.

Bobby kept his face relaxed, knowing that if he tensed, Martina would read the lie easier than writing on a wall.

Standing, Martina started to pace. "He's still looking for it."

Tucker and Bobby exchanged a quick glance.

"Tell me what he's looking for," Martina demanded. "Tell me what you know."

"The Grandfather's Weapon," Bobby said.

"Ona is looking for it too," Collette added.

Martina flinched at the mention of Ona. "What else do you know?"

Bobby stood and studied Martina's face for an intense moment. "That you sent the Ragnarok to the sphinx city. We

127

know they attacked the Hall of Art and destroyed paintings. We just didn't know why."

Looking impressed, Martina smiled. "Why do you think I would be involved with the Ragnarok?"

"You wouldn't," Bobby said. "But you needed a way to weaken the sphinx and all they protect. There's too much risk involved to use your own people to attack the city. It would just implicate you from the beginning."

Martina laughed. "You are very much like your mother. I always did like her."

"You liked her well enough to not harm her sons?" Tucker asked.

"Friendships mean very little when we stand on the brink of war."

"War?" Collette repeated.

"You are but children in a very grown up game," Martina said. "I did not inspire the Ragnarok to attack the sphinx. I would never risk anything in that city to the fiery fingers of those beasts."

From the door where Geraldine had left, they heard a violent rustling and screams. Several heavy items fell, crashing loudly, followed by more screams. Martina took a step toward the door, then backed up quickly as Geraldine burst through. "Madame Minister! It's a plague! A plague!" She ran out the front door.

Bobby, Tucker, and Collette quickly climbed onto the table, knocking over their chairs as a wave of frogs crashed through the doors and onto the floor. Along the walls, salamanders skittered. The room quickly filled with the croaks and plops of hopping amphibians and Martina's screams. Her cool threat to be judge and jury lost all its clout as she danced from one foot to the next with salamanders in her hair and frog's clinging to her robes.

Tucker came to a plan quickly. "Now!" All three jumped off the table and ran for the door. In the courtroom, the frogs were just emerging from the back rooms and they were able to slip through the large, black doors with the growing crowd of panicking people.

"This way," Collette took the lead and ran down the hall.

"Where are you going?" Tucker asked.

"Back to the Painter. Those guards will be too busy to stop us. We can get through the gateway."

Frogs, salamanders, and lizards hopped and skittered along the floor and walls. Collette screamed when a salamander landed in her hair, but she quickly brushed it off and kept running. The only people happy with the unwelcomed guests were the employees at Salamanders Restaurant, who collected the amphibians in bags for future meals.

"There!" Tucker pointed to the little studio. They slid to a stop just outside the Painter's alcove and stared in horror at the demolished paintings. Scattered, ripped, and broken canvas and wood cluttered the ground. Bobby ran over it all and went into the back room, returning only a moment later, his expression dark. "Nothing."

"Time to go," Tucker pulled Collette away from the studio.

Collette glanced back to make sure Bobby was following.

What did you see? Tucker asked as they dodged down a different corridor that led to a ladder to the outside.

She's dead.

Death by frogs?

Unless these frogs carry knives? No.

Outside, it took a moment to adjust to the blaring light. Tucker started running toward the stables. Nervous horses whinnied, but they calmed under Collette's soothing voice. Two horses were already saddled, so she grabbed the few canteens that were full off a table and tossed them to Bobby.

"Hey!" a man called as he ran into the stable. "What are you doing?"

Collette turned toward him calmly, her voice heavy. "We need these horses. Do they belong to you?"

The man slowed to a walk, then stopped altogether. "No. I just care for 'em."

"Then you'll tell the owners that in the confusion, they ran away."

"Ran away," he repeated.

"You won't be in trouble. You know how skittish horses are."

He nodded dumbly. "Skittish horses run away."

Collette raised her eyebrows and turned toward the brothers, whispering, "That was really easy." She indicated with a nod of her head that they should get on the horses.

Bobby and Tucker had ridden a handful of times with their father, but it took a few attempts to climb up into the saddle. By the time they were both settled, the man had helped Collette saddle a third horse and grabbed a bag of supplies. She swung her leg over the horse's back. "Ready?"

"Which way?" Tucker said.

"Let's just get out of this crater first," Collette said. "If we're caught, they can add 'horse thief' to our list of crimes."

Tucker smiled. "I think you are enjoying being a rebel."

"It's growing on me." She laughed and dug her heels into the horse.

They rode quickly away from the chaotic scene of panicking people who flooded from the hundreds of openings in the crater floor and toward the endless spans of desert.

Judge and Jury

Victoria finally had to stop, and she was angry with herself for it. It was more important to move on, to do what needed to be done, but her knees gave out and sobs escaped her before she felt the earth under her hands.

Once again she had been separated from those she loved. That seemed to be the theme of her life. The elements and their presence were of little comfort. She couldn't cry on Air's shoulder. Water couldn't tell her that everything was going to be okay. Earth simply scorched the soles of the boots, heating her feet and raising blisters.

Fire? That was tricky. If she had the other three elemental gifts, it stood to reason that she could call upon Fire as well. But she didn't want to. Fire was too risky an element with a mind of its own; a dangerous, hungry friend to have, feeding on anything from plants to animals to people.

And the lightening? She still didn't understand that. The bolt had worked with her, somehow, but still managed to serve its own purpose. The energy of the lightning—the source of it—was something to figure out, but not now. This was a time to survive the heat, to find water, to find help.

She thought this was the same place that Bobby, Tucker and Collette had slipped away to, but when she came through she was alone. When she arrived, the sun was high and the warmth of the day was well established. The trees of Bear Mountain were gone, replaced with scrubby plants and flat, scorched land.

Her run away from that spot began with the discovery of a dead body. As her mind sorted through the blinding after-effects of lightning, a pungent scent crept into her awareness. She knew the smell, recognized it from Ona's garden when she zapped the guard who touched her. Burnt flesh. Had she electrocuted everyone?

She feared the worst, knew she had killed someone and didn't want to see the body. But her own body didn't listen to her thoughts. She kept moving forward, scanning the landscape, praying that whomever she found wouldn't be anyone she knew.

The body was only a few yards away from her and once she saw it, she didn't understand how it wasn't immediately obvious to her. Twisted and bent around a scrubby bush, a young man lay dead. Victoria could see that he had been a handsome man with his long hair braided in tight rows over his head. But death drained him of beauty, leaving the horror of his last moment etched on his face. It wasn't Bobby and Tucker and that was a relief, but that feeling lasted only a moment. She turned quickly and was sick.

☜✿☞

Hours passed.

I think I killed him, she kept repeating in her mind. *I'm a murderer. But does it count if you didn't mean to?*

How many people had done just the same thing; tried to save one person only to kill, accidentally or not, someone else? She knew that life was fragile, that everything could change in a heartbeat. It was one thing to know it and another thing to see it. The man probably had a mother and father. He came to the desert for a reason and now he's dead. He won't be going home. Someone will miss him.

And her stomach reeled again. She knew how that felt. Her father had not come home one night. Her mother waited, but he didn't return. Had he been killed? Did someone try to save a friend and accidentally kill Victoria's father in the process? How different would her life have been if her father had come home that night? Would she still know Bobby and Tucker? They were such an important part of her life. But to think of having a father or having Bobby and Tucker in her life—which would she choose if she had a choice?

She grabbed the hair at her temples and pulled, trying to pry those thoughts out of her mind. Hopeless tears seeped from her eyes. She had only one choice—keep walking.

And walking.

The sun was hot. Her lips chapped, which seemed strange because every other part of her body was drenched with sweat, and as much as she wanted water, she also wanted chap stick. The thirst tried to stop her, to push her down like a bully on the playground. Her throat, her face, her feet burned. The canteen that the man had with him hung from Victoria's shoulder. She felt terrible about stealing from a dead man, but she reasoned he didn't need it any more. Small sips had sustained her, but she didn't know how far it was to water and didn't want to run out completely. That seemed worse.

With the water in the canteen, she felt safer. No, not safer, alive. Air surrounded her, Earth burned her feet through the leather soles of the shoes she had from Bernadette, and she carried Water in the canteen. So she walked on and on, thinking of the past, her mother, the twins, and the strangeness of being a mage who can call lightning from the sky. Strange. Very strange.

As the sun set, Victoria searched for shelter. It was all scrubby plants and dirt. Far off to the horizon, she saw a rise in the earth. A mountain. Had the man walked this far? She had obviously chosen the wrong direction. But what was the right direction? Air pushed her forward.

This is right, it told her. *Keep on.*

Sometime during the night she stopped and didn't feel badly about needing the rest. It must have been two or three o'clock in the morning, but time didn't matter. Water did. She cautiously sipped from the canteen. The only shelter, she reasoned, was the lack of sun. She lay down under nothing but the moon and slept.

In her dreams she walked through her garden. It wasn't much of a garden now, just a field with stubbles of grass. The devastation from Ona's cruelty filled Victoria with a heavy grief. Her ring of trees was gone.

Out of habit, she walked toward where the circle of trees once stood. Small rises in the ground were the only marks that trees had once stood there. It was too much. She had lost everything: her mother, Bobby, and Tucker. Or had they lost her?

In the center of the lost trees, Victoria lay on the ground and looked at the sky. It was dusk in her garden. She closed her eyes and prayed for sleep—deep sleep.

It wasn't to be.

She stood on cool green grass, the sweet aroma of green enriching her. What she saw next was completely unexpected and yet familiar. A small cottage stood in a clearing backed by towering pine and oak trees. A rather large barn squatted among a collection of pens and animals. Victoria could smell animals inside the barn and saw a large swine rooting in the hummus of the yard.

She had been here before. The baby's birth, the storm, the sudden clear sky.

A woman came out of the cottage, her dress and apron dusty with flour, her hair covered with a cloth and tied at the nape of her neck. It was the woman who had given birth. She looked tired and a shock of white hair at her temple aged her, but her face was untouched by wrinkles.

"David?" she called.

A young boy, no more than eight years old, came out of the barn carrying a bucket.

"I asked you to bring in the milk before you brought the pig in."

"No you didn't," David said. "At least not today." He walked toward her, hauling the bucket of milk. "You tell me that every day."

The mother sighed. "I do, don't I? I sent your sister out to help you. I asked her to remind you."

David stopped walking. "Sarah didn't come to the barn."

His mother's expression fell and she was as white as the flour on her hands. They both turned toward the woods. The boy gasped. "The lake!" He dropped the bucket of milk and ran, his mother not far behind. Victoria followed.

David ran effortlessly through the woods, leaping over fallen trees and ducking under low branches without slowing his pace. His mother wasn't as fast. Her long skirt caught on the brambles.

Victoria watched the mother struggle and felt the panic within her own heart for the little girl. As in dreams, Victoria wasn't bound by space or time. Her concern took her instantly all the way to the lake's edge where David emerge from the woods yelling, "Sarah!"

The water was glassy smooth. The only response to David's call was the splashing of several startled frogs. A small, scrap-quilt doll lay abandoned near the edge of the water. He picked it up and looked out over the lake. His mother caught up to him just as he dashed into the water.

135

"David," she called. "Is she there?"

He didn't answer, but ran up to his waist into the water and set his hands gently on the surface. Victoria felt the water respond to David, drawing toward him and churning. Soon, the surface bubbled wildly and Sarah's limp body was carried toward him.

Their mother screamed at the sight of her body, stumbled into the water, and helped David carry her to the shore.

Without hesitation, David pressed on his sister's chest and water spilled out of her mouth. "Breathe," he whispered, "make her breathe."

Victoria was holding her breath. "Make her breathe." She didn't ask the Air but prayed to God.

Sarah's face was pale, her lips blue. Victoria didn't know this family at all, but having been there for David's birth, knowing how much fear pumped through her own veins, she felt what must be a fraction of what David and his mother felt.

David pressed on her chest again. Victoria felt the air around her zing as sparks of static electricity popped between David's hands and Sarah.

"Breathe!" David's voice cracked as he commanded his sister to take in a life-saving breath.

The mother watched in awe as her daughter gasped. Coughing and crying, Sarah reached out for her mother, who snatched her up quickly. She looked at her son with tear-filled eyes. "You saved her."

David's shoulders relaxed and he let out a shaky sigh of relief. Mother and son stared at each other for a long moment, neither able to put into words what had just happened.

Victoria knew. David was like her.

ଏଠଃ

Victoria's eyes snapped open. She lay still for a moment,

trying to decide if she was really awake. The landscape was not familiar, but she had stopped walking in the blackest hour, so it wasn't a surprise that she didn't recognize anything. Bernadette's shoes were not on her feet in the dream and now they were strapped tightly to her feet.

She sighed, partly relieved to be able to wake herself and partly sad that the scorching heat had returned. There was nothing to do but stand and keep walking. She tried not to think about hunger or thirst, but the more she tried not to think about it, the more she dwelled on her aching stomach.

Just as the sky was turning from pink to blue and the landscape became sparse, she felt the footsteps. She scanned the horizon for people, for she knew the vibrations belonged to people; there was something familiar in the pace. Wilderness people.

Several minutes passed before Victoria saw the five silhouettes coming toward her. It did occur to her to run. Weighing her odds, she decided that wasn't an option. There was so little water left in the canteen that she would never survive. She hoped these people would give her water and help her find her way back to a village where, if her luck held out, she might find a mage.

Five men neared Victoria with weapons of wood and stone balanced menacingly in their hands. These were not mages, but men. Like the Native Americans of Victoria's terrace, these men were strikingly beautiful: dark skin, dark eyes, and wiry muscles. Their hair was long and braided like the dead man's. Their skin glistened with sweat. As they surrounded her, she could smell the earth coming through them. They may not be Earth mages, but they obviously lived closely with the land.

Trying to stand in the most non-threatening pose, Victoria kept her hands by her side. She did look them in the eye; she didn't want to appear submissive, but also something in the way they looked at her lead her to believe she had been hunted. One man pointed to the canteen hanging on Victoria's shoulder. He walked up to her, his eyes filled with a frightening blend of anger and fear, and asked her something in a language she didn't understand. He pointed from the canteen to Victoria. She knew three things at that moment: the canteen marked her as the murderer of the man struck by lightning, these men had indeed been hunting her, and she had no way to communicate with them.

She looked at the men, trying to think of what to do. There was nothing, she realized, but the man who spoke did have a plan. He slapped her. She saw it coming, but didn't try to dodge his hand.

The stinging throb on her cheek helped to dull the guilt she felt. Her innocence could not be proven at the moment, not with her in possession of the dead man's canteen. But she would prove to them, somehow, that it had been an accident.

When she didn't fight back, the men looked confused. They looked at one another, trying to decide what to do. Another man behind Victoria pushed her back the way they had come. She followed.

She hadn't missed the village by much. They followed a trail for several hours, and then turned south. Low prickly bushes grew everywhere, leaving small winding paths. The men did not let the bushes touch their skin. Victoria had learned this the hard way earlier. She thought her long skirt would provide enough protection from the plants, but instead the plants pulled at her clothes and found her legs. Biting thorns brushed her legs, releasing oil that stung relentlessly.

Hope drove her forward. It was possible that someone in their village would recognize her for what she was, would understand that she hadn't meant to hurt anyone. It was a slim hope, but it was enough to keep her feet moving.

(Mourning Songs

The men who found her would be gold medalists in marathons. They pushed her on, ignoring her obvious need for water and rest. She feared that justice was their main objective and it would be well-deserved. She accepted the discomfort of running, the pain in her side, and the burning of her feet as punishment for releasing the power of lightning.

The village was surrounded by a tall wall of thorny sticks, looking like a ring of mud and cacti. Inside the walls, the homes were earthen brown, sun-dried mounds. Lean men stood outside the village, stoically watching Victoria and her guides approach. As they neared the encampment, a group of people walked toward the entrance from the heart of the village. At first, Victoria thought it was a group of young boys, but as they approached, she saw the feminine features. Their heads were completely bare with their scalps shining brightly in the sun. Several of the women had painted patterns on their heads with thick lines of charcoal. No one smiled. No one offered Victoria water. Everyone greeted her with dark eyes and fearful trepidation.

The air, tense with high emotions, was rich with a strange

smell. The familiar scent screamed a warning, but Victoria felt helpless against it. Whatever was causing the lingering stench, it was dangerous. That much was obvious in the pained expressions of the people.

More eerie than the sight of the village was the sound of singing. A thin woman, wrinkled by the sun with her bare scalp marked by charcoal in swirling twists, stood atop a large boulder and sang a melancholy song as the group bringing Victoria crossed over the threshold to the village. Her voice matched her thin stature. The melody rolled like a flat cry. Another call to the left startled Victoria. Snapping her head in the direction of the closest caller, Victoria saw a younger woman, her face shining with tears. She was as beautiful as her voice and her baldness added to her beauty. She was dressed in soft leather, adorned with beads and feathers. Together, the two women wailed the sadness of the people in a mourning song.

The dead man had been brought home. Victoria passed his still form and was forced to stop. Standing a few steps away from the dead man's body, Victoria searched him for any reason for his death. A blackened burn on his chest confirmed it. Lightning.

Another slap across her cheek ended Victoria's assessment of the dead man. A tiny, wrinkled woman with a hand like steel smacked her again. She yelled and screamed at Victoria and hit her again.

Anger radiated off the woman in her hot breath and stinging palm.

Victoria heard the screaming. The words were foreign, but she recognized the emotion on the woman's face. No one stopped the woman's assault on Victoria. Never before had Victoria been the victim of rage. She had seen news reports on school bullies and believed that if she were ever a victim, anger would give her strength to fight back. It didn't. Fear, stronger than anything she had felt before, kept her still. There was no anger in Victoria's heart, no stirring of emotions to pull her strength together and fight.

For a moment, there was silence. Victoria kept her eyes respectfully down, but she sensed that the woman was exhausted by her outburst of emotion. Several women came forward and gently led the woman away, all whispering to her in loving voices. Victoria wanted to whisper to her too, but fear of another attack kept her silent. Keeping her eyes down, Victoria saw the feet of the women surrounding her part and a small man came forward, walking slowly with the help of a tall stick. He stood in front of Victoria for a long time, but she didn't meet his eyes until he lifted her chin. Victoria's mouth fell open in surprise. He was one of the Red Men from the kiva, the oldest man that had given her one of the silver pieces to the key. The man spoke to the people, and they bowed respectfully. Her fate had been decided and she was the only one who didn't know what it would be.

Another woman began the song again, lower and more melodious than the first, drawing their attention back to the heart of the village. Dread surrounded Victoria; her legs felt like lead, causing her knees to buckle. Pulled up and forced to stand, Victoria was pushed forward. Women, young and old, followed Victoria like ghosts, all joining in the song, the air vibrating with their tones. They walked through the village, out an opening in the fence and toward a filthy river, with the river banks littered with dead fish and birds. It looked like an oil spill at first, but the smell was far more organic. A fish twitched in the thick mud, gaping at the sky. It wasn't oil, she realized. It was blood. The entire river had been filled with blood.

The circle opened and two women came forward holding clay pots of blood.

"What are you doing?" Victoria asked.

The old man spoke. "You are Original. Our people die from lack of the gift."

"Gift?" Victoria wasn't sure what he meant. "You mean a mage? A mage did this?"

"You didn't respect the number. My people have guarded the gate for generations. You were there to collect the key. You failed. My grandson is dead. My people will not survive this."

"I didn't kill him," Victoria said. "The key was taken from me. The woman who took it is dead."

He shook his head. "You used light that tears the sky. It tears life away. Or it can tear you away."

"I don't understand."

Tears dripped down his wrinkled cheeks. "I know."

The mourning song began again, tearing apart the little sanity to which Victoria was clinging. Whatever or whoever had screamed had all the emotions Victoria felt building within her. Spinning from terror to beauty, the scream lost its horror and became a melodious hymn, sung not with words, but with emotions that surpassed the need for language and drove straight into her heart. The women surrounding Victoria began to stomp their feet in the dirt, raising rings of dust.

Left foot.

Right foot.

Left.

Right.

The mourning circle grew intensely more rhythmic and desperate. They danced around Victoria in great sweeping circles, bending, rising, and twirling in moans of agony and anger and despair. The ground quivered under the beating of their feet, the chills of the earth rising through Victoria in the language of the land.

A woman put her hand on the back of Victoria's neck and forced her to the ground.

Victoria covered her eyes with her hands and put her forehead on the ground. Dust choked her and settled on her sweaty skin. Women shrieked and cried. Victoria took it all in, embraced the guilt. She was a murderer. However unintentional it had been didn't change the outcome.

Hands snatched her to her feet and dragged Victoria back to the center of the village to a ring of charred earth surrounding a tall blackened post. A burning stake.

Tied to the post with her hands wrapped tightly behind her back, the circle of mourning women brought their dance to surround Victoria again.

It seemed a good time to pray. But what could she pray for? God had directed Joan of Arc in battle; she had listened to his word and had been burned for it.

She sent a prayer off with all the hope left in her heart. She hoped it would be enough, hoped that her story didn't end at the stake.

The women stopped their chanting dance and stood staring at Victoria. Through teary eyes, Victoria saw their expressions. It was an eye for an eye. Revenge was sought, found, and about to be executed.

Ever since she entered the world of mages and discovered that her elemental intent was not the same as with other mages, she knew that her life would be different. Why not her death, too? It made perfect sense. These desert people knew nothing of the mages.

Nothing?

The old man. He called her an Original. He was at the kiva. He handed her the silver triangle. He must be a mage.

In a flash, Victoria realized that the old man, if he really was a mage, must have had a mentor. Maybe he was someone else's mentor. With the desperation of one who stands on the gallows, Victoria searched the people around her for help, for something familiar.

There had to be something that would indicate a mage. What

was the same? Victoria searched the women who surrounded her for a hint of sympathy, an inkling of sameness.

Eyes.

Her eyes. Anna's eyes. They were the different colors. It was a small thing to hope for, that there would be a Painter in this tiny village, this insignificant place, with no need for gateways.

All the same, Victoria searched the eyes of the women. Brown eyes stared back at her with emotions that made Victoria's stomach flip. If this was the end, the last moment before the fire was lit beneath her feet, she was going to study the faces of her executioners.

A man walked through the band of women and spoke. Maybe it was a prayer or an announcement of what was going to happen. His eyes wandered over her face, down her neck to the silver chain from which the locket hung. He carefully lifted the chain, pulling the locket out from the neckline of her dress. His eyes gleamed when he saw the bright silver. Turning it carefully in his hands, he smiled. With a sharp pull, he yanked the locket, breaking the chain and cutting the skin around the back of Victoria's neck. The man backed away from Victoria, smiling. Another man untied her shoes and took them. She didn't need them after all.

From behind him, a girl walked toward Victoria. She held a shallow bowl with an iridescent oil. Victoria looked at her face. One dark brown eye, one gray eye. A mage. She too, saw Victoria's eyes and hesitated for a moment. She leaned in and whispered something in Victoria's ear. It was urgent and desperate and Victoria understood none of it. They stared at each other a moment longer. The girl looked up at the sky and whispered a few words. Tears dripped from her eyes as she dipped her thumb in the oil and marked four horizontal lines on Victoria's forehead, cheeks, and neck.

"Please," Victoria said sobbing. "Please don't let them do

this."

The girl understood. Victoria could see regret in her face as she struggled with what to do. But if the girl were to help Victoria, she would most likely find herself tied to a pole next to her. It was useless. The girl looked up to the sky, then at Victoria. She looked at the ground, then at Victoria. She looked at the lit torch in the hand of a villager, then back at Victoria.

Victoria nodded ever so slightly. The message was clear to her. *You must use what gifts you have to save yourself. I cannot help you.*

Her gift. Victoria almost laughed at her stupidity. She had more than one element. But the last time she had tried to save herself and her friends, she had killed the young man of this village. A battle like this could not be fought alone. She closed her eyes and prayed. *God. Are you here? I never knew that the elements were entities to communicate with. Part of me wishes that I still didn't know. Please help give me strength to get away from here. I don't think my life is supposed to end here. Please, help me escape and not hurt anyone.*

Before her prayer was finished, Victoria felt the wind pick up. Tiny specks of sand pelted her legs and arms as the Air rushed across the ground, raising the minute rounds of ammunition and casting it against the people. Victoria opened her eyes. The people were no longer looking at Victoria, but protecting their eyes from the blowing sand and looking at the sky. Black clouds rolled in, covering the sun and casting the village into cold fear.

God responded loudly in Victoria's heart. *I'm here. Don't be afraid.*

Victoria gasped. She looked at the village girl who still held the bowl of oil. Her eyes were wide with awe as she looked at the sky. Victoria looked up as lightning seared a path through the air and found a target near the village. The people ran and screamed, but the girl and a few other men stayed close to Victoria.

The girl looked at Victoria, her face asking, *Are you doing this?*

Victoria honestly didn't know. It was her element, but also

146

her prayer. Could Air, because of a prayer, act on its own? Or was the Air a messenger, a soldier for God?

Then the energy shifted from the sky to the ground. A wave of ground rolled toward the village from the distance, uprooting small bushes, knocking over the livestock and smaller structures. The men standing around Victoria yelled at each other and then ran toward the wave of earth with long spears. What they were going to do to stop it, Victoria had no idea. But she understood their need to fight this strange phenomenon.

The girl dropped her bowl of oil and ran to Victoria, cutting lose the ropes with a small knife that she pulled from her belt. She was speaking urgently to Victoria, the words foreign, but the meaning clear. *You must leave. Quickly.*

Once free, Victoria didn't know which way to go. The girl pulled her through the village, darting past the small houses with families huddled inside. They came to a stop at the fence. It was the only protection the village had against invaders. The girl motioned for Victoria to go over it. When Victoria started to climb, the branches bent under her weight, revealing cactus spines that were strategically embedded around the branches and in the mud. The girl pulled Victoria back and motioned with her hand that Victoria should jump over the wall of tangled wood and thorns.

"What?" Victoria stared in disbelief at the height of the fence. "There's no way," she looked at the wall. "Wait." She did know how to do this. She had lifted Anna off the ground the first time she communicated with Air. This was the same thing. The girl squeezed Victoria's hand and nodded, tears in her eyes. "Thank you," Victoria said. Risking her life, this girl had helped Victoria, a stranger. Elemental intent was all they shared, but it had been enough. Victoria's prayer for help as she was tied to the stake had been answered. They stared at each other for a moment. Victoria worried that she would be punished for freeing her, but the girl shook her head. *Go!* She motioned.

Turning to the fence, Victoria started running, but she was pulled back by a strong hand. The man who had taken the dreamwalker yanked Victoria away from the wall of thorns and timber, yelling at the girl. Victoria reached desperately for the girl as she was dragged across the ground and brought back to the burning post. The girl picked up a stone and threw it at the man's head. Air helped; Victoria felt the energy guiding the stone increase as it struck the back of the man's head. He hit the ground and didn't move. Victoria pulled the dreamwalker off from around his neck and gripped it tightly. The girl pulled her away from the man and urged her to the fence.

Calling the Air to lift her over the fence was easier than stepping over a speed bump. With the wind still blowing fiercely, she felt her body grow lighter as she ran toward freedom. She knew the Air was behind her and under her, lifting her easily as she jumped over the fence. Little rhymes of cows jumping over the moon and the stories of Peter Pan flew through her mind.

Her feet hit the ground and a new sensation filled her entire body. The energy from the earth was still boiling madly. Off to her right, she could see the villagers stabbing the ground with their spears, trying to stop the vibrating chaos that surrounded them.

Victoria wondered who had created this distraction. She ran to a patch of low, scratchy bushes and hid behind them. Maybe it was Bobby.

Her feet burned when she ran. The boots gone, the hot sand scorched her already bruised and blistered feet.

The earth pulsed under her touch and she searched for that familiar pulse of Bobby's elemental intent. She had studied it, memorizing his gift, curious and timid.

This was not Bobby. This mage was fierce and experienced.

Victoria reached further and found the other mage, who

immediately tracked her back to where she hid. Pulling her hand away from the dirt, her heart thumped stiffly. Whoever this earth mage is, he or she knew where Victoria was hiding. She moved behind a grouping of tall plants. The earth mage would probably know that she moved, but she hoped that if she could see who it was first, she would have a few seconds to prepare to fight if needed.

A minute later, she saw a figure crouched low, running toward her. It was a man. He stayed hidden behind the shrubby trees and bushes and watched the villagers continue their attack on the ground just outside the village. He wasn't dressed like a Green Mage. He wore clothing she recognized from home: cargo pants, a t-shirt and a long-sleeve shirt over it, protecting his arms from the sun. He wore a brown hat, making him look like a desert-bound Indiana Jones. He was perfectly camouflaged for this terrain. This man ran right to where Victoria had been when he tracked her. When she wasn't there, he scanned the surrounding area for signs of where she had gone.

Victoria gasped. She did know this man. She had known him since kindergarten but never expected to see him here. Especially here.

His eyes followed her tracks to where she stood, leaning out from behind a tree.

"Principal Wood?"

Lost and Found

Crouching low, he ran toward her. "Are you hurt?"

"Principal Wood?"

"Are you hurt?" he asked again.

Victoria opened her mouth to answer, but she didn't form any coherent thought. "You—what are—I thought. Wait— how? Is this—? I mean—where?"

"Hmm..." He assessed her condition. "Shock. Here." He handed her a canteen of water. "Drink. Then we need to run."

Victoria took the canteen but didn't drink. "What are—*you* doing?"

"Rescuing you." He pointed to the village. "But it looks like you didn't need much help."

She shook her head. "No. What are you doing *here?*"

"As you can imagine it's a very long story, but a really good one." He assessed her ragged appearance. "Probably not as good as your story, though. We can swap tales once we are safe. Now drink."

Victoria obeyed her principal and drank. The water was warm and stale, but the wetness on her parched tongue was bliss.

"Satisfied?" he asked.

"No."

He glanced back at the villagers. They had stopped their attack on the soil and were looking around for the source. "I'll distract them. Then we'll run for those hills." He pointed behind them.

"Do you know how to get out of here?"

He shrugged. "It's been a long time since I've been here, but I know where we need to go. Get ready."

"I can't," Victoria said.

"I know you're tired, but we must."

"My feet," Victoria moved her feet so he could see them. Red and blistered from the hot sand, they had been protected by Bernadette's boots, but running here had reopened blisters. Several cuts bled freely.

"Oh." He looked over at the villagers then pulled off his backpack and rummaged through it.

"Please tell me you have shoes in there," Victoria whispered.

"Just bandages. Can you manage wrapping your feet while I throw them off course?"

Victoria honestly didn't think she could, but she nodded. She wasn't about to be caught again.

Principal Wood handed her the bandages and left, ducking away behind the sparse greenery. Victoria knew she didn't have much time, but really didn't want to look at her feet. She knew if she looked at them and saw the blisters and the ground-in dirt, they would hurt worse. She didn't have a chance to look before a sound a few feet away startled her. Lying down to hide, Victoria peered around. It wasn't Principal Wood; these movements were cat-like. Holding her breath, Victoria waited for a sign that it was safe.

Whoever was near her was moving painfully slowly. Victoria's heart pounded and her ears filled with the rushing of blood as she felt the adrenaline course through her muscles. A face emerged from the shrubs and Victoria raised her hand, ready to make her request to the Air, when she stopped. It was the girl, the mage from the village, who had helped her escape. Victoria lowered her right hand and the girl let out a long sigh. She crawled toward Victoria as if approaching a lion with a thorn in its paw, speaking soft words. Although Victoria didn't know what the words meant, she felt reassured that the girl meant her no harm.

She held out a clay bowl with an oily substance, pointing from the bowl to Victoria's feet.

Victoria nodded. She couldn't remember the name of it, but it looked like the same ointment Tucker had used on her feet after the dream in which Lucian gave her the locket. When the girl rubbed the oil on Victoria's feet, hot pain shot up from her ankles to her knees and then straight to her head. Covering her mouth with both hands, Victoria lay back and fought the urge to scream. Fire. That's what it felt like—hot oil searing through the blisters and dirt. Several minutes passed before the pain lessened. And then Victoria remembered the heat that accompanied a healing. Sweat beaded on her forehead, her back, and even on her legs. Her feet didn't feel like branding irons any longer and when she finally looked she saw ten red toes on two red feet, the color of boiled lobsters. The blisters left white circles on her feet, but the healing made them look like no more than white pencil marks.

"Thank you," Victoria whispered.

The girl looked up from wiping her hands on a cloth and smiled. She pointed to Victoria and asked, "Anku?

"What?"

"Anku?" The girl pointed to Victoria, then put her hand on her chest and said, "Erankus."

"Oh," Victoria understood and put her hand on her chest. "Victoria."

"Veek-tur-ea."

Victoria smiled, "Close enough." Remembering the bandages, Victoria wrapped her feet while Erankus watched closely.

From a distance, the shouts of villagers erupted and the ground vibrated. Victoria peeked through the leaves of her hiding place to see if Principal Wood had been captured. Erankus, too, leaned forward and saw the men of her village stabbing the ground with their spears. Whispering to Victoria, Erankus quickly removed her sandals and tied them over the bandages around Victoria's feet.

Moments later, Principal Wood's face peeked through the barrier of branches. "Ready?" He startled when he saw Erankus. "Who's this?"

"A friend," Victoria said.

Erankus placed her hand on Victoria's arm, squeezed it gently, then slipped out from the bush and disappeared.

"You always did make friends easily," Principal Wood said as he helped Victoria to her feet, but she swayed, reaching instinctively for Mr. Wood to steady herself. "What is it?" he asked. "What's the matter?"

"I'm just tired," Victoria said.

"Alright. There is a mage in this region who can help us." He placed his hands on the ground and sent out several vibrations through the earth. Victoria watched the men as they felt the earth tremble beneath them. It was enough of a distraction to allow them to slip away.

Victoria cringed as they ran, hoping they weren't going to run the entire way. Despite Erankus' healing, her feet pulsed painfully. She stumbled, falling to the ground with a loud grunt. Mr. Wood turned and helped her up. "I can't run," she said, her voice quivering. "My feet hurt too much."

"You won't have to run much farther," he said. "I have

horses just over there." He pointed to the distance, but all Victoria saw were short trees and a long distance between them.

She wiped a tear from her cheek and tried to sound brave, but her voice didn't agree. "I'll try."

He didn't let her stop. Although every inch of her aching body wanted to, Victoria did her best to stay on her feet. Mr. Wood held her arm, practically lifting her off her feet as they ran. Memories of gym class came to mind, those horrible days when the coach walked them to the track and held a timer, announcing for all to hear how long it took each student to run a mile. Her gym teacher would be impressed today. She was jogging to keep up with Principal Wood, doing so to avoid being burned at the stake. If coach had a bonfire on the football field and threatened the slowest runner with a toasting-roast, all of them would have finished the mile in eight minutes.

She paced her mind with small goals.

I can make it to that tree. When she passed the tree, she would select a new target to reach.

That boulder. Then, that tall shrub next to the little tree. With each target reached, she knew she could go farther and farther. Her mind succumbed to the rhythm of her feet. Her breathing and heartbeat matched and on she went.

When he slowed down, Victoria hoped they would stop and that he would have food in the bag that slung across his chest. But more than food, she saw the horses—beautiful creatures tethered to a tree.

"Drink more. Looks like you need it," he said, handing Victoria the canteen.

Victoria only nodded. Talking took her breath away and with the change of rhythm in her step, her mind and lungs needed to catch up. Knowing that she would soon be riding and her feet would no longer have to carry her weight, she found the motivation to take a few more steps.

"You'll be on the brown mare," Mr. Wood told her. "Have you ever ridden a horse?"

"Mom took me once."

"Just hold on. We won't take this at a run, but we do need to stay ahead of them. I don't think these people have horses, so we have an advantage."

He helped her onto the horse and they were off again. For hours they rode swiftly across the land. For some time, Victoria was relieved to be riding instead of walking, but that slowly wore away as a different discomfort increased. Sleep whispered tantalizing words in her ears, sending chills of possible nightmares down her back. To sleep on the back of a horse gave her only a few minutes of delightful rest, but it abruptly ended when her head fell heavily onto her chest or when her body started to slide off the horse. At some point in the deep darkness of night, Mr. Wood slowed down and stopped. They were in a slightly wooded area now, the trees sparse and small. "We'll sleep for a few hours."

Victoria slid off the horse and sat down hard. Her legs just wouldn't support her at all. She crawled to the base of a tree, curled up, completely unconcerned with the dirt.

"Do you want to eat first?"

Victoria wanted to tell him that she was too tired to chew, but she was asleep before she could say anything more.

It seemed like seconds later when the sun's rays woke her. It felt like her heart had dropped to her feet, they throbbed so badly.

"Good morning," Principal Wood said. He sat a short distance away, eating something.

"Uh-huh." Victoria's stomach jumped at the thought of food.

"Here." He handed her water and a granola bar. "Eat up."

"Haven't seen one of these in a while."

"I packed in a hurry."

Victoria ate everything he handed her except the water. The

canteen felt very light. Her head swam a bit. Dehydrated.

Mr. Wood noticed that she didn't drink the water. "There used to be a stream that would swell in the spring just a few miles that way. I'm hoping it's still there. Finish what's there and we'll fill up."

Victoria hesitated. "Shouldn't we save some?"

"You need it. Drink up."

She obeyed and was grateful.

"And the people," she nodded in the direction of the village. "Are they following us?"

"Yes."

She started to cry. "I didn't mean to kill anyone."

Mr. Wood leaned forward and held her hand. "I know. You saw the blood in the river?"

Victoria nodded.

"That's why they are afraid. They don't understand what's happening."

"You do?" Victoria asked.

His expression was grim. "I do. I'll explain later. Ready?"

She looked at him as he stood and strapped his bag to his horse's saddle. "Do I look ready?" Her sarcasm was rude, but it seemed obvious that she couldn't keep up this pace much longer. Sleep had been a sweet respite, but it mostly just made every muscle stiffer and more tender. At least her sleep had been dreamless and she woke up in the same place she had fallen asleep, so she would count that as a small victory.

"Today will be better." He held out his hand and helped her up. "Once your body warms up, you'll feel better."

Victoria didn't think anything less than a week at an all-inclusive spa with a hospital wing for the recently-tortured would be enough. Instead, she tried to find comfort in the fact that she hadn't been roasted like a s'more.

They rode until the sun reached its peak, and Mr. Wood

slowed his horse and dismounted. The area was slightly greener and the spring that Mr. Wood had promised Victoria bubbled gently from the ground over rocks and down the sloping land. Feeling the ground, he closed his eyes. "They've stopped."

"They've given up the chase?" Victoria asked hopefully.

"At least for now no one is following us. A little shade and lunch should do us both some good."

Easing herself to the ground, Victoria stretched her legs out and sighed. Never before had the hard ground felt so comfortable. As her former principal refilled the canteens, Victoria asked, "Do we have time for a story, Mr. Wood?"

He laughed. "We do. Where do I start?"

"Start with my mom. Is she okay?"

"She and Adam Martin left to gather up the other mages who left the society."

Victoria frowned. "Adam Martin? You mean Mr. Martin's name is Adam?"

"Much changes when you go into hiding."

"How many are there?"

"No one knows for sure. We all stayed isolated." He handed her a canteen, some dried meat, and some fruit from his bag. "But as far as I can tell, we all know one or two other mages in hiding."

"Why did they leave the society?"

"That's part of the story. But first, you may stop calling me Mr. Wood."

Victoria blushed, "What should I call you?"

"Well, I guess that's part of the story, too. I'm not sure what you know, but I'll start from the beginning. My beginning anyway. My first mission as a Green Guard was to stop a small band of mages from finding the Grandfather's Key."

"Lucian told me."

His face brightened. "He's alive?"

"No. That's a long story. You finish yours, then I'll tell you mine."

"Fair enough," he said, although it was obvious he wanted to know that story immediately. Leaning back on an elbow, he continued. "We were asked to find the Grandfather's Weapon to protect it, but we discovered a bit too late that a few of the Council Mages had other plans. They wanted to find and use the Weapon."

"Wait." She remembered Lucian's story. His sister, Leora, had died in the kiva, leaving three: Lucian, Alexander and Foley. "You're Foley."

"That's what they used to call me. As an Earth mage, I can work with the trees. Having a name like Wood, well, it seemed clever when we were kids."

"What is your real name?"

"Doesn't matter anymore. I'm not him."

Victoria knew *that* story was probably a really good one. "Why does Ona want the Grandfather's Weapon?"

"The Grandfather's Weapon is like the Holy Grail of the Mage Society. No one is sure it exists or where it is or what it can do. What is agreed on is its power."

"So, what is the Grandfather's Weapon?"

Foley shrugged. "That's part of the mystery. And part of the protection around the Weapon. If no one knows what to look for, no one can find it easily. But we uncovered a few truths behind the Weapon, and our task was supposedly complete. Except that the few Council Mages who were searching for it realized if we ever shared with others the purpose behind our first mission, their motives might be discovered. We became a risk to them and they decided to eliminate us." He took a bite of dried meat and chewed slowly before continuing. "Your mother discovered their plan and alerted us. Just in time, too. We hid in the Fourth Terrace among all the static."

"Ambrosia told me that it's very difficult for mages to find their elemental intent in terraces with electricity."

"Very true. There were four of us in hiding. Lucian, Xander, your mother, and myself." He paused again, and Victoria knew why. She knew a part of the story from Lucian—how Ona had used them to try to open the Earth Gateway and how Leora had been killed. Foley's version of the story was missing a few details, but she decided it would be better to pretend not to know and learn something new then throw out all her knowledge and miss new information.

"The Council Mages never stopped searching for us. Lucian was found. A fluke really, but found and captured all the same. It was decided that Xander would go after him. He was a Fire mage and very strong. He was a great man. A bit of a fool at times, but we all were."

"And you never went looking for them?" Victoria asked.

"I did. I was on my way back to the sphinx city, but luckily, I met with a friend before I was discovered by the wrong people. That's how I learned the Xander had been cast away."

Victoria looked down and fiddled with the dried meat. Her appetite was gone.

"Are you okay?" he asked after a moment.

Victoria took a breath. She felt the tears building behind her eyes, stinging her throat and nose. "This means my father didn't abandon us. It means that everything my mother did that I thought was crazy was just an effort to protect me from the Mage Society. And it means that you have a lot of explaining to do." She pointed at him, feeling the sparks tingle her skin. Taking a deep breath, she tucked her hand under her leg and tried to prevent a freak bolt of lightning from doing the electric slide across Foley's skin. More calmly, she continued. "You welcomed Anna Witherspoon to the school, knowing that she would discover that I was a mage."

"We all knew that someday you would discover your

elemental intent. We thought it better to do so under the guidance of a mentor."

"We?" Victoria asked.

"Your mother, Adam, and I."

"And you knew Anna would be my mentor?" Victoria asked.

"It was luck that it was her," Foley said. "You see, Anna Witherspoon was there when we received the orders from the Council to find those trying to locate the Grandfather's Key."

"But Anna imprisoned Lucian," Victoria reminded him.

"Yes." Foley wiped his forehead. "That does throw a wrench in the works, doesn't it?"

"What do you mean?"

"Lucian and Anna were to be married."

"Oh," Victoria said, remembering her vision from Ophidia of Anna and Lucian holding hands. "That does complicate things."

"When she came to see me about teaching, a masquerade to search for something the Council wanted, she recognized me. She had been told that we had been killed. She didn't want to believe that the Council had lied to her."

"She told me that she was on a mission to find the Lost Painter," Victoria remembered.

Foley nodded. "Just another pointless mission from the Council. You see, if the Council can keep mages in the Society looking for legends that don't exist, those same mages won't see what the true goal of the Council is. But with her finding me, I saw it as an opportunity to open her eyes to the fact that it is possible to hide from the Council, an idea that mages assumed could never happen. It blows a big hole in their idea of the Council being 'all-knowing'. I told her everything that happened, but I left out Xander's role and that I knew where the Martins had been hiding."

"So, Anna's mission to the Fourth Terrace to search for the Lost Painter was just a distraction?"

Foley nodded.

"But when I met the Council, they scolded her for searching for a legend. It sounded like Anna was actually going against their orders."

"It's all an attempt to cover up their true goals," Foley sighed. "One Council Mage will secretly give another mage an order, under the guise that the rest of the Council forbids such an action, but in reality, it's a mission to keep eyes focused on something other than the Council."

"A conspiracy."

"Yeah. Which makes me sound crazy, but you've seen the imbalance for yourself."

"But Anna did find me."

"Anna found a mage in hiding. She found the truth about our disappearances and now she knows that the Council has lied. Having Anna on our side is a huge step. Especially after Lucian."

"What do you mean?" Victoria asked.

"She imprisoned her fiancé on order from the Council." Foley smiled ruefully. "Anna is nothing if not a staunch rule-follower."

"And the Lost Painter legend?"

Foley waved his hand as though the idea was nothing more than a pesky mosquito. "Victoria, the Lost Painter legend is ridiculous. It says that a mage will have full elemental intent. That hasn't happened since the Grandfather himself. It also says that this Painter will step between the worlds."

"Sounds like any Painter, except for the full elemental intent part."

"Step *between* worlds, not through the doors that link them. I can't remember the original text it was written in a rhythmic verse and I can barely understand Shakespeare. It stated that the Lost Painter will take a step in this terrace and with the second step be in the next terrace. That's why the legend is called 'Lost'. She can do what a Painter can do but without the painting. Lost. Never found. The way between the terraces is never found by anyone except that mage."

"Which you say is impossible."

"So much must be in place for this to happen. We are protected from this legend because if it were to happen, the entire Mage Society could fail."

"Hypothetically speaking, what would need to be in place?" Victoria tried to ask casually, but she feared she already knew the answers.

"Well, the Grandfather's Weapon would be in danger."

"I think we've already established that. What else?"

"This Painter would need a device that could weaken the boundaries between the terrace and the mind. But it's a device that must be given in a dream. To take this from someone would mean death."

Victoria held out the dreamwalker, which was still in her hand. The broken chain dangled uselessly. "I'm sufficiently freaking out."

He didn't speak for a moment. "I spoke to you yesterday through the earth. Back at the village after you had escaped the village fence. How did you get outside that fence?"

"I jumped."

"With bleeding feet? That wall was over six feet tall!"

"Air."

Foley's shoulders and jaw dropped. "Water and Fire, too?"

"Water. Too scared to try Fire."

"Can't blame you there." He stood and walked around nervously. Victoria didn't feel nervous at all, but relieved. There was a name for her abilities, a diagnosis for her freakishly uncommon elemental intent. She didn't mention lightning and Foley didn't bring it up, which was just as well. That would take away her newly acquired sense of comfort.

"You're the Lost Painter?" he finally muttered.

"I'm not lost anymore." Victoria smiled. "What does that make me now?"

"You've really stepped from one terrace to another without a painting?" he asked.

She nodded.

"Who else knows you have a dreamwalker?"

"Bobby and Tucker. Anna and Worthmere. The Sphinx. I tried to keep it hidden from Ona, but I'm pretty sure she knows."

Foley paced. It made her nervous to see him nervous so she changed the subject.

"Then Mr. Martin is a mage too?"

"Earth."

Victoria remembered his uncanny ability to know who was at the front door and when the twins tried to sneak out of their room. "Then what was your plan for when Anna did discover me?"

"Our plans didn't matter when you and the twins disappeared," Foley said. "I checked on Anna in the art room and saw the broken door and easels. That's when Diane and Adam decided to find others who might be able to help."

"And you came here?" Victoria asked.

"I tried to get to the kiva in the First Terrace, but the Council instituted a talisman passage. I did manage to travel two terraces up. A bit of luck from a mage whose sister is also in hiding. She knew of other mages who had successfully left the Society and let me pass through and gave me a talisman. I came west to check the kiva here."

"So this is Terrace Two?"

Foley nodded. "I knew that if Ona found you, she would take you there to try again. I watched the man walk into the kiva and saw the lightning. I assumed that you were successful."

"If by successful you mean that we found what Ona was

after? Yes. If you mean that we all escaped alive? No."

"Lucian. How?"

"I'm not sure," Victoria rubbed her eyes trying to remember everything that had happened in the kiva, but so much had happened so fast. There was no way she could sort out the intricate details in order to determine what had gone wrong. "Maybe Bobby would know."

Foley's attention was diverted to the vibrations coming from the ground. Victoria could feel them too. They were still being followed.

"I think we should get started. It's a long ride, but if we start now, there is a shelter we could reach by night."

Victoria didn't move.

"There's a bed and a hot meal," Foley said.

"You win." Victoria stood, stretched, and walked to the horse. Foley helped her up and she winced as every muscle protested. "Do these horses have names?"

"Yours is Marlis. This is Osef." He patted the neck of his mount.

"Good girl, Marlis." Victoria stroked Marlis' neck. "You are saving my feet." To keep her mind from her aches and pains, she kept the story going. "What did you hope would happen when Anna discovered I was a mage?" Victoria asked.

"I hoped that she would be persuaded to join our cause," Foley said as he mounted his horse and started riding west again.

"And what exactly is your cause?" Victoria asked, pressing her heels gently into Marlis' sides, trying to urge it to follow. The horse finally did, but Victoria was certain it had nothing to do with her skills as an equestrian and all to do with Marlis' tendency to follow Osef.

"There's a little history involved in this, so bear with me," Foley warned Victoria. "There have always been mages that have wanted to leave the society. They fall in love with someone outside the society, they are mistreated by another mage—any number of reasons. But until recently, Society mages were hunted down and returned."

"And by 'returned', you don't mean a welcome home party." Victoria feared the answer, knowing that her mother was one of these mages.

"More often than not they are arrested, tried before the Council, and cast away. But times are changing. There are two terraces that have been launched into an age of technology. And while those terraces makes life very easy for the ungifted, life as a mage among the constant energy hum and pollution is extremely difficult."

"The electricity interferes with the elemental intent," Victoria said.

"To the point where I stopped trying for several years," Foley said. "It was like having a constant fuzzy television. The messages were never clear. I finally turned it off."

"So it's a safe hiding place," Victoria said.

"Safer." Foley corrected her. "There was always the threat of just running across a mage. It happened to Lucian, so we were always on the lookout."

"What about the mages in that village?"

"They aren't a part of the Society, so the Council doesn't worry. Any mages in that village can live apart from the benefits of the Society, but they also live apart from everyone. Mages are different. Those without elemental intent never really understand or trust what it means to be a mage. The trust a neighbor has with another is vital to the success of communities. That little village obviously has some respect for their mages. Others don't have the understanding of what it means to be a mage or to have the help of someone with elemental intent. Now, with the Council seeking the Weapon, I don't trust them. That's why I told Anna what happened in the kiva and Ona's true purpose for using us."

"She believed you?" Victoria asked.

"No."

"But she didn't turn you in either."

"We had hoped that with someone as influential as Anna on our side, we could reenter the Mage Society and restore the balance."

Victoria thought for a moment. "I've heard that, about the balance. The balance between what?"

"Good and evil."

"That sounds a bit—medieval."

Foley laughed. "I suppose it is. But think about the very first story mankind ever knew."

Victoria rolled her eyes. "I knew this would turn into a lesson."

"Yes, well," Foley chuckled, "I did warn you this would involve some history. Might as well make it a learning experience. Besides, all lessons should take place in the wild and on the back of a horse."

"With an angry tribe of men with vengeful hearts following us?"

"It's better motivation to listen than just doing well on a mid-term." He winked at her. "Back to the lesson. First story of mankind?"

Victoria thought for a moment. "Outside of the creation story which involves mankind, it would be the story of Adam and Eve."

"Exactly!" Foley said. "God and Satan. Good and Evil. Adam and Eve were God's creation and Satan hated that God had made something as beautiful as he once was."

"So he deceived them to sin so God would banish them."

"And ever since, the world has been pulled between the two. Some of us fight for what is right and others succumb to what is easy and pleasurable."

Victoria shook her head. "I understand that, but I don't get how this fits into the Mage Society. What does the balance really mean?"

"When the Grandfather, the first mage, divided the terraces—"

"I know this story too," Victoria interrupted, "he did so without the consent of God. He went against the divine plan."

"Right. Think of it like a balance." Foley held his hands out with his palms up, lifting one then the other with each set of opposites. "God created the heavens and the earth, man and woman. There was day and night, earth and sky. Each thing He created had balance and it was all good. Satan added sin and destroyed that balance. It became a third ingredient to the mix. When the Grandfather divided the terraces," he lowered his right hand, "it was man splitting the worlds. Seven different terraces. No balance."

"It's an odd number," Victoria said, seeing where Foley was going with his story.

"Yes, an odd number. And not just three terraces. Seven."

Victoria yawned.

"Am I boring you?" Foley teased.

"When I tell you my story, you'll understand."

Foley looked at her with concern, but continued his story. "The dragons were sent to the Seventh Terrace, but no one goes there because it's too dangerous."

She knew what the Council did with mages who worked against them. To be 'cast away', Lucian had told her, meant to be sent to the Seventh Terrace. That's where her father had been sent: to the land of dragons. Survival over the last sixteen years would have been impossible.

"How can you hope to restore the balance? If it's always been imbalanced, what hope is there? Wouldn't it be better to just get rid of everything bad?"

167

"I know what you mean," Foley said. "The term, 'restoring balance' has really just become a phrase that means to overcome evil. It will always exist, but so will the Creator's good. The balance is in place when evil can't get the upper hand."

A chill shook Victoria. Her skin hurt and she yawned. Her eyes wouldn't stay open. She could hear Foley talking and she knew that her head was bobbing. Before she fell asleep, she leaned forward, resting her head on the warm neck of the horse.

Ɑ⳨

"Do you see that tree?" Foley's voice snapped Victoria's mind awake. "When we reach that, we'll stop and rest."

"Are they following us?" Victoria asked, struggling to form words in her mind and her mouth.

Foley looked at her. Even in her foggy mental state, Victoria knew he was concerned. But she didn't understand why. Her mind tried to tell her, but she couldn't stay alert long enough to connect her thoughts.

A memory tickled Victoria's mind—a story of terrace traveling. It was a dangerous story, but her mind wouldn't pull together the details. The light feeling in her gut and the lack of complete thoughts both should have warned Victoria what was happening.

She struggled to stay on the horse. She felt as though she was filled with helium and wanted to soar through the air. If she allowed that feeling to take over her thoughts, Foley would pull her back down with his words. For awhile that worked. She heard Foley say, "Just to the tree," but the lighter-than-air feeling was stronger and the words no longer made sense.

For fleeting moments her eyes absorbed the scene in front of her—tangles of brown branches clothed in leafy gowns dipping into the earth then leaping out again like frozen serpents in the ocean. Just as Victoria was about to remember the name of the tree or where she had seen such a snake, her mind wandered away, sometimes back to the pain in her feet or the man holding her and talking, but other thoughts dripped through, leaving a trail of disconnected images: one face on two people, a handsome face with a friendly smile and stern eyes. She saw gold and silver frames filled with mountains and hills and she wanted to climb through and stay there. Other moments were filled with a darkness so wild and thick she didn't think that the sun ever really existed. Nor did she care. The moments of darkness started to stretch until the only reality that she felt was nothingness.

DAVID

"You're not asleep," a man's voice warned her. He sounded far away, but Victoria could feel someone checking her pulse on her neck. She tried to open her eyes, but the light was too bright. "Keep your eyes closed." A strong hand lifted her head and gently pressed a cup to her lips. "Drink this."

Doing as she was told, she recognized the spicy flavor of limenterra. She pulled away and made a face.

"I know it tastes terrible," the man said gently. "You must drink it."

He held the bowl to her lips again and encouraged her to drink until he was satisfied. "That should work. Now you can open your eyes."

The light didn't seem as bright now. A dim, lantern-lit room greeted Victoria's blurry vision. Slowly, it cleared, revealing an older man's worried expression.

"Where am I?"

The man gestured to the room. "My laboratory."

Beyond the light of the flickering flame, she could make out stacks of books, bubbling pots over blue flames, and several high windows along the walls. Lost in the dark recesses of the room, she could hear a metal windmill whirling.

"Who are you?"

"You don't remember me?"

Victoria tried to focus her eyes, but the best she could discern from him was that he was sitting next to her. "Sorry."

"David."

"The boy from my dreams?" Victoria couldn't believe her ears.

He laughed. "How many times I wish I had heard girls say that about me. Perhaps you have been dreaming when I see you, but you've been stepping in on my life for as long as I can remember."

"Am I dreaming now?" She absently reached for the dreamwalker, but it was gone.

David held it up. "It was clenched in your fist. I fixed the chain." He placed the locket in Victoria's hand and she pulled it close, relieved that she would not be stuck here. Without it, she was certain she would never wake up, let alone return to the place where she had fallen asleep.

"What is it?" David asked.

"A locket," Victoria told him. "It was a gift."

"The markings on it are remarkable. What do you keep inside?"

Victoria slipped the locket over her head. "I've never opened it."

David raised his eyebrows. "Why not?"

"It's sealed shut."

David thought about that for a moment. "You asked if you were dreaming. You were never really there the other times, then?"

"Not really. But," she rubbed her forehead, "oh, it's hard to understand."

Standing, David took the bowl of limenterra to a table. "What city is yours?"

"You mean, where am I from?"

He nodded.

Sleepiness was wearing Victoria thin. "I can't remember."

"Near Rome?" he asked. "Or Greece? You have very pale hair. You might be from the Scandinavian or Germanic provinces."

She shook her head. "Farther."

"To the north?"

Victoria could feel tears forming in her eyes. "I can't remember."

Smiling kindly, David brought Victoria some food. "It's not important. Just trying to make conversation. Here." He helped Victoria sit and propped pillows behind her. The bed was just a cot. Not particularly comfortable, but it was covered with a simple, hand-sewn quilt.

David handed her a wooden plate with a piece of flat bread and some kind of vegetable mixture. He picked up a plate for himself and Victoria watched him as he used the flat bread to scoop up the vegetables. It was delicious and warm.

While they ate, Victoria looked around the room. A small painting of a woman with four little girls caught her attention. "Is that your family?"

"It is." David smiled proudly. "They've grown since that painting was completed and my wife has had another daughter. She's expecting again." He blushed. "It will probably be another girl. My house is very much filled with delicate clothing and emotions."

Victoria giggled. "I can imagine." An awkward silence filled the space as David stood and took his plate to the table on the far side of the room.

"Do you know how long you'll be staying?" he asked.

"I don't even know how I got here."

"A friend brought you to me. He and I usually meet—in a garden—but today he was here and asked me to help you. Said it was important that you and I meet."

"Who is your friend?"

"I'm sure you'll meet him. In the meantime," he gestured to the room, "this is my passion." David pointed to the various items in the room. "I think you and I are alike. We can do things other people can't."

Victoria nodded.

"Well, our mutual friend won't tell me the purpose of my gifts. He says that I must figure out why I can do what I can do and how to use it to help mankind. I'm trying to do that."

There was nothing in the room that looked like anything to help mankind. Different solutions bubbled over a small fire and an assortment of wooden structures hung from the ceiling looking like models of future devices. Several books were stacked on the shelf and others were open on the table. Nothing seemed to go together, as if David was searching blindly for a way to use his skills.

"What is it you're trying to create?" Victoria asked.

Scratching his head, David searched for words. "There are times when I'm very clear in my purpose and I have no doubts about what He wants me to do. But then my device doesn't work how I expect it to, so I try again. Maybe I can find a way to keep crops from failing. I created a system that keeps water near the crops, but then the growing season had too much rain and the crops drowned. I tried to construct a way to prevent homes from being destroyed in severe storms, but they tumbled during an earthquake. When I tried to temper Air with a more consistent weather pattern, Water levels underground fell and the crops dried out. My best success so far is the medicine I gave you. You were near death when you arrived. My friend said my medicine was what you needed. I'm glad something I've made works."

"Me too," Victoria smiled. "Could taste better."

David laughed. "Well, my mother always said that some of the best medicines in life were bitter."

Outside, a bell rang. David stood. "That means I have to go. My wife insists that I be there to tuck the girls in for bed."

Victoria smiled. "Thank you for your help."

"I'm sure we'll meet again. Sleep well." He left the lantern burning on the table and walked out the door. There was nothing else to do but close her eyes. Sleep well, he had instructed. She intended to do just that.

Black Lake

Victoria felt completely rested. The lingering taste of the limenterra was nasty, especially after sleeping, but the exhaustion and the feeling that bits of her were dissolving away had passed.

The early morning sky was a pale pink. Foley sat nearby tending a small fire. When she stirred, Foley moved toward her and put his hand on her forehead, checking for a temperature. "You're awake."

"Where are we?"

"A few hours from that shelter and hot meal I promised you."

"What happened?"

"You needed limenterra. Jo will have some, but I managed to find a few of the ingredients and brewed a weak tea for you. As soon as you are feeling up to it, we can keep moving."

Victoria sat up and stretched. "Any granola bars left?"

He reached into his bag and handed her a foil wrapped bar and watched her while she ate.

"Why are you staring?" Victoria asked.

Foley looked away and cleared his throat. "I—um—I

thought you were dying."

Victoria stopped chewing and tried to remember what had happened before her dream of David. "Maybe the tea you made was strong enough."

"That would be a miracle." Foley sighed and Victoria had the feeling that he had prayed for just that.

"I feel fine." She didn't know how to explain her visit with David so she stood up and stuffed the last piece of the granola bar into her mouth. "I'm ready when you are." Picking up the blanket she had been lying on, she shook it out and wrapped it around her shoulders to keep the cool morning air off her arms.

Foley shook his head in disbelief. "Alright. Let's get moving."

That's exactly what Victoria wanted, needed. Every sensation was alive. The air smelled of summer; a mix of flowers, rotting leaves, and dew, which sparkled on the grass, releasing a clean watery scent as it evaporated. She could almost taste the warmth of the coming day. The energy within her mind and the strength of her elemental intent was intoxicating. She was aware of so many things as they rode on: the vast network of ant tunnels beneath the earth, the dampness in the westerly wind.

Victoria told Foley, "It's going to rain."

He looked up at the cumulus clouds and shook his head. "Those aren't rain clouds. We'll be fine."

Victoria didn't argue. She knew the clouds above them weren't storm clouds; any idiot could see that. It was the clouds to the west that were already discharging sheets of driving rain just a few hours in front of them. Victoria felt the air zap with lightning bolts even though she couldn't hear them. Hours later when the sky darkened and the lightning screeched across the sky, Foley looked at Victoria as if to ask if she were calling the storm. She shook her head. "It's the rain I told you about."

Foley looked around the open land. If only they had stopped three miles back, there had been old barns they could have found protection in from the rain. He pulled the hood of his coat tightly over his head and urged the horse onward, shoulders slumped under the weight of his bag and the weather. Victoria didn't mind riding in the rain. It was unlike anything she had felt before. The raindrops were so thick, it was more like walking through walls of water. Every drop washed away grime and sweat. She was soaked to the skin and loving every moment. The rain drove into Foley's eyes, blinding him. From the expression of pain on his face, it seemed as though the drops pricked his skin. But Victoria felt nothing but joy. Her skin was cool and her spirits high as she drank her fill.

It was hard to ignore the look of concern on Foley's face. "No one should enjoy rain this much," he told her.

"You don't melt in rain, do you?" she teased.

"I didn't think so, but this is likely to wash me away."

Not likely, Victoria thought, although the ground was becoming quite saturated.

The rain did eventually stop, followed by a blazing sun that heated the air to a thick humidity. Just as their clothes were almost dry, the trees opened up to a bleak scene. A large crust of obsidian and pumice rock covered the ground like a scab. Around the edge of the dark rock, small, shrubby pine trees were still dwarfed by several tall and blackened tree trunks. Many of the charred trees had fallen, but a few stubborn ones remained, looking like giant toothpicks.

"This used to be a beautiful lake," he said. "My family had lived along its shores since my mother was a child." He pointed to the eastern edge, but there was nothing there except black dirt. "Being mages, my parents were often away. But when they were home, we were here and playing, fishing and doing all the things any child loves."

Victoria looked at the barren scene in front of her. Nothing of what Foley said seemed possible. There was no water, certainly no fish, and this seemed like a place to send criminals for punishment, not have a family get-a-way.

"The earthquakes in our terrace stem from this terrace's volcanic activity."

"How often does a volcano erupt?"

"More often than you'd think," Foley said.

The earth suddenly felt fragile as if she were riding on porcelain and a heavy footstep would break through to the red depths below. She had seen video footage of volcanoes boiling angrily, spewing hot destruction and marring the landscape. This land wasn't like that, at least not until they reached the black, stone lake. Foley stopped at the edge of the lake and stared. No water lapped against the shore. Instead, black and brown crusted rock—a frozen lava flow—formed a petrified river, perfectly still, absolutely barren.

Foley stared at the black lake and sighed. Victoria glanced at him. Although she had known Foley most of her life, all that time he had been Principal Wood, a friendly school administrator, not her missing father's best friend or secret body guard.

"My father was a Water mage and my mother an Air mage. , they were home when the volcano blew and the fires started. They got everyone to safety."

"Were the other people they saved mages?"

"No. Our friends saw what we could do and were afraid. They were good people, but when you see something that you can't explain, it's hard to accept." Foley turned away from the black lake and led the horses away toward an unburned and vibrantly green forest.

The trees closest to the burnt lake were small and scrubby pines, whose needles had fallen for years, making a quiet cushion for the horse's hooves. Deeper in, the trees were taller. Not all pines, but oaks and maples, poplars and hickory. High above, hidden within the leaves in the canopy, birds chirped a warning cry that someone had entered. Victoria knew it was a warning, for as soon as she heard it, the other birds and creatures were silent. But not for long. Just as all creatures, they tired of being silent and still, and soon continued foraging for food and frolicking fun.

Deeper still, the trees became massive. Trees, with trunks broad enough that five grown men could have scarcely stretched their arms around it and still reach each other's finger tips, stood like giants. Victoria stretched her neck back to see how far up the trunk towered, but the leaves protected the tree from full view. She pulled Marlis to a stop and reached a hand out to the thick, rough bark of the tree. Within, she could sense the vibration of a thousand different inhabitants. From ants to beetles, birds and squirrels, a mother cat lay sleeping on a high branch, and a family of some furry type of animal lay huddled under the roots, waiting for nightfall. She pulled her hand away and saw that Foley had stopped ahead and was waiting for her.

"It's almost become a legend, these woods," Foley said when Marlis caught up to Osef, bringing Victoria side-by-side with Foley. "There are people who want to experience nature at its fullest. Most people who enter these woods are never seen again."

"Sounds dangerous. Why are we going in?"

"To visit an old friend."

"A mage?"

Foley nodded. "Jo is bitterness personified. Left the Society years ago." He rode on, not saying anything more about Jo or the Society or why anyone would live so far from any other person.

Jo's home was hidden deep in the woods. Victoria, when she was little, had been captivated by the Grimm's Tales—the original fairy tales with death and destruction and sad endings, not the fluffy animated versions. These woods reminded her of the tangled woods that Little Red Riding Hood walked through on her way to her grandmother's house. The sounds of animals were clear, but the creatures remained hidden. Not even a flash of fur or creepy yellow eyes were seen. It was just darkness, bark, dense leaves and the sound of the horses breathing and steps.

"How do you know we are going the right direction?" Victoria asked. From all she could see, one tree looked the same as another.

"I'm an Earth mage."

Victoria had been communicating with Earth too, but she felt nothing other than the old trees, a million insects, and animals. There was nothing in her senses that led her in this direction. "Is there something in particular that you are following?"

"In the Air, do you sense a disturbance?"

"No. There's just stillness. The trees are too close together for any wind."

"That's your clue. These woods are called the Silent Woods. The valley surrounding the woods keeps most of the wind at bay, so even the sound of rustling leaves isn't heard. But there is something here that shouldn't be, according to Earth."

Victoria didn't reply because she didn't understand. The next question was almost out of her mouth, but she knew he would just tell her to think it through.

Air was quiet; she turned to Earth. The constant movement of all the creatures moving among the dirt and stones underground filled her ears with an energizing hum.

She remembered being separated from Bobby and Tucker at a concert. With all the noise, she couldn't hear them calling her until she focused on the one sound that was different. The music was loud and steady. People singing along matched that beat. Sorting out various sounds, she listened for the short shouts and the familiar voice. From across several rows, she heard Bobby's voice calling her name. Once she focused, she was able to walk right to him.

No sooner did she think about searching for the different

sound that it came to her, an irregular pattern. Having never heard, or more accurately, felt, a sound like this, Victoria was surprised to discover that she knew what it was. It was immediately clear what Foley was following, what didn't belong in these woods. Human. Another human. And not only that, a woman. It was obvious from the lighter rhythm of the footsteps. She was sweeping.

"I can't imagine living in these woods, let alone being a woman and alone," Victoria said.

Foley stopped and turned in the saddle. "You can tell it's a woman?"

"Sure. She's singing." Now that she had identified that it was a woman, she could hear a soft voice on the air.

"When we fled from our village after—" he paused, "we went to Jo's. She is a bit of a hermit, but she took us all in. Mages and people and animals."

"That was nice of her."

Foley snorted, laughing.

"It wasn't nice?"

"Not really. She's the grumpiest woman I hope you ever meet."

"But she helped you," Victoria pointed out.

"She did, the way you feel obligated to help a dying man or to shoot a horse with a broken leg."

"And you think she will help us?"

"I don't know. She left the Society long before I did. Her information may be old, but she'll have limenterra for you and she's a damn good cook."

SIMETRA

Foley had described Jo perfectly. She was rough and weathered, but she retained a defiant beauty that lay just beneath the surface, like a lollipop that had fallen in the dirt. If she would just smile, Victoria thought, she would shine, but it was as if her face had been created to express sadness. The lines on Jo's face were the markers of years of sorrow. Her square shoulders and chin challenged the world to just try to take her on.

She stood outside of a small cabin nestled up against tree trunks and Victoria immediately thought of the witch's cottage that Hansel and Gretel discovered. Although it wasn't crafted from gingerbread and candy canes, it was the tidiest home Victoria had ever seen. Tall, slender logs had been carefully planted in the ground, forming the walls of her cottage. The roof was moss. Victoria couldn't tell what held it up; it could have been pure will-power for all she knew. The grass under the tree and surrounding the cottage was trim, courtesy of a few lingering sheep. Circular gardens were planted in the small pieces of earth that actually saw sun.

Jo held the broom like a staff, put her other hand on her hip and looked at Foley as if she were choosing which limb to devour first. "And where have you been for the last twenty years? Your mother watched your father die. No son to console her."

Foley looked hard at Jo. "Don't put your own fears on my mother. She knew what was at stake when I left. She knew that I might not return."

"Still fighting for a people that cast you out and left you for dead."

Foley shook his head and forced a laugh. "You are still as lovely as ever. We've come a very long way. I don't suppose you have a little extra food?"

Jo ignored Foley and turned to Victoria. As if she was inspecting a piece of meat at the butcher shop, Jo looked Victoria up and down. "You've the eyes of a Painter."

"Yes, mam. So do you."

"And judging by that lovely dress, you've been an unwelcomed guest to a Council Mage."

Victoria nodded.

"Hmm." Jo looked back at Foley. "How bad is it out there?"

Foley's eyes twinkled. "What makes you think it's bad? Maybe we've just come here for a visit and some of your warm hospitality."

Not softened one bit, Jo retained her harsh glare. "That bad, huh?"

"Worse."

"Fool." Jo frowned and leaned the broom against the wall. "Well, you're probably as hungry as you are foolish. Luckily for you I made some bread yesterday and I put on a pot of stew. Bread's on the table. I have work to do." She walked toward a small barn, leaving Victoria and Foley to serve themselves.

Foley watched her go. "Just as lovable as I remember." He opened the door to the cottage for Victoria.

Inside the cottage, Victoria smiled at the simplicity of the furnishing. A narrow bed stood in the corner behind a curtain that could be drawn shut. A heavy wooden table sat in the center of the room with a platter of fresh bread. A small cup of wilting flowers sat next to it. Behind the door, another table stood beneath an open window. Here, a pitcher of water and a wash bowl stood next to a bowl of potatoes and a dish of berries.

In the corner, an easel held a half-finished painting. The wall behind it was lined with narrow shelves holding jars of paint. Walking toward the painting, Victoria saw Jo's painting of the sphinx city in all its white marble glory.

"It's beautiful," Victoria said. "But it's not a gateway. What are we doing here?" Victoria asked as Foley spooned some stew into a cup and handed it to her.

"Well," he rubbed the back of his head, thinking. "When you fainted, I thought you needed limenterra. But you seem fine."

"I feel fine."

"How? Don't get me wrong," Foley said. "I am—well, amazed and thankful." He picked up a bowl from the shelf and scooped stew into from a small pot hanging over the fire. "I just don't understand how you overcame that without limenterra." He handed Victoria the stew.

In truth, she didn't really understand how she had overcome it either. In the dream, David told her that his friend brought her to him. Who was his friend? Was David even real? Or was the dreamwalker messing with her mind?

"You don't have to tell me," Foley said, interrupting her thoughts, and she realized that she had been silent for a long time, still standing and holding the stew.

Sitting at the table, she tasted the stew. Jo was brilliant in the kitchen. "It's not that, I just don't know how to explain it."

"I imagine there is a lot going on that is hard to explain," Foley said. "So, I'll just chalk that up to an amazing miracle and move forward. We have a mission."

"To find Bobby and Tucker?"

"We have another task first."

Victoria tossed her hands in the air. "What could be more important than helping Bobby and Tucker?"

Foley reached into his pants pocket and pulled out a worn piece of paper. "We can't help them without help."

He reached across the table and set the paper in front of Victoria.

"What is it?" She didn't reach for it. It was only paper, but the way Foley handled it, she knew it was extremely important.

"Before your father left to try to help Lucian, he gave me this."

The paper felt old and soft, folded and unfolded many times, carried in a pocket until it was here, now. She slowly opened it. It was just a piece of paper, just a note, but it was the closest she had ever been to something her father had touched. His handwriting was short and choppy, as though he couldn't decide whether to write in print or cursive.

Help is with Simetra along Oath Shores.

"Oath Shores?"

"It's not a real place," Foley explained. "There is a ceremony when you are released from your mentor. A Council Mage pours water over your head and rubs earth on your hands as everyone stands in a circle around a fire. It's really a meaningful event: a coming of age, a graduation of sorts. After our ceremony, Lucian, Leora, Xander, your mother, and I left. Diane had painted her first gateway that took us to an area north of here, a river valley that's home to a string of small villages, near where your mom worked with her mentor. We had our own graduation party along that river. We pricked our fingers and mixed a few drops of our blood onto a piece of driftwood and sent it downstream."

"A blood ceremony? Like becoming blood brothers?"

"The meaning was there, but we didn't allow the blood to mix within us. Too dangerous to risk that."

Victoria rubbed the scar on her thumb, the thin scar barely visible. "Why would becoming blood brothers be dangerous?"

"It's actually a ritual performed by mages long ago, called the Sanguis Ceremony. In the sharing of blood, the mages became linked and their elemental intent increased in power, which is why mages used to perform the ceremony. But there's a catch. If one of the mages dies, the other loses their elemental intent."

Victoria looked at Foley. "My mother lost her intent, didn't she?"

Foley nodded. "She and Xander kept their Sanguis vows a secret until after Xander disappeared."

"That's why she didn't go to a doctor," Victoria remembered the day her mother collapsed. "She knew what it was." She stared at the note her father had written. So much history she didn't know about.

"Who is Simetra?" Victoria asked.

"I don't know."

"Do you know where to start looking?"

Foley sighed. "We need to go to where we were that night and find someone named Simetra."

"What help will she be?"

He shrugged.

Victoria waited for him to continue and was furious that he didn't freely offer his opinion about what might be waiting for them if they found Simetra. "Is she another mage in hiding? Does she have a secret weapon? Tell me why you want to go there instead of looking for Bobby and Tucker! Protect your own hope, but give me a little. I've lost everything."

Foley looked at Victoria for a moment before looking away. "You're right. And I will. Let's eat and get some sleep and I'll answer all your questions in the morning. I'm tired. You may have slept on the trail, but I didn't."

The Old Ways

Jo gave Foley and Victoria space on the floor in front of her fireplace to sleep. It was pleasant, cozy and snug, much how Victoria imagined a house should feel. She and Bobby and Tucker, before they started kindergarten, spent hours in the woods behind their houses in a little house Mr. Martin built. It was there that Victoria first hung dried flowers from the rafters to dry, the scent filling the little room with sweet aromas of summer. Jo did the same, but for practical purposes. Dried flowers, roots, and herbs hung from beams in bundles. Lavender, dill, and rosemary mingled with her senses, softening the worry creases on Victoria's forehead. Jo had hung another bunch of herbs over the fire just before they extinguished the last lantern. Whatever herb it was, it had tiny white flowers and a slightly pungent scent. Victoria was about to ask Jo what the plant was called, but her eyes were too heavy and the need to learn the plant's name was defeated by her desire to sleep.

As her breath evened and sleep came, she dreamed of her garden. Grass covered the earth like peach fuzz and a spindly tree, no taller than Victoria, sprouted in the center. She walked to it and felt the young bark and examined the budding leaves. Oak. Victoria felt sorry for the little tree growing all alone in a field of weak grass. She touched the bark. A light breeze ruffled through her hair and lifted the tiny leaves.

When I'm alone I can grow taller and stretch my roots.

Victoria pulled her hand off the bark. Those were words she heard, not images or a faint understanding, but words, groaning and creaking words from the wooden fibers of the tree.

"We'll keep this conversation between the two of us," Victoria said aloud to the tree. It was silent, but she thought it understood.

This dream was pleasant. She left her garden and walked through the surrounding land, soft grass under her feet, gentle leaves brushed against her skin. This sun was high and bright and shone on her skin with caressing warmth. Laying down in the short grass, Victoria curled up to sleep. Sleeping within a dream. Probably the safest place to sleep.

☜☜☞☞

The atmosphere at breakfast the next morning was tense. Jo stomped around the house doing chores with the energy of a lumberjack: chopping the bread, sawing through dried meat and felling eggs into the pan, picking out the broken shells. When Foley offered to help, she sent him out to the barn with a wide shovel. Foley sighed in disgust, but did what she asked. Victoria saw through the window that he was cleaning out stalls. Jo came up behind her and said, "You can help, too. I won't make you clean out the stalls."

Victoria relaxed gratefully and Jo set her to work crushing herbs.

"I want to know what the two of you are doing."

Nervous that she would unintentionally share something she

shouldn't, Victoria feigned ignorance. "We're just trying to find my friends."

"Where are they?"

"I'm not sure."

An ugly smirk crossed Jo's face. "Hard to find when you have seven terraces to search." Picking up the bucket of water that Victoria had used to draw water from the well, Jo walked passed Victoria to the table and stumbled. Water splashed toward Victoria, but she held out her hand to stop it and caught Jo with Air to prevent her from falling and hurting herself.

As soon as Jo looked at Victoria, she realized that the stumble was staged. Victoria blushed fiercely and secretly wished she had just let the old woman fall.

"You're the one then, aren't you?" she accused Victoria.

"What do you mean?" Victoria asked.

Jo shook her head. "Well, I'm not going to educate you on something your mother and mentor should have." Jo's eyes narrowed. "Who is your mentor?"

"Anna Witherspoon," Victoria answered.

"Then you no doubt know that you are expected to save us all." Jo rolled her eyes.

Victoria's jaw dropped. "I—I—what?"

"Jo," Foley said from the door, "legends are tricky. The Lost Painter may or may not be a part of what we are in the midst of. You know firsthand that the Society is losing its hold on the Old Ways."

Jo turned her venom on Foley. "I do. And no one came forward to save my family. If such a person does exist, then why is my family dead?"

"They knew the dangers, Jo," Foley said. "They fought for what they believed."

"To what end?" Jo yelled. "What was accomplished?"

"Mages joined our cause."

"They hide in the shadows of their elemental intent, waiting for a legend to emerge and march us all off to war."

Foley sighed. "Hopefully not, but I will fight for the Old Ways."

"You'll die for the Old Ways."

Foley nodded. "Probably." He leaned the shovel against the porch wall and told Victoria to gather their bags. "It's time we go. Thank you for feeding us and giving us a place to sleep. If you change your mind, you know where to go."

"You won't see me there," Jo said, walking sharply out of the cottage and toward the barn.

Foley watched her for a moment, then sighed resignedly. "Wasn't wrong about her, was I?"

"I just hope she's wrong about me."

Foley winked at her. "She might be right." When Victoria opened her mouth to protest, Foley interrupted her. "But now isn't the time to worry about legends. Let's go find this Simetra and see what help she can be. With any luck, this whole mess will be over soon."

A Little Kindness

It didn't take as long as she expected to reach their destination, but she wouldn't have known they were anywhere if Foley hadn't told her.

"This is it." He pulled the reins on the horse and stopped at an overlook to another valley. It was beautiful, but not much different from any other valley they had seen. From her viewpoint, she saw tall grass waving in the breeze and white birch trees and pine trees in small clusters throughout the landscape. Birds swooped through the air and the entire scene looked like an all-American, amber-waves-of-grain kind of national park.

Victoria noticed several ribbons of gray smoke rising from the trees. A narrow trail wound its way down the side of the valley, wrapping back and forth down the steep hill until they reached the lush green floor. The stinging heat that followed them as they rode along the top of the river valley lessened as they descended but was replaced with a sticky humidity.

"Town looks different. I hope those changes aren't the brain-child of Simetra."

Victoria agreed. "That has got to be the ugliest town I've

seen yet."

Foley nudged Osef forward. "It wasn't always like that. I wonder what happened?"

The town had a sloppily constructed fence around it, looking as though it had been constructed after a mad clearing of trees. Surrounding the fence, newly cut stumps of slender trees stood like small tombstones in a field of tall grass. The dirt road led to a gate that matched the shoddy construction of the fence. The two men guarding the town were busy using shovels to dig holes to support the tree posts. Turning the shovels so the blades were held like wide swords, they stopped Foley and Victoria.

"None may enter," said the older of the two guards.

"Why? What's wrong?" Foley asked.

"Illness."

"How bad?"

The guard shook his head. "Terrible. Blistering sores, high fever. Nasty business."

Foley looked around for a moment. "We are looking for someone, someone who can help us. Where does Simetra live?"

The guards exchanged a confused expression. "I don't know no Simetra."

"Are you sure?" Foley said. "We've come a long way."

The other guard scratched his neck as he thought. "Our town is bigger than most along the valley, but I've lived here all my life and never met anyone by that name."

"You can't go into town anyway," the first guard said. "Even if this Simetra did live here, we can't let you through."

"Agreed," Foley nodded. "Maybe it's a nick name?"

The guard lost his patience. "No one. Not a name a nick name or even a dog's name. Now, if you don't want to catch the plague, I suggest you leave before you catch my fist."

Foley nodded. "I hope your people recover." He pulled the reins and led them away from the village.

When they were far enough away Victoria asked, "Is this the wrong place?"

"Maybe." Foley said. "There were times when I really appreciated your father's mysteriousness. Today is not one of those days."

"What do we do?"

Foley smiled weakly at her. It was obviously meant to be encouraging, but it fell sharply flat.

"Nothing drastic. Let's find a place to sleep, maybe a hot meal, and then we'll make a new plan."

Foley's plan for that night was to rent a corner of a floor from a very young, and obviously a recently married couple. They were nice enough, but Victoria quickly tired of Mrs. Normance's giggles. Mr. Normance had introduced himself and his wife as 'Mr. And Mrs. Normance', leaving out their first names.

Foley wasn't taken in by the newlyweds. "I'm Woodson and this is Nike."

"Oh, what unusual names." Mrs. Normance's eyes widened. "Are you from the North?"

"No," Foley answered. "We are just simple folk without first names."

The jab was delivered but not received graciously, Victoria believed, as they were just given a corner of the main room of the house to sleep. As she helped Mrs. Normance clean up the dinner dishes, she realized that the corner of the floor nearest the fireplace was the only extra space the couple had. Their barn was unfinished, although there was enough room to tuck Maris and Osef under the eaves of the roof.

"Is Woodson your father?" Mrs. Normance asked Victoria as they worked to set down a few blankets for them to sleep on.

"No. He's a friend of my father's," Victoria said, keeping her eyes down.

Victoria had overheard Mrs. Normance warning her husband

that they shouldn't help them. "She's one of them," she'd said.

Mr. Normance shook his head and smiled at his naive wife. "That's all just stories. Don't worry. She just has different eyes. Don't let them differences scare you."

Until then, Victoria never realized that stories of mages and their abilities would be known to those outside the Society. The villagers who had tried to burn her were not mages, but the girl and the old man were. Apparently, in this place, mages were nothing but the stuff of strange stories.

If only.

Mrs. Normance continued her seemingly innocent questioning as she and Victoria lay out make-shift beds. "And you are traveling to see your father?"

"My mother."

"Where is she?"

Victoria sighed. "I'll be honest, we aren't sure."

"That must be difficult."

Victoria agreed that it was very difficult and swiftly changed the subject. "Thank you for giving us a place to sleep tonight. I hope we aren't too much trouble."

"Not at all." Mrs. Normance waved away Victoria's concern. "It wouldn't be decent otherwise. There isn't much room, but there is enough. With the sickness—" She stopped and swallowed.

"Do you have family in town?"

Mrs. Normance's face suddenly streamed with tears. "My sister and her family."

"I'm sorry. I'm sure they will be okay."

Sniffing and wiping her eyes, Mrs. Normance smiled. "That's what Marcus says."

"Marcus? Oh, your husband."

Mrs. Normance smiled. "I'm Laurel."

"Victoria."

"Well, Victoria," Laurel said, her youth shining through her smile, "I hope you sleep well tonight. The floor isn't very comfortable. I wish we could offer you more."

Marcus and Foley entered the house, continuing a discussion they had started while doing chores in the barn. "...it's certainly been a strange season," Marcus said.

"Any strange weather?" Foley asked.

Marcus hung his coat on a peg and kissed his wife. "Not here. Heard rumors about problems with the water in the south. I imagine that would explain the insect problems."

Laurel sighed. "More talk of problems." As she looked at her husband, tears pooled in her eyes.

Marcus reached from behind Laurel and pulled her into his arms. When Laurel covered her abdomen with her hands, Foley smiled. "Congratulations."

Laurel blushed and Marcus smiled widely. "Baby should be here mid-winter."

"Wonderful!" Foley said. "I have just the thing to celebrate." From his bag, he pulled out a bottle of wine. "Of course, Laurel won't want but a sip."

Marcus took four tin cups from the shelf and they poured celebratory drinks for the new baby. Laurel and Victoria had just a splash in their cups, but Marcus and Foley both had seconds.

All four fell into easy conversation over dinner. It was an enjoyable evening for Victoria and she realized that their presence took the young couple's minds off their troubles, if only for a few hours. When the moon was high and the little farm was dark, the peaceful quiet stirred strong emotions in Victoria's heart. She prayed that the illness would remain in town and resolve itself quickly. She hoped that Laurel's sister and her family would stay healthy. In the midst of her third prayer for Bobby and Tucker, and for her mother, she drifted to sleep.

DAVID'S ISLAND

She was back in a meditation garden. It wasn't her garden. This one was a tiny island, water splashing on a shore in every direction. She could have walked around the entire shore without breaking a sweat. The sky was close. Tiny clouds hung just out of arms reach, reminding Victoria of the crayon drawings she made in kindergarten. There was still one of these drawings in her mother's room—her and her mother reaching out of the second-floor window and squeezing rain drops out of clouds.

Just out of reach of the salty waves, a crackling fire blazed in the center of a ring of stones and large sea shells. David stared into the flames. He was much younger than in her last dream— now younger than Victoria.

He looked up and smiled as a man walked into the light of the fire and sat with him. The man had short black hair and a handsome face. He was tall and slender, not too muscular but clearly strong. He wore similar clothing as David: homespun pants and shirt. Both of them were barefoot.

"You have a question brewing," the man said.

"Is it true that I can ask you anything and you won't be

angry?"

The man laughed. "Very true."

David's shoulders relaxed. "I'm different."

The man waited, but David didn't say anything else. "That isn't a question, David."

"Why am I so different?" David wiped a tear off his cheek.

"Is this about what happened this afternoon?"

David looked at the man in surprise. "You saw that?"

"You know I did. Tell me about it."

"Why?" David frowned. "If you saw it, why do I need to tell you about it?"

"Good question. Why don't you tell me about it and maybe you'll understand why I want to hear about it from you."

Sighing, David shared his story. "I guess it started a while ago. My mentor was trying to help me figure out which element I could communicate with. I asked him if it could only be one element. I guess that was the wrong question to ask, because he scolded me and made me clean up the latrine."

"Why do you think he was angry?" the man asked.

"He told me that it was wrong to think that a mage could have more than one element. He said that terrible things have happened to Air mages who tried to communicate with Fire or Water mages who try to speak to Air. Is that true?"

"It is."

"But—" David started, but the man held up his hand.

"Finish your story."

"Today when I cleaned the latrine, I asked Water to help."

The man smiled. "Why is that so terrible?"

"I'm not a Water mage."

"Your mentor discovered your secret."

David nodded. "Father is furious. He's afraid they'll send me away."

"They will not send you away. I'm certain of that."

198

David struggled to keep the tears from spilling down his cheeks. His chin quivered. Finally, he hid his face. "Will terrible things happen to me?" he asked, his voice muffled behind his hands.

"Yes."

David's mouth fell open in shock as he looked up at the man. "I thought you would say something to make me feel better!"

"Lies serve no one." The man put his hand on David's shoulder. "Do you believe me?"

David nodded.

"Do you trust me?"

"I do."

The man appeared relieved when he smiled, but a hint of sadness kept his expression tense. He squeezed David's shoulder, patted it and let go. "The answer is yes. Terrible things will happen. But I promise that for every ounce of suffering you endure in faith, the rewards will greatly out-weigh the bad."

"Will the bad things happen to my family?" David wiped his nose on his sleeve.

"If they do, it will be their duty to endure them for the good outcome I can make of it."

Victoria's ears perked up. *For the good outcome I can make of it.* Who did this man think he was?

"Why did you make me this way?" David asked.

Victoria wondered if this man was his father. Perhaps this dream, of her being in David's prayer garden, was a moment when David talked openly with his father. But parents don't *make* their children a certain way. Who was this man?

"I have special plans for you."

"Why? I don't feel special."

"That's why I chose you. You are not stricken with pride like so many others. Many mages use their elemental intent to intimidate others. That is not its purpose. No gift granted to any person, mage or not, is meant to increase pride or power. All gifts are meant to bring knowledge of me to others. You know who I am, David. That's all I want from anyone, but especially you."

"I'm just a boy. I can't do anything great."

"Boys and girls, just like you, can cause great storms. You can save lives. It's in the small things that I make myself known. I love the little things of the world. You may be a boy today, but today is not forever. Someday you will be a man. If you keep your faith in me, you will be a great man. If you lose your faith, you could still be a great man among men, but that power is not the same. Power is not a strong arm or a mighty ruling from a throne of gold. Power is meek. It's a gentle touch in a moment of anger. A blessing instead of a curse."

"My mentor tells me that we have power over the elements."

"Your mentor is wrong. The elements *cooperate* with you by my bidding."

"What if I try to make the elements do something bad? What if I hurt people with Water or Fire?"

"Then it isn't the elements doing the hurting, it's you. Mages who make that choice will have to answer for it."

David thought about that for a long moment. The fire cracked and sparks burst into the air. The man waited patiently for David. Victoria's mind burned with a thousand questions. Who was this man? What was elemental intent? What was it really? What was the purpose behind it? Why was she like David? What happened to David? Was he a real person or were these just dreams?

"Will you tell me what it is that you want me to do with my elements?" David asked.

"Do you think I should?"

Again, David was silent for several seconds as he stared intently into the flames. "No."

"Why?" the man asked, smiling at David's answer.

"You made me this way. I trust you. Even though that doesn't feel like enough," David looked at the man, "somehow it is."

Victoria watched as David stood and left his garden. He didn't walk away or swim off the island, he simply wasn't there anymore. The man remained sitting with his back to Victoria.

She was furious with David's answer. She wanted clear answers. Why had she been given more than one element? Who was this man and why hadn't he talked with Victoria? He was clearly responsible for David's extraordinary elemental intent. Was he also responsible for Victoria's?

All the trouble Victoria had endured: the paintings, the elemental intent, the dreamwalker, her father's death, her mother's loss—it was all because of the Mage Society. It would have been so perfect to have someone to blame for everything. If it wasn't Victoria's fault for the way she had been born, if someone else had gone after Lucian instead of her father, if Anna hadn't found her at school, if Lucian hadn't died in the kiva, if Victoria hadn't taken the dreamwalker from him—if none of those things had happened, she would be a normal kid at a sub-average high school doing normal things that teenagers do. Instead, her principal was a mage who had saved her from an execution at the hands of natives who believed she had killed a boy and turned a river to blood. Definitely not the normal problems that come with hormones.

Watching David sit at a snug fire with this gentle man was a jab to Victoria's soul. David had two parents, a mentor and, from the sounds of it, conversations with God in his prayer garden.

"Are you angry?" the man turned toward her. It surprised Victoria that she wasn't surprised by his knowing she was there. Instead, it confirmed who he was. He wasn't just a he. He was He.

"Why?" Victoria faced him. "Why did you show me all these

moments of David's life?"

"Don't you know?" he asked.

"Don't pull that on me," Victoria pointed her finger at him. "You've given me all these elements, taken away my father, and denied me a mentor. And then when Anna found me, you gave me a dreamwalker that pulls me all over the place. What the heck!"

The man laughed.

Victoria wanted to punch him, God or not.

"You think I am responsible for all of that?"

"You're God, aren't you?"

"I am."

"How could you let that happen? Do you have special plans for me like you have for David?"

"I *had* plans for David," the humor disappeared from his face. "And I didn't let *all* of that happen."

"But you're God!"

"Victoria," He spoke softly and walked toward her, "I know. Let my work be done. Your part isn't finished yet."

Ashamed, she lowered her head. "I'm afraid." She started sobbing uncontrollably. She felt his arms around her and leaned her head onto his chest.

"I know," his voice was soft and assuring. "If you will trust me, the fear is just a pest, not a defeating enemy." He kissed the top of her head and wiped the tears off her cheeks. For a moment, his eyes grew distant and his expression darkened. "It's time for you to go. What happens next is not your fault."

The Way is Small

A rushing roar stirred the back of Victoria's mind. The island she had dreamed about was gone. She and Tucker stood in an alley of an old city trying to tame a fire that was in the shape of a wild dog. Tucker was telling her that the fire-dog was hungry and needed to be disciplined to wait for an appropriate snack. Typical of Tucker to make it seem so simple, and yet here was a ravenous fire-dog consuming wooden buildings just from his dripping drool.

"Just tell him to sit, Victoria," Tucker instructed as he watched from a distance.

The fire-dog, at the sound of Tucker's voice, turned to Victoria. With a tip of his head and a raised eyebrow, the dog seemed to say, "Really? You're going to tell me what to do?"

"Victoria!"

It wasn't Tucker's voice that roused her from her sleep, but Foley's. "Victoria! We need to go!"

"What? What's happening?" She rolled off the thin blanket that was her bed. She had fallen asleep with Eranku's sandals still on. After walking for so long with bare feet, she didn't want to be

203

caught unprepared again.

Foley pulled his shirt on over his t-shirt. "I don't know. I hear yelling coming from town." He turned toward Marcus and Laurel and pointed a finger at them. "You stay here."

"I can help," the husband said.

"Not this time," Foley called back as he opened the door. "Keep your wife safe."

Victoria ran to follow Foley, but Laurel caught her arm. "Please be careful."

Touched by her concern, Victoria hugged her. "I will. Thank you."

By the time Victoria left the house, Foley was already running from the barn toward town. "Aren't we taking the horses?" she called.

"Too skittish. They know something's wrong."

Victoria knew instantly what was wrong. She could sense it in the air as much as she could smell it. "Fire."

By the time they reached the town, the two guards who had turned them away were gone. The gate was unguarded.

Flames crackled in more than half of the buildings. People ran through the streets, shouting orders, calling for loved ones, hauling buckets of water. A young child stood screaming in the street. Victoria scooped her up and carried her to a group of children who stood a good distance away, watching their parents fight the flames. "Stay here," Victoria told the little girl. "All of you, stay here!"

Running back, she assessed the damage. Foley worked among a group of men with shovels as they tried to smother the flames with dirt. Massive amounts of dirt flew from Foley's shovel. The flames slowly lost their edge and he left the men to finish the job while he started on another building.

Victoria felt the hot Air around her gather its strength in anticipation for her direction. Reaching toward a burning roof, she snuffed it out by thinning the Air around it. Building after building, she extinguished the flames as easy as if they were candles. People started to notice.

The townspeople, she realized, were no longer working the bucket brigade and the men with shovels stood still, watching Foley and Victoria work. Hesitating, Victoria didn't know what rule she had just broken, but it was clear by the looks on their faces that it was a big one.

A scream tore through town as a building collapsed, a rolling cloud of debris and sparks darkening the road.

A man ran down the street and pointed to another building that was burning hotly. "My wife!" he shouted. "My wife!"

People sprang to work and followed Foley and Victoria.

"Can you stop it?" Foley asked her.

She shook her head. "I've been using Air. But this—" she didn't finish. This fire was different. It was feeding on something inside the building. A fuel surged the inferno beyond a simple wood fire. The flames were almost blue and the heat singed the skin of anyone who dared to get too close. "She can't still be alive," Victoria said, although no one could hear her over roar of the fire. Glancing at the man whose wife was trapped inside, she knew she had to try something.

Raising her hands, she worked against the heat to pull the air away, to make a pocket in which the fire couldn't survive. The flames lessened, but the fuel inside the building was feeding the flames with or without oxygen. Closing her eyes, she focused on her other senses and her elemental intent. The earth hummed with the energy of the fire. Air swelled and dipped in rolling heat waves. Between the two elements, Air and Fire, it was clear that the strength of the heat and the foulness of the fuel had left no one inside the building alive. This was a losing battle.

Just as Victoria was about to let go over her hold on the Air, the feel of the fire shifted. A strong wind kicked in from the west and pushed toward the building. With the sudden surge of air reaching the flames, the fire exploded. She saw it coming but was unprepared for the intensity of the sound, which she heard and felt. Everyone near the building was lifted off their feet and thrown backward.

Victoria lay dazed, her body aching from the impact. Foley pulled her to her feet and they started running. She didn't understand what he was saying, but she did understand the urgency.

"It's not your fault," he said.

"What isn't?"

"The explosion," Foley said as he ducked under a low tree branch. "The wind picked up and who knows what was in that house."

It was a chemical of some sort. Victoria remembered smelling something unfamiliar.

As they ran, Victoria could hear people behind them shouting in anger and fear at what she had done. They were blaming her. Just like the people in the previous village who had tried to burn her at the stake.

"This way." Foley pulled her through a wall of greenery and toward the river. In the moonlight, the rush of water replaced the roar of the town's fire with an ironically calming presence. Foley moved closer to the tree-line where there was still some soil and not ankle-breaking rocks.

"What's your plan?" Victoria asked.

"Run."

"We can't run forever." Victoria's breath was ragged from the smoke she had inhaled.

"I'm open to ideas," Foley said, slowing the pace.

Victoria stopped running. She knelt and felt the ground, feeling for vibrations that would tell her if they were still being followed. She knew eight men had followed them through the woods and were just about to the river. Hoping to send them in the other direction, Victoria sent a surge toward a small hill. The stones skidded down to the bank and the men were quick to follow. "That should buy us some time."

"I'm going to state the obvious," Foley breathed, wincing at the pain in his side. "We're in trouble."

"It's my fault," Victoria started, then held up her hand to stop Foley's protest. "I know, the wind picked up and there was something in there that was burning like crazy. I had a hold of the Air and when it surged from the wind, I let go."

"A back draft," Foley said. "It wasn't your fault."

"The back draft was. The woman inside," Victoria wiped tears from her eyes, "she was already dead."

"You could tell?"

She nodded. It was a strange moment when she sensed the presence of death. Maybe that's what caused the Air to slip past her and into the burning building. The death was similar to the sensation she had when she came through the gap between terraces into this world. It wasn't a cold feeling, but fleeting, as if the world really had no hold over her at all and she simply could leap off the face of the earth and be free forever from gravity. "I just hope no one else was hurt when it exploded."

"Me, too."

"Now what?" Victoria asked. "We didn't find Simetra. How are we going to search for someone we aren't sure even exists in a place filled with people who fear us?"

"I don't know."

"Why would my father send us here?" She stood and looked around. "Is this where you had your celebration?"

Looking around, Foley shrugged his shoulders. "One riverbank looks like the next, especially in the dark. It was near here." He studied the area. "It was over twenty years ago." Foley turned toward the north where the townsmen had followed

Victoria's decoy. "We should get moving."

Scrambling along the river, they walked slowly, trying not to make any sound. "I think we should walk through the night. We can keep to the river all day tomorrow. Too bad we don't have the horses. That would help. The sky is clear, so the moon will help, but we'll have to be careful not to be seen."

Victoria wasn't listening. Leaving Foley behind, she was walking quickly over the rocky shoreline.

"Where are you going?" Foley followed.

"I see something." She stopped a few steps later and pointed. "Look." A birch tree leaned over the water, the trunk creaking in the wind, leaves rustling, reaching out beyond the others as if to shout, *See me!*

"Of course!" Victoria ran forward and touched the tree. "It's just like the painting at home. The one in the living room."

"Wasn't that painting of a palm tree on the beach?"

Victoria continued searching for a way through. "Yeah, but this has to be it."

"That isn't a gateway. It can't be."

"It has to be," Victoria said, searching the tree for a way through. "There's no other reason to be here. There's no Simetra and the people in town are not mages. Why else would my dad send us here?"

Foley stared in disbelief. "I don't—"

"My parents were here. Maybe mom painted the tree for more than commemorating the night you all graduated—or mentor-ated—or whatever." She scrambled over the ground and her voice grew from excitement. "You said you came here through a gateway. Everything about this tree and the water is perfect. It's just a different tree."

Perhaps, just like all mothers, she had provided exactly what Victoria needed now: a way home. It would make perfect sense. Her mother had created a link to this place. All she needed to do was find the opening. Victoria remembered the first painting she fell into and Lucian's prison.

The way out was small.

Painters could open it.

She only had to find it. Settling her mind on the task, she tested the space along the tree trunk but found nothing. It could be anywhere, Victoria realized. The opening could be a foot away from the tree or four feet off the ground, reachable only from on specific direction. Without the right spot in mind, she would never reach it.

"They're coming," Foley felt the ground. "I hoped they would follow the river north further. Can you find the way through?"

"Oh, sure," she held her arms out wide and gestured. "Just pick a spot anywhere from here to six feet up."

"Well," Foley stretched, "it wouldn't be like Diana to make it easy."

Victoria's mouth fell open as the answer struck her mind. "I know where it is! I know how to get home!" She ran forward and dug into the dirt near the base of the tree.

"Down there?"

"Yes! When I finish a painting and add my signature, I always sign it in the lower right corner. But my mom put her initials near the middle of the painting and right in the sand. I asked her why the artist had done that and she told me that every single stroke of a painting is committed to canvas with a purpose." As she dug, she felt a familiar opening. "I found it. Take my hand."

Foley sighed. "I hate traveling through gateways. That pouring feeling that makes me vomit."

As soon as Victoria had a firm hold of Foley's hand she reached further into the hole she'd dug and felt her body slip through.

When she stood up, she turned and saw the familiar painting, the tan carpet, the brown leather couch, the dining room table with her untouched homework. She was home.

GUARDIAN'S HOME

It was just as it had been; even the dishes from her last dinner were in the sink, untouched all these weeks. It smelled the same, a mix of oil paints and her mother's favorite scented lotion. A musty smell had settled in as well. Through the open drapes, eddies of dust swirled in the sun rays from the late morning sun. The painting was still there, the palm tree leaning out, that one visual clue that tripped Victoria's memory and led them back home. She didn't know that the painting didn't have to be an exact copy of the location to which it led. She wouldn't forget that precious piece of information.

"I thought all gateways had gold or silver frames." Victoria looked closely at the black frame.

Foley leaned in. "They should." He scratched the frame with his fingernail and smiled as gold was uncovered. "Smart."

"I always thought that frame was ugly. Now that I know it is solid gold, it's beautiful." Victoria imagined how much her parents had to pay for such an item.

Foley lifted the painting off the wall and tore the brown paper from the back. "Gold frame or not, this is just paper."

Tucked squarely into the lower corner of the frame was a package wrapped in burlap. Victoria carefully lifted it out and unwrapped a worn, thickly folded paper.

"Is that what I think it is?"

"It's a Map of Art." Victoria confirmed, unfolding it carefully on the dining room table. The blue lines of the town's roads, hills and the small lake to the west surfaced as she unfolded the thick paper.

"How did Xander get a hold of this?" Foley wondered aloud.

Victoria looked at the painting again. In the center near the bottom were the initials 'A.N.' They were just letters on a painting that had hung in her living room ever since she could remember. Her mother dusted it regularly, which always struck Victoria as odd since all other surfaces in the house were dusted only when the thickness couldn't be ignored any longer.

Her mother had been a Painter. She had loved a man so much, she performed the Sanguis ceremony to try to protect him. Her mother had sacrificed so much, had lost much more than Victoria had known.

"Why did my father's note tell us to look for Simetra?" Victoria wondered.

Foley smacked his forehead with the palm of his hand. "I'm such an idiot!"

Victoria didn't think he was, but she waited.

"Simetra." He pulled a scrap of paper from the counter and wrote S-I-M-E-T-R-A. "Your father loved secrets and secret messages. This is backwards." Below Simetra, he wrote A-R-T-E-M-I-S. "And Artemis is—?" Foley waited for an answer.

"Yeah, I'm not Bobby. You are going to have to tell me." Victoria crossed her arms.

"Artemis is the Greek goddess of the wild and hunting." Foley paused. "Diana is her Roman counterpart."

"Diana Nike."

212

Foley smiled. "Your mom gave us a way home and the Map."

As exciting as it was to discover what Xander had left behind, Victoria didn't linger long over the Map. Leaving Foley in the kitchen, she showered, scrubbing off weeks of grit. She took her time, enjoying the hot running water, the soap, a washcloth; it all seemed so luxurious. In fresh clothing, she joined Foley in the kitchen wearing jeans and a t-shirt and tennis shoes. Comfortable shoes were a must. She had taken a little time to pack a few things into her mom's old backpack. She was prepared with a bar of soap, toothbrush, hairbrush and a change of clothes.

Walking into the kitchen, she wrinkled her nose. "What's that smell?"

"Everything in the refrigerator is rotten. Really wish I hadn't opened the door." He pushed a box of crackers toward her and nodded toward a bottle of water. The map was on the table, but still folded. Foley stared at it as if it had teeth and an appetite for flesh. "When did he come across this?"

"It must have been before they went into hiding." Victoria dug through the cupboards and stuffed several granola bars and another water bottle into her bag.

He shook his head. "I can't believe he didn't tell me."

Victoria understood why her father hadn't. "It would have put you in danger. If something happened, you would have been pressured to give it up."

"Where's the nearest gateway?" Victoria asked.

A sound at the door stopped them both. Someone was picking the lock.

"We need to go," Foley whispered. "Come on." He grabbed his bag, stuffed the Map in and quietly slid the back door open, slipping out and easing the door closed. Racing to the tree line, they paused to see if they could identify the intruder. Three men walked quickly through the house, noticing immediately the painting on the living room floor with the paper on the back torn off. Victoria recognized one of them from Ona's dwelling.

"We need a gateway out of here," Foley said. "Let's go before they search the yard."

Victoria followed him through the small woods behind the house, along the sidewalk, and down to the corner grocery store.

"What is that smell?" she asked Foley.

"Exhaust."

"Are we near a highway?"

"Probably, but it always seems worse when you first come into the terrace. You'll get used to it."

"I don't think so."

"It never bothered you before," he said.

"It's always this bad?" Victoria asked.

"Always."

She expected him to walk to one of the cars in the parking lot. It wouldn't surprise her at this point if he stole a car. Instead, he walked around to the back of the store where a lonely, old shed stood in the far corner. Behind it, under a tarp, was a motorcycle. "Here." Foley handed Victoria a helmet.

"Is this yours?"

"I stashed it here before I went looking for you. Always have an escape plan. A really fast one." He winked at her. "Just don't tell your mom that I let you ride this. She'll kill me."

"Right. My mom is going to worry about me on a motorcycle after everything I've been through."

Foley laughed and his leg over the bike and sat down. Taking the key out of his pocket, he turned the ignition and the engine roared to life.

"Do you know where to find a gateway?" Victoria shouted over the engine noise. "Shouldn't we check the Map?"

"I know where to go. Climb on and hold on."

He drove a little too fast for Victoria. Maybe it was because she hadn't traveled faster than a horse's trot for weeks. Perhaps he was speeding a little. Now that they had what Xander had left behind, she felt more rushed than ever to find a way to the sphinx city, so she just closed her eyes and held on.

Her senses were bogged down. As they rode, she tried to see by using her elemental intent, but the Air was too busy. The drafts from the vehicles on the road and the pollution confused her because Air wasn't moving on its own, powered only by the sun's solar energy. Racing cars and massive trucks caused eddies to swirl in the atmosphere and in Victoria's mind. The stench of the exhaust was sickening. She didn't open her eyes until Foley turned off the engine.

Opening her eyes, she was delighted. "The art museum?" she asked. "Perfect!" She climbed off the bike, unclipped the helmet's latch at her chin and handed it to Foley.

"It was your mom's idea. She donated a piece years ago."

"Seems dangerous to have a gateway here. What if someone falls in?"

Foley looked surprised. "How much do you know about gateways?"

"Another lesson." Victoria rolled her eyes.

He laughed and started walking toward the museum entrance. "Gateways are very elemental in their construction. The Painter must paint a real place and include soil from that location in the paint. That's part of what makes the connection. As you know, small changes can be made to a gateway, but only a few painters are good enough to do that. We were blessed that Diane was one of them."

"And the gold or silver frame," Victoria added so she didn't look like a complete idiot.

"And the blood of the painter."

Victoria's mouth fell open. "Blood? Why?"

"Elemental intent is in the blood. It must be added to the canvas before it will become a gateway. Otherwise it's just a prison."

"Anna mentioned that part. About the prison. Not the blood."

"It's an older tradition. Gateways painted more recently are left open to any Painter, making the passage more open, the traveling freer. This gateway is special. Your mom's blood seals it."

"But my mom—"

"—isn't here. And she's no longer a mage. Her blood won't work."

"You're hoping mine will."

"It's slim, but it's all we have. Diana told me this gateway will take us very close to the sphinx city."

"Alright," Victoria said, walking toward the entrance. "What do we have to lose?"

Foley took her arm and stopped her. "Everything. We could lose everything. If this doesn't work, we can't get to the sphinx. Without their help, we can't find Bobby and Tucker or your mom. Without their support, the Council will find the Grandfather's Weapon. Then we lose everything."

"Well," Victoria set her chin in determination, "I'm glad I don't cave under pressure."

◌

Foley paid their admission and the woman at the desk smiled at him. "Ah, Mr. Wood. Good to see you."

Foley smiled, and returned the greeting. "Good to see you, Lila."

Victoria glanced around the atrium and Foley joined her. "The last time I was here was with my freshman art class." She nodded to Lila. "You obviously come here often."

Leading the way, Foley pocketed the museum brochure. "I

216

like to check on the painting. Sometimes the museum will move pieces to make room for special exhibits. It's a good idea to know exactly where the escape hatch is."

Through well-lit halls, up a winding staircase and around two more corners, they came to a narrow corridor in a corner of the art museum dedicated to sculpture.

"Oh no."

Victoria looked around. "They've moved it?"

Foley quickly walked toward a security guard. "Excuse me. Where are the paintings that are usually here?"

"This sculpture's name is Eleanor." The young guard pointed to the room. "Just Eleanor. One name."

"Fascinating," Foley muttered. "But the paintings that *were* here. Where are they now?"

The guard shrugged. "Probably in storage."

"I need to check on a painting. Can you take me to the storage room?" Foley asked.

The guard looked down the hall at two towering doors marked with a "Museum Employees Only" sign. "Um, no. Maybe Lila could help you. She's at the front desk."

"Thank you," Foley said and dashed off toward the stairs.

Victoria walked quickly to keep up with him. When she recognized the men climbing the stairs, she pulled Foley's arm and hid behind a column. "Those are the men from the house."

Foley peeked out. "How did they know?"

"Could they have a Map, too?"

"At this point, anything is possible." Foley peeked out again and watched as they walked toward the sculpture exhibit. "We don't have much time. Come on." Dashing from one column to the next, Victoria followed Foley toward the double doors.

"Is this the storage room?" Victoria asked.

"This is where the guard looked when I asked to see the painting. It's as good place to start as any." He touched the handle and was relieved when it wasn't locked.

On the other side of the door, a hallway stretched from left to right with a large elevator lift large straight ahead.

"Basement?" Victoria asked.

Foley pulled the door to the elevator up and they both climbed onto the platform. His released the gate and pushed the button labeled 'B'.

At the bottom, they were in near darkness, but Victoria knew they were in the right place. It smelled of dust and dried paint and felt massive. Foley fumbled along the wall searching for a light switch. With a series of four clicks, four rows of lights illuminated the depth of the storage room.

"How are we going to find it in all this?" Foley asked.

"I know how." Victoria walked toward three tall file cabinets. "It should be listed in here somewhere." She pulled open a drawer and looked at a few files. "These are listed by the name of the piece. What did mom name the painting?"

"Guardian's Home."

Scanning the drawers, Victoria opened the F-H drawer and searched. Within a minute, she pulled the file. A single page listed the artist: Artemis Nike, and that it was a donated piece. A post-it note read: "D-149." Victoria tucked the file back in place. Beyond the file cabinets, long corridors of shelves and storage rooms lined the room like massive shopping aisles. The ends of the rows nearest them were labeled: A, F, K, P, T. Starting between the A and F corridors, they walked quickly toward the D section.

It was easy to find. Stored in a box labeled D-149, Foley struggled to open the lid. "We'll need a crow bar. Have one in that backpack of yours?"

Victoria smiled. "I focused more on food."

"Be back." He ran back toward the elevator and returned quickly with a crow bar. The squeak of the nail being pried from the wood echoed through the basement. Hopefully they were alone. They quickly cleared off the shredded paper and leaned the painting against the shelving.

"That looks so familiar." Victoria leaned in and examined the long, shallow valley her mother had painted. In the distance, in front of a back drop of rolling green mountains, an oval lake glistened. Clusters of trees stood among a prairie of grass. One round of trees spread out almost like a star with four arms. Another was almost perfectly round. "Hmm."

"You don't like it?" Foley asked.

"It's a little rigid. The groupings of the trees seem too orderly." She straightened. "No way!"

Foley frowned. "What?"

"It's the sphinx city. Look." She pointed to the star-shaped grouping of trees. "That's the Hall of Art. This cluster of rocks must be the Library. These other trees are the smaller buildings. The layout is perfect."

Foley's mouth dropped open. "All these years of looking at this and I never noticed. Gotta hand it to your mom. She is going to get us very close to the sphinx city. We can have a real meal tonight."

"Let's go," Victoria said, remembering Ambrosia's stuffed grape leaves.

Foley handed her a pocket knife.

Victoria sighed. "More blood. How much are we talking, here? A finger prick or a palm slice?"

"Let's start small."

Holding her finger against the blade, Victoria prepared to quickly slide it across the pad of her index finger when a shout startled her and the knife deeply cut her finger.

"Who are you?" a man called from the end of the corridor. "Museum employees only!" He reached into his pocket for his cell phone, but was lifted out of the way with a yelp.

"Victoria!" Foley said. "Don't hurt him!"

"I didn't do that."

The three men who had followed them from the house walked around the corner, then started running as they finally saw their prey.

"Now!" Foley yelled.

Taking Foley's hand in hers, she pressed her bleeding hand against the painting, Victoria spoke to her element. Air, still sounding dull under the hum of electric light, was slow to respond.

"Victoria! Now!"

Desperate to get away, Victoria bowed her head and pulled all the elements to her mind: Air, Earth, Water. Not Fire. The Air thickened a little catching the men as they ran and slowing them down. Water pipes above their heads rumbled and burst, spraying them all. The ground shook and the shelves of priceless art shuddered and fell.

The way in is small.

She could hear Anna's instruction from the first time she entered a gateway.

The light bulb above their head burst just as Victoria fell forward into the painting pulling Foley with her.

Tainted Trust

Tiw heard him approaching her guest suite, as she had come to call her prison. She and Freya were in neighboring cells, not able to see each other, but they could hear each other. Deep in the mountain and far away from the activity of Kivavallis, they were kept in small alcoves hollowed out of the rock. Their doors—doors with no hinges—were made of iron bars. Food, unfit for pigs, was slipped through a narrow slit between the bars where it fell to the dusty ground. They didn't dare eat it at first, but hunger prompted them on the fifth day. They picked at it.

"Here he comes," Tiw warned Freya.

"It's about time. Can't wait to hear his excuse for this."

Caladrius turned the corner and stood where he could see them both. "I hear you aren't eating much." When neither sphinx spoke, Caladrius continued. "I'm sure you are angry, but you see, your situation requires this type of housing."

"Our situation." Freya eyed him coolly. "Would that be the situation of your betrayal? Or the fact that we are sphinx in a human terrace?"

Caladrius raised his eyebrows and nodded knowingly. "Both,

I suppose."

"Where is Sebastian?" Tiw asked. "Is he also a guest here?"

"Ah, no. Sebastian is on an errand. I don't expect he will be troubling us any longer. Which, I admit, brings a great amount of relief."

Tiw sighed and leaned against the wall. "If you plan to kill us slowly with infested food and boring conversation, I think your efforts at torture are quite pathetic."

"There will be no torture. I'm not a barbarian, am I? I simply need information."

"You believe starving us will break us?" Freya asked.

"I believe with the right motivation I can learn what I need from you." He stood with his hands calmly clasped in front of him.

"Well," Tiw spoke when Caladrius didn't ask them anything. "You aren't very efficient at acquiring information. It typically starts with a question."

"Where are the scrolls?"

Tiw laughed. "At the Library of Ages. Now release us."

Caladrius shook his head slowly and spoke with his deepest voice. "The scrolls that were taken twenty years ago. I know you've been traveling with Adam Caius' twin sons. I want those scrolls."

"Adam's their father?" Freya asked. "*That* explains a few things."

"It doesn't explain why you want the scrolls," Tiw added.

"Do you know what those scrolls contain?"

Neither sphinx answered.

"Well, you either know what Adam took or you are as clueless as that bumbling bunch of Elders."

"You started this to find the scrolls?" Tiw asked.

"I started nothing. I hope to finish this upsetting time as swiftly as possible."

"You don't seem upset by our imprisonment," Freya said.

Caladrius pressed his lips together, thinning his already slim features. "The plagues have been unleashed. The search for the Grandfather's Weapon has begun. The only way to ensure success before the final plague is to have those scrolls."

"Who opened it?" Freya asked.

"Ah, so you are aware of what the scrolls contained." Caladrius smiled. "The clock started when your sweet Victoria helped Ona open the Earth Gateway."

"That was Ona's doing," Freya said. "Victoria is innocent. She helped Ona only to protect those she loves."

"You think the Weapon can decipher between the intentions behind the act?" Caladrius laughed darkly. "She's marked. And now she's dangerous." He breathed in deeply, then bowed to the sphinx. "I see you need some time to think this over. I will return, but not soon. Enjoy your time."

Tiw waited for several minutes after the sound of Caladrius' footsteps faded. "Is Victoria dangerous?"

"Without the information on the scrolls? Yes." Freya confirmed.

"Do you know what the scrolls contain?"

"Only one sphinx has that knowledge."

Tiw thought for a moment. "Elder Parnassus."

"I pray that he can help Victoria through this. It will take both of them; Victoria's abilities and Elder Parnassus' wisdom."

TRINA

Parnassus sat patiently in Elder Aurum's office, waiting for him to return. No longer an Elder, he was restricted from using the mirrors to communicate with the Council Mages. The six other Elders had been in the mirror for almost a half hour when the door to the office opened. Surprised by who entered, Parnassus smiled and bowed.

"Trina, you are a sight for these sore eyes."

The Council Mage from Terrace Three smiled and bowed in return. "Elder Parnassus."

"Surely you've heard. It's just Parnassus now."

"I've heard. News of the arrogance of the Sphinx Elders reached my ears months ago." She winked. "Other sources confirmed your fears."

Parnassus glanced at the doorway which led to the mirror room. "The other Elders expected to speak with you today."

"I decided a face-to-face conversation was necessary. That, and I want to see Anna. How is she?"

"Recovering. Worried about the young mages."

"And Worthmere?"

"Restless."

Trina paced the room. "How long have they been in there?" She pointed to the door leading to the mirror.

"Some time now. They will be taken aback by your visit."

Trina laughed. "I'm not following their rules. I'm sure my absence from the Hall of Mirrors is raising questions."

"How delicate is the situation?" Parnassus asked, his face set firmly in anticipation.

"There is much news to share and time is running short," Trina said. "There have been wide-spread reports of plagued waters, and frog and fly infestations. "

Parnassus walked to the window. Trina followed. They stood side-by-side, staring at the Hall of Art's fallen wing. "And the rest of the Council?" Parnassus asked the question he dreaded hearing the answer to. "Have they come to a conclusion on why the Ragnarok have joined the Minotaur?"

Trina's face reddened. "Bureaucratic obstacles."

"What about the young mages? Young Victoria showed incredible skill."

"There is talk that they were with Ona." Trina gripped the stone of the window sill so tightly her knuckles turned white. "If that's true, hopefully the Map is giving them some help. I have it on good authority, however, that they are not with Ona, but lost."

"Dead?"

Trina shook her head. "No. Caladrius found the young mages a few days ago, but claims that Ona is dead. There's no body or anything convenient like that to help prove that she's dead." Trina waved her hands at that pesky truth.

"The mages are not with Caladrius? How did he lose them?"

Trina shifted her weight to one hip and looked at Parnassus with a raised eyebrow. "Ready for this? Through lightning."

Parnassus' mouth fell open, most unbecoming for a sphinx, Elder or not. "Do you believe him?"

"There are many things that I don't trust about Caladrius. This, I believe."

Parnassus raised his eyebrows. "He continues to be on your list of suspicious characters?"

"Oh, that hasn't changed. Reggie confirmed it. He said that they were trying to arrest Victoria and the twins when lightning zapped around the inside of the room. When the dust settled, Victoria and the boys were gone, along with Caladrius' student." Trina watched Parnassus digest this new information. "You are thinking the same thing I am."

"If you are thinking that we need to find those young mages, then, yes."

Trina rolled her eyes and sighed. "Parnassus, you know what the lightning suggests."

He paused. "That a myth, a legend that would be better left to the pages of a child's book, is walking among the terraces, completely unaware of the indications behind her uncanny skill."

"And she's lost." Trina paced the room. "Time is short."

Parnassus turned away from the window. "You mentioned that."

"My Guards have been watching for signs of the Ragnarok. A few small skirmishes here and there, but mostly the Ragnarok have been difficult to find. The Minotaur even more so."

Parnassus frowned at the information. "Despite their appearances, the Ragnarok are highly advanced people."

"You see past the appearance," Trina said. "Many don't. They see a primitive people who can't possibly know as much as those who are educated." She nodded to the Library. "With the Minotaur as new allies, they are stronger. They found a target and accomplished what no other group has succeeded at in all of history."

"They attacked the Guardians." Parnassus finished her statement.

226

"You are one of the few who remember your purpose," Trina said. "Once the purpose of existence is forgotten, all is lost."

"We haven't all forgotten."

"Will that be enough?" Trina asked, looking back at the Library of Ages.

"You believe that's their next target?" Parnassus asked

"My mentor told me that the Mage Society was as strong as an oak tree. But if we allowed the ants of dissension to gnaw away at the interior, our strength would be hollowed out." Trina turned to Parnassus. Tears pooled in her eyes. "What would happen if our history was demolished? If the proof of our purpose was allowed to dance carelessly on the lips of fools, what would our people do with their gifts? If those who were assigned the task of protecting our roots felt demeaned by that task," She left the question unasked and watched a small group of Junior Elders walk along the grass, away from the Library, ignoring the training fields, holding their noses up at the stench of the decaying frogs, doing nothing to help clean up the mess.

"Then new trees will be planted," Parnassus finished. "Much will be lost in this battle. Much can be gained. Everything will change."

Just then, the door opened and Elder Aurum entered, looking downtrodden. When he saw Trina, his frown deepened. Three other Elders followed him out of the room; only one, Elder Amberson, looked pleased to see Parnassus and Trina.

"Lady Trina," Elder Aurum bowed his head ever so slightly, "we were concerned when you weren't present in the Hall of Mirrors for this morning's meeting."

"I felt I would be more useful here."

Elder Aurum walked passed her, toward the wall of glassless windows overlooking the city. "This view used to be beautiful. Now it's a reminder of the destruction of our society, from within and from our enemies."

Lady Trina looked at Parnassus and shrugged.

"Old friend," Parnassus spoke, "you can no longer deny my warnings." He turned to the other three Elders. "None of you can."

"I bring another warning," Trina addressed the Sphinx Elders. "A battle is coming."

"We are not in Council," Elder Aurum stopped her. "We cannot discuss such things without all in attendance."

Trina stood her ground. "Gather them now."

"To pull the entire Council and the Junior Elders—" Elder Aurum started, but Trina cut him off.

"I have no interest in the musings of your Junior Elders," she chided him. "I came here to share news from my Guards, news of a coming battle."

"The Ragnarok?" Elder Amberson asked.

Trina nodded. "My Guards have seen evidence that they are gathering in large numbers. The Minotaur have left their homes."

"It's not against any law for such creatures to journey," Elder Rufus said. "We all know that both the Ragnarok and the Minotaur are nothing but hunters and gatherers."

Trina's voice hardened. "They hunt *you*! They've already gathered gateways into their burning clutch, preventing escape and limiting those who would come to your aide. They gather your arrogance as easily as children plucking flowers from a field." She walked to the window and pointed at the training arena. "Where are your soldiers? War is upon us."

"She's right," Elder Niveus said. "Parnassus and I voted against these changes. Look at what has become of our way of life. We cannot hide behind the pretense of being anything else than what we are: guardians and secret keepers. It's time to reform. We must replenish our city by returning to the ways of our ancestors."

Elder Rufus scoffed. "Our ancestors sat around, keeping their secrets so well, that none of us can remember their purpose. It's time we make our own destiny."

"You presume erroneously," Parnassus said. "I may have been stripped of my wings and cast out of the Elders, but my knowledge remains. I know our purpose. If you have forgotten that then you have no right to be among the winged guardians."

Elder Rufus puffed up his chest in preparation to debate with Parnassus, but Elder Aurum interrupted. "Enough!" Turning away from the window, he faced the small audience in his office. "Lady Trina, I thank you for coming. You are correct to believe that we are unprepared. Never before has one of our own acted against the vote of the Circle. Parnassus' trial is set for three days from now. We had hoped in that time we might find the young mages who set this whole debacle in motion."

Shaking her head at the Sphinx Elder, Trina sighed as though she spoke to a misbehaving child. "I'm disappointed. I'm not surprised, but still, disappointed. I had hoped you would see reason. Now I see that reason has been set aside along with your ancestral rights."

Elder Rufus lowered his head, smiling ruthlessly. "Then I will bid you farewell, Lady Trina. I'd hate to witness your exasperation spent in trying to educate us, the Sphinx Elders, leaders who have outlived your small lives ten times over."

"Not at all." Trina smiled sweetly. "I wouldn't miss the opportunity to witness your education."

"Due to the circumstances," Elder Rufus indicated the mess of dead frogs outside the window, "I'm afraid the only place we can provide for you now is where our prisoners are staying."

"Perfect." Trina spread out her hands and smiled as if the whole matter was settled. "I will require a bed, of course, and meals should be sent three times a day. And I'm familiar with what you serve to your prisoners. That will not do."

"Lady Trina," Elder Rufus interrupted, "I don't think it's proper for a woman of your position to stay in a prison."

"Well, considering that Anna is there and it is, from what I hear, the only dwelling in this city that was spared from the frogs, I don't see any other options, do you?"

His silence indicated that he didn't.

"There we are then," Trina smiled. "Parnassus, would you walk me to the dwelling please?"

"Ah, yes," Parnassus nodded. "My entourage and I would be glad to escort you." As they left, two sphinx soldiers joined them as they walked toward the fenced prison.

Just Out of Reach

After they left Rockheart, Bobby had suggested they turn north. He tried to sound confident in his decision, but he wasn't sure. Being the Earth mage with the expectation of knowing which way to go, Tucker and Collette needed to believe that Bobby knew what he was doing. If he was honest with himself, he chose to go north because he hoped they would eventually find a way out of the desert. They pushed on, enduring the blazing heat, then the biting chill of the desert at night.

Early the next morning, Collette found water underground and they were able to dig down and fill up on gritty water. As Bobby studied the earth, he discovered that he could hear the water flowing underground. "If it's an underground river," he told Tucker and Collette, "we can follow it and maybe find fresh water at the surface. If this river continues to go north, we would have water the entire way."

"That's good enough for me," Tucker said.

The next afternoon, the river did emerge from underground, but it was nestled deep in a ravine, completely out of reach. Following it, they rode along the edge of the cliff for several miles. The sound of rushing water teased their parched mouths and cracked lips.

"Can you bring some of that up here?" Tucker asked as they stood at the top, staring down at the life-giving water.

Shaking her head, Collette's eyes filled with tears. "I'm not that strong."

Victoria would at least try, Bobby said to Tucker.

Agreeing, Tucker sighed. "How far is it until we can reach the water?"

Bobby rested on one knee and pressed his hand to the stony earth. After a moment of studying the land, he pointed north. "A ways that way."

"At least we don't have to walk," Collette said, returning to her horse.

The horses were a blessing to their feet, and traveling was faster. Heat from the sun was intense, so they rode early in the morning when the first rays of light brightened the terrain until the sun reached its peak. Seeking shade was tricky. They rested in the shadow of a cliff for a few hours until the sun was closer to the horizon and rode until well past dark. Several times that day, Collette dug a shallow hole and tried to pull water to it. She was usually successful, but it was always sandy. The horses didn't seem to mind.

On the fourth day, the ground started to slope downward and the river was in reach by evening. The horses quickened their step when they realized the water was in reach and walked right into the water, drinking their fill.

"Take the blankets off," Collette said and she quickly dismounted and pulled off her bedroll. "I had a horse once that would swim. I don't think we want to sleep on soaked blankets."

Bobby and Tucker were grateful for her foresight. Once Bobby had removed his bedroll, his horse did walk all the way in the water, enticing the others to do the same. It was still hours from sunset, so Collette didn't hesitate. She joined the horses in the water, knowing that in this arid heat, their clothes would dry quickly. Even if they didn't, their blankets were dry.

Collette's saddle bag contained a tiny pot that had been strapped to her saddle, so she made a bit of stew. That's what she called it, at least. It was very salty and the powder she also found in her bag made it pasty. They huddled around the pot, scooping out hot stew with their fingers. Whoever had packed the pot forgot the spoons.

After they ate, Bobby spent hours studying the landscape, hoping to discern a direction based on anything he could sense through the earth. "I think we should continue to follow the river. I can hear a forest. The woods are too thick for me to venture far enough with my elemental intent. Too many animals keep distracting my tracking."

"I think if we find a city it will be near a river," Tucker said.

Collette's eyes were closed as she tried to picture the map of this terrace in her head. "You're right. Far to the north of Rockheart," she traced her finger in the air as she spoke, following the path of the river on the map in her head, "is Springs Forest. It covers the land on the east side of the lower mountains. Closer to Saber Mountain Pass, we'll find a city, Delta-something."

"Any chance there are mages there?" Bobby asked.

"There's always a chance," Collette said, smiling as she used a phrase that Caladrius had used frequently.

"At least we'll be out of this desert," Tucker said as he scraped his finger along the pot, licking off the last bits of stew.

"Springs Forest will be a difficult journey," Collette warned. "There are all kinds of wild animals. And the ground is really soupy in parts."

"I miss roads." Tucker leaned back, clasped his hands behind his head and rested. "Paved roads and billboards marking the next restaurant and rest area."

"What's a rest area?" Collette asked.

"A building just off the road with toilets and sinks and snacks."

"Ew," she wrinkled her nose at the idea. "They have food in the same building as toilets?"

"Well, it's in a machine. You put money in the machine and the food comes out."

Collette frowned. "I don't understand. What's a machine?"

"A vending machine is a tall box. Inside the food is wrapped up. You just put money in, select the food you want and it comes out."

Tucker could tell Collette still didn't understand, but she just shook her head. "I can't believe they have food so close to the toilets. And it sounds like these machines—excuse me for being a little vulgar—but it sounds like the machines poop out the food."

Bobby laughed. "Even worse, some of that food has been in the machine for months."

"What? How? Doesn't it spoil?"

Tucker sighed in exasperation. "Machines don't poop out food, they dispense it."

Bobby winked at Collette. "A fancy word for pooping."

"That's not—you're ruining vending machines! I just miss roads and cars and traveling fast."

Collette laughed and Tucker's temper flared a bit. The flames of their small fire flashed brightly then died completely, leaving only smoldering coals.

"Wow." Bobby leaned back.

"Sorry." Tucker's shoulders slumped.

Collette was still laughing as she wiped out the pot with sand. "Let's keep going. It would be nice to find that forest."

Tucker covered the coals with dirt. As the smoke drifted skyward, he hoped no one would see it. They hadn't seen anyone

234

since leaving Rockheart and hoped their luck would hold out. Of course, that would all change when they finally did reach a city, but that was a problem for a different day. Right now, he felt content with water to quench his thirst, gritty stew to fill his stomach, and a horse to spare his legs.

The moon was almost full, providing perfect light. After riding through blinding sunshine for days, which dished out headaches and parched tongues, the moonlight felt cool and dull. Muscles around the eyes relaxed as the sweat on their bodies dried up. They pulled out blankets from their saddle packs to keep off the chill.

A line of blackness loomed ahead of them, barely distinguishable in the dark. Bobby dismounted and pressed his hand to the ground. He smiled at the thick network of tree roots and animals burrowed in and around the root systems.

The tree line started abruptly, almost as though the bordering trees had been planted in a neat row. A few steps beyond the first trees, the neatness ended in a mass of branches and trunks. It was too dark to venture forward. With the horses tethered nearby, greedily munching on the nourishing grass, the mages nestled into the cool earth of Springs Forest.

Tucker sighed as he leaned against the rough bark of a tree. "The grass is cool, the bark isn't made of sand, and the sun isn't trying to bake me like an egg. This feels like heaven."

The usual habit at night was to decide who would take first watch to make sure they weren't attacked or eaten by wild animals. No one said anything. They were all too tired to think about not sleeping, and before anyone even offered the idea that they should all just sleep, that's exactly what they were all doing.

Fiery Footsteps

Victoria stood on a hill just behind a tree looking over the sphinx city. The gateway her mother left for them did indeed bring them very close to the sphinx city, but they didn't receive the welcome they had hoped for. Instead of Ambrosia's sweet pastries and something healthy wrapped in grape leaves, Victoria saw firsthand the destruction the Ragnarok had inflicted on the Hall of Art. Until now, it had only been a rumor, a possibility. Now, seeing the burnt remains of a once fabulous building, she felt sick. The remnants of paintings were scattered around the tall grass. The lawn, once meticulously green and trim, was now a meadow of weeds and litter, and it was victim to a constant cloud of flies.

"What is that smell?" Foley's face twisted in disgust. It didn't take long to discover the source: dead, rotting frogs. Everywhere they looked, frogs lay on the grass in various stages of decomposition. The smell was overwhelming, but the flies and birds that swarmed around the carcasses, feasting and fighting over the abundant death, was nauseating. Using Air to push the flies back, Victoria created a pocket of fly-free breathing, but it didn't do anything to stop the smell.

Foley studied the scene before them. He pointed to a small house with a tall fence around it being guarded by two sphinx. "That's strange."

"What are they doing?" Victoria asked. "That's where we stayed with Anna."

"Looks like they're guarding it. But why?" His eyes scanned the city. "The Library looks unchanged and unguarded. So does the Elder's Circle," he pointed to the circular building with two trees growing from within, topping it with leaves. "But the training field is empty." To the south of the city, a wide field, rimmed with a gravel track and filled with posts, jumping fences and sparing circles was neglected. Based on the number of scavenging birds, Victoria assumed that the grass there was littered with more frogs.

As they studied the sphinx city, Foley's expression darkened and Victoria began to believe that the bloody river water near the village where she had escaped was somehow connected to the dead frogs. She didn't know how that could be, but she couldn't shake that growing sense of foreboding.

"Something tells me this place is no longer safe," Foley whispered.

The sun was setting behind them, casting long shadows across the city. A different sensation tickled Victoria's senses. Was it Air or Earth? She looked down and turned her head a little, concentrating on what it might be. From the west, behind them, she felt a scrambling heat, as if burning torches were walking toward them.

Foley turned to her, his eyes wide. "Do you hear that?"

She immediately tapped into her Earth element to focus. Footsteps. Thousands of footsteps were approaching the city. The Air rushed into her mind, bringing images of fire. The scar on her side flashed in anger. "Ragnarok," she whispered.

"Quick." Foley pointed to the high branches of the tree. "Go!" Victoria scrambled up into the tree, thankful for her jeans and sneakers, and stood on a branch clinging to the narrowing trunk.

She looked at Foley who was still on the ground. He nodded and turned his gaze toward a tall stone that stood closer to the city. An elemental cairn. The lines on it indicated that it was an Earth cairn.

Good, thought Victoria. *We can both do some damage.*

Victoria nodded back and Foley held up one finger then pointed to himself. He would act first.

She watched in awe as the ground around his feet churned and spun. Foley sunk into the earth as if it was nothing more than pudding. When the top of his head disappeared, the grass didn't cover the newly disturbed ground as Victoria expected it to. It looked like someone had recently dug there. Hopefully the Ragnarok wouldn't notice.

Moving as little as possible, Victoria slipped her backpack off and tucked it into the nook of a branch. The last thing she needed was to lose her balance and topple onto a group of fire-tattooed warriors.

A moment later, the first Ragnarok warriors stalked passed the base of the tree. Their already pale skin was painted with a white clay. Dark charcoal lines were drawn in vertical stripes on their faces. As they passed the tree, Victoria saw the tattoos of fire permanently etched into their skin on their back. Each man held a long piece of rope. Something about the way they held it told Victoria it was more than just rope, but a weapon.

In the slowly fading light, their approach toward the sphinx city would not be noticed right away. The light from the torches blended with the setting sun. With no sphinx guards posted around the city, they would reach the edge of the trees with no confrontation.

It was a strategy, she realized. The first group of warriors ran down the hill, charging the city and awakening the sphinx to the undeniable destruction that would result from their lackadaisical border security. The second wing waited to reinforce the first and to capture anyone fleeing from the fight. She watched as sphinx emerged from doorways, wondering at the commotion, then either turning to flee or charging to fight.

Victoria couldn't imagine what Foley was going to do from underground. Moments passed and Foley didn't act. More and more Ragnarok marched toward the city. As the seconds ticked by, Victoria realized that two mages against this army would do little.

Little Hopes and Small Seeds

It was almost evening and Anna was trying to ignore the noxious odor of the frogs just to stand in the sun for the last few minutes of the day. Ever since the frogs had invaded the city, time outside in the small, fenced yard was worse than remaining inside the crowded dwelling. Now that Trina was staying with them, the already cramped space felt even more so. Trina had brought with her news from the outside. While Anna was grateful to know more of what was going on, the hopelessness that clung to the back of the news oppressed her spirit. The thickness of the air was just as depressing.

"There still is a little hope," Worthmere said as he followed her outside.

Anna, despite her mood, smiled. "Reading my mind now?"

"Well," Worthmere shrugged, "spend enough time with someone, and you start to understand their body language."

Anna relaxed her clenched fists and brought her shoulders down from around her ears. "I could use a little hope right now. This whole—" she gestured toward the fence, "situation feels like a boulder pressing on my head."

"Victoria and the boys are still out there. Even a massive rock can be cracked in two by the growth of a small seed."

"Such wisdom," Anna teased. "You've been spending too much time with Parnassus."

"Believe it or not, I've been enjoying it." Worthmere walked toward her. "I also," he paused, he eyes drifting toward the ground. He knelt, placing his hands on the ground and studying the Earth element for a moment.

Alarmed, Anna looked skyward and spread her thoughts into the Air. "Do you feel that?"

"It's big."

"Flames. Lots of flames."

Worthmere stood and shouted, "Parnassus! Trina!" They ran out of the dwelling, joining the elemental study of the strange disturbance.

"Oh." Trina paled as she turned toward the woods. "Ragnarok."

A Late Warning

Ambrosia stepped out of the Library of Ages and instantly wished she didn't have to leave the safety of the walls. The familiar scent of the scrolls and paper covered the stink of the outdoors. Tomorrow she would return and continue her search. She was close. The scrolls she read today alluded to a possible answer. She just hoped she had enough time before her father's trial.

Keeping to the stone paved walkway, Ambrosia went the long way around the sweeping lawn that had once been the pride and joy of the sphinx. Now it was littered with small, decaying carcasses. A peaceful stroll through the soft grass was a thing of the past as squishy frogs and legions of flies ruled.

A sudden movement in the trees along the western rim of the city caught her attention. When she realized what it was, Ambrosia's skin rippled with fear. Turning back toward the Library, she dashed inside and raced up the stairs, breaking every rule about etiquette in the Library.

"What is it?" Clio called after her.

"Get to the lower levels. Ragnarok!"

On the fourth level, built into a stone balcony, a warning horn had been mounted into place to warn the sphinx soldiers of invasions. It hadn't been used in centuries. It was law that only a soldier under the orders of a Sphinx Elder could use it. There were no soldiers currently training. Warning the city of the imminent attack would be useless, but she had to do something. This was her home and she would fight.

Escape

At the sound of the warning blast from the horn at the Library, a determined frown etched Parnassus' face as the others gathered around him. "I say we've spent enough time in captivity."

"I'm in." Worthmere agreed.

Anna and Trina held hands and squeezed tightly, both silently encouraging the other.

They watched as a thick line of Ragnarok warriors ran toward the city, carrying bright torches and shouting a war cry. The lead warrior slid to his knees on the grass and jammed the post of his torch into the earth. With a savage scream, he sent a wave of fire toward the city, intending to stop anyone who dared challenge him. A wave of heat swept over the city, but the damage was minimal. Only the thorn fence around the prison caught fire.

Worthmere stomped his foot toward the fence and shouted out his own war cry, sending the flaming pieces of wood and twig back to the invaders. Now free of the fence, they faced a great army. They ran forward, joined by the few sphinx soldiers who knew how to fight. Ambrosia, although not a soldier, joined her father. Together they ran toward the smoldering army.

THE TARGET

Victoria watched in amazement as a Ragnarok cast a rolling rim of fire toward the city. She pulled it back, directing it away from the buildings and carefully toward the dwelling surrounded by the fence. There, it quickly caught hold, but the wall didn't burn for long. She could see Worthmere within and knew that when the fence structure blew apart, it was his doing. Many of the sticks pierced the Ragnarok warriors, landing the first casualties of this battle. Victoria cringed. Despite the fact that these people were the enemy, lives ended at that moment. It wasn't like Worthmere to allow an opportunity to end an attack go, and he had used the situation well to lessen the numbers against them.

Foley, on the other hand, remained hidden below the surface of the grass at the base of the tree. He had said he would act first, but it wasn't fast enough in Victoria's opinion. The first wave of warriors had already clashed with the sphinx. The second string still stood below the tree, waiting.

A slight tremor in the tree told Victoria that Foley was preparing to do something.

About time, she thought.

The waiting Ragnarok felt it too. Nervously, they looked at the ground, asking each other questions, stepping cautiously away. Then, the ground split open like the mouth of an earth giant, swallowing a large group of Ragnarok. The fissure in the earth, steered by Foley, continued to cut across the land, eating Ragnarok like any good earth giant would.

Just as quickly as it started, the earth closed. Foley had not emerged. In a panic, Victoria jumped from the tree, using Air to soften her landing, and went right to the spot where he had disappeared.

She was not the only one coming to check on a friend. More than a dozen of the pale warriors followed the sounds of commotion to find their companions missing and the earth chewed up. They stared at her, obviously in disbelief that such a young woman could have defeated more than one hundred of their own.

Victoria was ready for their disbelief. They each held a torch. With only a thought, Air snuffed them out like candles on a cake. Surprised shouts scattered through her would-be attackers, but it didn't last long. Despite the sudden loss of light, the sun hadn't yet set and they could see each other clearly. One threw the rope he carried at Victoria and it wrapped around her arm. She felt the heat from it as it tried to burn into her flesh, but it was only hot to her touch. She calmly untangled her arm and held the rope out, silently daring him to come claim his useless weapon.

She smiled at his hesitation, which further unnerved them. Then, far in the background, she recognized something familiar. Her smiled darkened from one of pleasure to one of confident intent against an enemy. She closed her eyes, something she couldn't believe she was doing as she faced over a dozen seasoned warriors. She didn't need vision. The entire scene was clear to her. Through Earth, she could feel Foley making his way underground toward an area thick with the second wing of warriors. She felt

Worthmere's familiar tone in his intent. She knew that Anna was fighting the fires cast toward the city. She also knew that just to the south of the city, a possible distraction was available.

Sending Air toward the south, she gathered together her intent and carried the flying beasts toward her.

She hoped Foley would stay underground.

A scream met her ears. The Ragnarok glanced skyward at the sound. On seeing what approached, they scattered, but the falling razor-sharp feathers of the stymphalids found their marks. Victoria kept the wind moving over the trees, felt the slicing sound as the feathers fell from the bellies of the stymphalids and dove toward their targets.

Little by little, the vibrations of the earth and sky lessened. Victoria opened her eyes and saw a sickening scene of desolation before her. She felt lightheaded, but managed to stay on her feet.

From behind her, she felt Foley approaching. "Are you okay?"

She nodded. "I don't like fighting."

Without any hesitation, he hugged her. "I know. You did well. You helped our friends."

Tears burned her eyes and she couldn't hold back a sob. It caught in her throat as she tried to keep her wits about her.

"Victoria," Foley said, his voice soft, "you did what you needed to do."

She nodded.

He lifted her chin to look him in the eye. "Do you think you can do it again?" He tipped his head toward the sphinx city where the sounds of fighting still raged.

Sniffing and wiping her nose on the back of her hand, she faced the city. Taking stock of the situation, she saw that the Ragnarok were making their way toward the Library of Ages. The Hall of Art, the Ragnarok's last target, still lay completely desolated. She knew that to allow them forward another foot toward the Library would mean their success.

With her hands held out, she drew together all the strength she had and rotated her hands as if she spun a great wheel. Little bits of grass, dead frogs, and dirt surrounding the Library were lifted into the air. Faster, the debris spun, forming a tornado-wall around the building. Those inside were safe from the invaders and the storm. Those outside either cheered at her efforts or screamed in frustration.

TIDE OF THE STORM

It was soon clear to Worthmere that the Ragnarok had one target in mind: the Library of Ages. Fighting madly, he was down to hand-to-hand combat. He took a torch from a fallen warrior and used it like a club against the head of another. A Sphinx soldier ran past, finishing off Worthmere's opponent with a single, crushing step.

The feel of the fight altered. As Worthmere ran toward more fighting, he noticed that everyone on both sides paused for a moment and turned toward the Library. He watched in amazement as a tornado developed, surrounding the Library with an impenetrable wall of roaring wind and debris. Scanning the field for the responsible mage, he saw that everyone was just as confused as he was.

Anna ran toward him. "It's Victoria! She's here!"

"Where?" he shouted over the noise of the wind.

Anna was smiling, but she shook her head. "I don't know. But this is her! I recognize it. She doesn't know she shouldn't be able to do this!"

"Well," Worthmere gripped the burning torch in his hand

tighter, "let's not waste it!"

Trina and Ambrosia ran toward them.

"Where are the soldiers?" Trina asked. "What about those so called Junior Elders? Why aren't they fighting?"

Ambrosia's frustration surfaced and she clawed the ground leaving deep gouges in the grass. "Those fools are hiding in the Library."

Trina shook her head in disgust. "Maybe they can throw heavy objects out the window."

"Maybe," Ambrosia said, "but I will fight."

HOPE FALLS

"How long can you keep this up?" Foley asked her.

Victoria gritted her teeth with the effort. She honestly felt like she would be completely spent in less than a minute. She also knew that if she let the tornado go, the Library would be lost to the Ragnarok. "I've got it. I can do it. Go help them!"

"I'm not going to leave you. If anyone comes near, you need protection."

That helped. Victoria had been sending her Earth intent into the ground at her feet to stay alert for anyone approaching. Her Fire intent, while completely untested, was tingling just beneath the surface. The rope that had wrapped around her arm when the Ragnarok threw it at her had ignited the first spark.

Because Foley would protect her, she could drop her connection with Earth and Fire and focus on the wind around the Library. As soon as she did, the tornado thickened, spinning faster.

She could feel Foley using his element to fight off attackers. She trusted him completely. She had to. If she let her attention slip for only a moment, the tornado would die. The Ragnarok near the Library were counting on that. She could see them gathering as close to the spinning storm as they dared.

Behind her, she heard Foley grunt and fall. Daring a glance, she saw that he had been hit on the head and his shirt was on fire. Victoria ran and fell to her knees by his side, patting out the flames with her bare hands. Just like the rope, the flames were hot, but they didn't burn her. When his shirt was extinguished, Victoria checked his head. A thick bump was already forming above his left ear. His eyes fluttered open and he groaned.

The Ragnarok were closing in on them as cautiously as they would a ravenous tiger. A few had sputtering torches and long pieces of the hot rope. Others held long, slender spears. Victoria knew those spears well. Her side and back itched with the memory. Never again would anything pierce her. Never again would she feel the hot breath of evil on her face while a spear broke her skin and threatened her life. The Ragnarok worshipped fire. She would give them a fire of her own.

In a flash, she stood and spun around with her arms out, shouting with all she had, casting every ounce of intent she had into all four elements. Fire rode on the back of Air in a ring that nearly tore the Ragnarok bodies in two. Earth pulsed in a rippling circle around her, burying them all. The storm that raged within her came to the surface as heavy rainfall fell from the sky, extinguishing the fallen torches.

Adrenaline coursed through her veins, making her shake and sweat. It was dizzying, using all the elements at once. Her legs felt like rubber and she felt the world beneath her shift. Fearful that she might faint, she dropped to her knees and put her head to the ground, hearing only the rushing of her blood.

"Victoria," Foley's voice was weak. "The Library."

"Oh!" Victoria scrambled to stand and staggered toward the edge of the forest and looked down at the city. Bright flames lit every window of the Library as all the precious documents burned at the hands of the Ragnarok. Millennia of written history in every language from every terrace were vanishing.

The Air hummed with the call of several Air and Water mages working together to pull enough rain from the sky, but it was useless. All was lost.

FALLEN

The tornado stopped instantly; the curtain of debris fluttered to the ground.

Anna tried to resurrect the spinning storm, but couldn't. The Ragnarok were engaging in close combat. She felt a burning pull on her arm as a warrior flung a hot rope around her wrist, distracting her focus to protect the Library. She shook the rope off and pulled her burned arm toward her. She hated ingis rope.

Worthmere grabbed Anna's other arm and pulled her away. With the tornado gone, the Ragnarok charged through their lines with ease. Sphinx were cut down by the spears, their bodies left as the invaders swarmed into the Library, their goal achieved.

Anna was crying. Tears ran freely down Worthmere's face too, but he knew he had to get Anna away from the fighting. They had lost. Retreat was the only option.

"Come on!" Worthmere held Anna's hand and ran away from the chaos with Trina and Ambrosia close behind. "Where's your father?" he called to Ambrosia. "We must leave!"

Ambrosia's expression hardened and she only shook her head. Worthmere's gut twisted. He faltered a step, stumbling.

Anna held him up this time and they all continued away from the burning city, leaving behind a legacy of history, but more importantly, a friend.

Exodus

Foley rolled to his side, stood on wobbly legs and walked toward Victoria. He put a shaky hand on her shoulder and watched the fire in the Library grow. From the windows, burning papers were tossed out. Every speck of history was turning to ash.

"We need to leave. It's over."

Victoria squeezed her eyes shut, sniffled and cleared her throat. "Do you think they were down there? Bobby and Tucker?"

"Any survivors will be headed to the caves," he said. "I'm sorry."

She shook her head. "It wasn't your fault." With one last look at the sphinx city, she asked, "Anna and Worthmere. Do you think they survived?"

"Worthmere is too stubborn to die and Anna doesn't have time for something that inconvenient." With his arm around Victoria's shoulder, he guided her away from the battle ground and deeper into the woods toward the south, away from the ancient city.

They walked most of the night, meeting up occasionally with

other sphinx who had survived and were going to the caves to regroup. Each time they encountered another survivor, they acknowledged each other as allies and forged on in silence with only the sounds of stumbling, sniffing back tears, and the occasional hushed voice. The ragged band were injured and singed, but alive.

Victoria's mind replayed the events again and again, trying to discover where she had made a mistake. If she had just continued at least her Earth element while she maintained the tornado around the Library, she could have warned Foley. It would have been difficult to do both, but she should have.

As the sun rose, turning the sky pink and sending the birds into a chirping frenzy, Victoria saw a stream of people heading in the same direction. Over a hundred sphinx and about two dozen people marched with defeated steps. Victoria stopped walking and scanned the crowd for familiar faces. The more she looked without finding Anna or Worthmere, the more her stomach soured. Desperation turned to panic when she didn't see Bobby and Tucker either. All this time, she had been hoping they had found their way back to the sphinx. Now she prayed that they weren't there at all, but somewhere safe in a different terrace.

Animal Attacks

Bobby woke suddenly. He lay perfectly still, listening and feeling for what woke him. One of the horses neighed loudly as the sound of scuttling startled him. Pressing his hands against the earth, Bobby tried to determine what was out there.

Another sound behind him was quickly followed by a louder scramble of feet to his left. It wasn't a question of who was out there, but how many? Bobby knew they were surrounded. Collecting his wits, he took a deep breath and prepared to fight. He knew that Collette was also awake and was likely just figuring out that they were in trouble.

Do you know how many? Tucker asked.

Too many. Bobby waited for a moment as a group of feet moved from the north toward the east. *Not people. Animals.*

Like, wild animals? Tucker asked.

Just hold still for a minute. I have an idea.

Bobby could see Tucker reach for Collette's hand, reassuring her that they knew what was going on. He could feel Collette's heartbeat racing, but it calmed a bit when Tucker took her hand.

The tension among the creatures surrounding them was

growing. Bobby knew he needed to act soon.

Get ready to run to the horses. I'll follow.

With a quick prayer that his plan would actually work, Bobby sent out a shock wave that rippled from him in a outward moving circle toward the animals, but not toward the horses. The last thing he wanted was to scare away their means of escape. The closeness of the trees absorbed much of his intent, but it was enough to give them a start.

Collette screamed in surprise. Tucker hauled her up by the hand and together they ran to untie the horses.

Bobby rolled from his back to his hands and knees and sent another shock wave, a stronger effort that toppled a few of the prowling animals off their feet.

Bobby ran toward his horse, mounted and rode after Tucker and Collette. He knew almost immediately that his distraction only bought them a few seconds. Racing between the trees with only the dim light of night to guide the horse, Bobby dared a glance back to what had surrounded them. The moonlight didn't reach beyond the canopy of leaves. It really didn't matter what they were, he realized. They had a voracious growl which meant they probably had sharp teeth. They were also running faster than his horse.

Just ahead, he saw sparks fly as Tucker dragged a flint stone from his pocket and cast the glowing bits toward the dry grass. Bobby realized that Tucker had run back the way they had come, back into the small grassy area just outside the line of trees. Within a breath's time, Tucker enlarged the small glint of fire into a raging circle which surrounded him and Collette. Their horses' eyes were wide with terror at both the fire and what chased them. Tucker lowered the edge of the flame for Bobby's horse to leap over.

"What are they?" Collette asked, struggling to keep her horse still while holding the reins of Tucker's horse as he controlled the flames. "They aren't dogs."

She was right. Too big to be dogs, too graceful for bears, too boxy for cats. Large ears poised upright flinched at every sound. Long tails brushed the ground behind them. They were almost laughable if not for their over-sized incisors. Their fur was sleek and brown, perfect camouflage for desert life.

"Some kind of hybrid killer rabbit?" Tucker suggested.

Bobby looked around the outside of Tucker's circle of fire. "Whatever they are, we've stepped from one trap to another. I count seven. Maybe we can fight them." As he said the words, five more walked into the ring of light.

"Now what?" Collette asked.

Tucker's flames were slowly losing their strength. "I'm running out of fuel for the fire."

They had nothing other than their elements to fight the rabbit-eared dogs. They already knew that out-running them was not an option.

"I have an idea," Tucker said as he moved the ring along the ground, allowing them to walk within the protection of the flames.

"Do we risk moving this toward the trees?" Collette asked. "Can you control it to keep from starting a forest fire?"

"Don't think so."

"This will work until we run out of grass," Bobby said. "Unless you can make dirt burn."

Sweat dripped from Tucker's forehead in the effort of moving the ring of fire. "We are about to find out."

The fire dimmed as the horses hooves clamped onto hardened soil.

One of the rabbit-dogs yelped in surprise and collapsed.

"Look!" Collette yelled, pointing to a long knife jutting from the side of the animal.

Another and then another fang-toothed dog-rabbit dropped,

felled with knives and several arrows, until only five remained. The remaining creatures nervously backed up, finally running off as one more arrow flew from the darkness to find its mark right between the eyes of the largest animal.

Tucker finally released his hold on the fire and it died immediately. He was spent. "I hope whoever just saved us is on our side."

"Oh man," Bobby sighed as he watched four men wearing black step toward them. In the eerie moonlight, these men looked frightening, but it was the spiked ball hanging from a chain on an iron stick that told them these men were not friendly.

Collette tightened her grip on the reins and her body tensed as she prepared to charge past them and run.

"I wouldn't," a man said with his bow tensed and arrow aimed right at her. "Your horse couldn't outrun the cunicanes. I'm sure you can't outrun my arrow." The man nodded when Collette dropped her reins. "Good choice."

"Not much of a choice," Bobby said.

The archer smiled. "I'm under orders not to kill you."

"Although nothing was said about maiming," the man with the spiked club said.

"Whose orders?" Bobby asked.

The man with several knives strapped to his belt stepped forward. "Your aunt wasn't happy with your quick departure." He pulled a knife from the side of a cunicane and wiped it clean in the grass. "It's rude to leave without saying good-bye. It's especially rude to leave without her permission."

"Well," Tucker shrugged, "we always did wonder what a family reunion would be like."

"That's the spirit," the man said with a smile on his face. "Lady Martina will be grateful. Now," he held out his hand and they all felt the Air around them tighten, freezing them into place, "to assure that we don't need to chase you across this Godforsaken desert again, you will be tied to your horses." Three men came forward with leather straps and tied their hands behind their backs and then to the saddle. "I'm sure you can imagine what will happen if you try to run. Bound like this, if you fall off your horse your shoulders will dislocate and you'll be dragged. It won't kill you, well, I don't think it would, but it would make a very uncomfortable ride."

"Are we going back to Rockheart?" Bobby asked.

The guard tightened the ropes around Bobby's wrists. "No. Despite what you might think, you aren't that important to Madame Minister. But you are important to her plans."

Tucker frowned. "What does that mean?"

Bobby looked to Collette and his brother. "We're the bait."

"For whom?" Collette asked.

The man only smiled.

Timeless Return

Nuri walked quickly through the streets of Kivavallis. He wanted to run. Bounding up the steps to Ona's dwelling, he brushed past the attendants, bumping into a guard but not taking the time to apologize. The message from Bernadette had been delivered in her racing, high-pitched voice. Nuri had only understood two of the words: *Ona* and *here.*

He charged into the room and saw her standing there, her green velvet gown strikingly dark against her skin.

He wanted to rush to her, embrace her, make sure she was real flesh and blood. That would never do.

"Where have you been?" he asked, wincing at the obvious emotion in his voice.

"I never left," Ona remained business-like, "but if what Bernadette tells me is true, then some weeks have passed."

"What do you mean, you never left?"

Ona sat down and indicated that Nuri should do the same. "Yesterday I walked to the kiva. Today I came home."

Nuri leaned forward, frowning. "That was almost three weeks ago. What happened?"

Ona lifted an embroidered cloth off the table, revealing three triangles of silver fused together.

"You have it."

Ona held it out for him. Nuri took it and closely examined it for a clue to its significance and purpose. It was lighter than he expected. For what it had already cost them, it should have weighed much more. "It looks as though there is one piece missing."

"Lucian kept it. Do you know what it is?" Ona asked.

Nuri turned it over. "No."

"There were four men from the terraces beneath ours," Ona told him. "They each had a section. It was really quite amazing."

Nuri turned the silver piece over, examining it further. "What was it like in the kiva? Were we correct?"

"We were. We had all the pieces we needed. I wasn't sure if she knew what to do, but Lucian did. He knew how to put this together. He must know what it is."

"And he won't tell you?"

Ona sighed. "Victoria did something when my guards tried to stop her from leaving the pueblo and again in the kiva. Lightning struck. I don't know where they are. Of course, no one knew where I was, so they might still show up."

"Caladrius found them in the mountains and brought them here. A few of the guards foolishly attacked and she did it again. I don't know where she went, but she and the twins, along with Collette, disappeared."

"Disappeared." Ona leaned back in her chair, thinking. "I wonder if she will suddenly show up here a few days or weeks from now."

"Only one other mage in history has been able to call lightning." Nuri saw Ona's pride-eating grin. "You knew. You knew who her father was."

Ona smiled. "No one could miss the similarities. Assuming

what we know of the late Alexander Veracitous to be true, I could venture a guess that her mother was Diane."

Nuri whistled. "Quite the lineage. No wonder the girl is so strong." Leaning forward, Nuri spoke quietly. "The twins' parents. What do you know about them?"

Smiling, Ona dismissed the challenge. "You obviously know. Stop gloating and tell me."

"Adam Caius."

Ona's eyes widened. "Impossible."

"That's what I thought. Parnassus made that known at his inquiry."

Breathing in deeply, Ona regained her composure. "You believe him?"

"I do. There would be no benefit to lie about such a thing. It certainly doesn't give the twins any credibility."

"It does give us a new target," Ona said. "If Adam truly did take the scrolls, then perhaps the twins know. They could be very useful."

"We'll be ready if they return." Nuri pointed to the hallway where Victoria's lightning struck, leaving a blackened burn on the floor. "We'll keep guards posted here at all times."

"We need to learn what this all means." Ona gestured toward the silver pieces. "Did you see Ophidia?"

Setting down the key, Nuri stood, shaking his head while he paced. "It was different. Normally Ophidia doesn't look at me, as if she just needs to pass along the vision without any concern for the recipient. But this time she never took her eyes off me."

"Tell me what she showed you."

"A woman in the middle of a series of circles, each one bigger than the next, like a target. The outer circle was all doorways. Stone, wood, some were more like open traps in the earth and a few were just there."

Narrowing her eyes, Ona bit her lip as she thought about

what that might mean. "Doorways? Or gateways?"

"Not paintings."

"Not all gateways are connected on both sides with paintings," Ona reminded him.

Nuri rubbing his hand over his face. "It's illegal, not to mention extremely dangerous, for a Painter to make a singular gateway."

Laughing, Ona took the silver piece from the table and held it up. "When did you become a law-abiding mage?"

Nuri shook his head, trying to stop his cheeks from turning so red. "Ophidia is dead. Right after, there was a swarm of insects with razor-like teeth."

"It's just another case of the imbalance."

"You are certain of that?" Nuri asked.

"You question my knowledge of this? You think I'm just like everyone else?"

"I'm asking if you are certain about the Weapon." He softened his tone, feeling proud that he could make her so angry. "No one has ever seen it. Entire wars have been fought over what the Weapon even is. Are you certain that you know what it can do?"

Setting the three, fused silver triangles on the table, Ona smiled. "I have no doubts."

"What of Ophidia?"

Ona rolled her eyes. "You are upset because of an insect swarm?"

"It wasn't natural," Nuri said in a low whisper, stepping closer to Ona. "A priestess of Apollo died of a snake bite. Those insects didn't fly in on the wind; they rose from the dust when the Python statue was toppled to the ground. The entire line of Greek gods is faltering."

"We have never believed in those little gods. Why would their demise affect me?"

Nuri shook his head. He wasn't worried about the Greek gods. He knew they were weak and ineffective. It was the God the Grandfather believed in that made him nervous. He knew that the Grandfather had defied the Creator and ruined all of Creation. The terraces were the punishment for his misuse of his elemental intent. Like the first man who ignored God's rule and was banished from the garden, the Grandfather's punishment broke that world apart. Not just toppling over a tower and dividing families by infecting them all with a different language, but clearly dividing each family up between the terraces.

"There's more," Nuri said. "I saw one of Martina's men talking to the priest right after Ophidia died."

Ona spun around. "Martina? What could she possibly know about the Weapon?"

"I'm sure she's wondering the same about you."

Ona fidgeted with the emerald on her necklace for a moment before she regained her composure. "Send four guards to Rockheart. Make sure they stay out of Martina's way, but tell them to keep their eyes open," Ona said in a determined tone. "If we expect to survive, we must find the Grandfather's Weapon." Straightening her posture, Ona breathed in deeply and pressed her lips together. "The visions are never very clear. Perhaps," she paused, "perhaps this is a wave of fortune in our favor. Ophidia's death is an indication that the balance is shifting in our favor. The Grandfather's Weapon can only be opened by one mage during a period of extreme unrest. Yes. This is a good thing. We are getting closer."

The Caves

By late morning, the caves came into sight. Victoria had been expecting a network of caves set into a mountain side. This was worse. The 'caves' were low, rocky hovels dug into the ground and covered with an abundance of grass and branches. The refugees silently started clearing away the over-grown weeds to uncover doorways. As soon as they were cleared, sphinx and men alike ducked inside. Foley and Victoria worked with an older sphinx whom Victoria recognized from her one trip into the Library of Ages. She looked haggard at the loss of her beloved books and scrolls. When the doorway was cleared, she nodded to Victoria to climb in first. She peeked inside at a dark and dusty floor covered with dirt and debris. It seemed everyone was just crawling inside their holes, hiding from the pain of the previous day. In Victoria's mind, there was still more to do.

"Shouldn't we get everyone together and make a plan?" Victoria asked.

The sphinx looked at her, so sad by this unfortunate child's lack of understanding. "All is destroyed."

Her mouth fell open. "Aren't you going to fight?"

"For what?" the sphinx asked. "Everything I've worked for was reduced to ash."

"So what?" Victoria almost shouted. "You are still breathing. We need to figure out who survived and what to do next."

The sphinx started to cry. "No, child. This place," she looked around, "this is where the sphinx first lived. These holes show you how far we've come. All our ancestors could do all those thousands of years ago, was to dig holes. Now we are back."

"These are not homes," Foley joined in. "These are graves. Go ahead and hide your head in the sand. Death will find you fast. Victoria and I are going to fight."

The sphinx stood there a long time, staring at the hole, then she turned to Victoria and Foley. "I know what you are saying is right. But for now, I am going to hide my head in the sand." She slid into the hole and disappeared in the darkness.

Victoria looked to Foley. "If that's the level of motivation of the sphinx, there isn't much hope, is there."

"They've lost everything." Foley wiped sweat off his forehead. "Everything except their lives. They will realize that soon. Let's look around and see who we can find. Once we know more about what just happened, we can make a plan."

Together they started wandering through the caves. War-shattered expressions devoid of emotion and filled with blank stares met them at every turn. Bruises and dried blood covered many of the survivors. Even Foley's neck was caked with dried blood, but he ignored it, focusing on the next task—finding their friends.

Despite the work of uncovering the rocky shelters, no one spoke much. The whispers were quick and strained. Victoria's heart ached for the sphinx and the people who just lost their home and livelihood. She understood completely. She had been home that morning. She, too, had been forced to leave; literally chased right out of her terrace.

Thinking of home, she glanced down at her jeans. They were filthy and had a tear at the knee. Her t-shirt was the same. Her backpack, she realized, was still stuck in the tree. So much for a hairbrush and a change of clothes.

"Victoria?" a familiar voice called from a distance.

Turning, Victoria saw Worthmere almost running toward her. Complete relief swept over Victoria as she reached out and was swept up in his massive hug.

"Oh, you made it. You made it." He held her a long time and only let go when Anna shouted her name and practically ripped her from Worthmere's grip and into her own embrace.

After several long moments filled with the sound of thanksgiving and sniffles, Anna stood back, but continued to hold Victoria's arms. "Let me look at you."

"Are you okay?" Victoria asked.

"We're fine," Anna said. "A little," she didn't finish, but the tears told Victoria that they had been through a great deal.

Worthmere wiped his eyes and tried to smile. "We are better for seeing you." He looked past Victoria toward Foley. "Aren't you supposed to be dead?"

Foley nodded. "I'm glad to report that my death was greatly exaggerated." He held out his hand and Worthmere took it. "Good to see you, Worthmere."

"Rumors," Worthmere smiled and winked. "Terrible things." Looking around, his smile faded. "The boys didn't find you?"

"They did," Victoria felt the hot tears forming. "I—I don't know where they are. I," she remembered the feel of the lightning as it ripped the sky and the terrace. The fear she endured as she was tied to the post and about to be burned ravaged her nerves. She remembered the sting of the fire at the village where the building exploded and how those villagers had chased her, too.

Foley put his hand on her shoulder and looked at Worthmere. "I think we should find a place to talk. There is much

271

to share."

Victoria was surprised when Trina, a Council Mage she had only seen once a few months ago when she followed Anna through a mirror, hugged her. "I'm so glad you're here." Trina smiled widely. Victoria had the sneaking suspicion that Trina's joy over her arrival had more to do with politics than emotion.

Worthmere started the discussion. "We are thrilled you are here, but I have so many questions. How did you get out of that barn? You said that you found the boys—or they found you. Where are they? Trina said something about lightning."

"Give her some space," Ambrosia said as she walked forward, smiling at Victoria.

Victoria quickly wrapped her arms around Ambrosia's neck. "I have so much to tell you." She looked at the group. "So much to tell you all."

"We have a shelter over there," Ambrosia nodded with her head. "In anticipation, of a disaster, I had it stocked with food and drinks. We can rest, eat, and listen to Victoria's story."

The shelter was much cleaner than the first one Victoria had peeked into. Small shelves carved into the wall of the cave held clay jars of food. Bundles of burlap cloth in the shape of loaves of bread and rounds of cheese lined another shelf. "I came out here shortly after the Elders named the Junior Elders. Nothing good was going to come from those changes."

"How like a woman to think of food," Foley smiled. "Without your foresight, we would all starve. Thank you, Ambrosia."

She blushed an bowed her head. "I just know how thick-headed men are. Especially when they are hungry."

"Agreed," Foley said as he unfolded a thick cloth with dried foods inside.

As they ate, Victoria told them everything that had happened. Lucian, the dreamwalker, Ona and her minions, the lightning. The events in the Kiva made Anna cry. Telling her story relieved Victoria from the burdens she had suffered. Foley smiled at her when she left out their visit to Jo. She told about them about the fire in the village, the explosion and how they were once again on the run. The story about her mother's painting seemed safe. Her mom wasn't a mage anymore and she hoped there wouldn't be any negative consequences for painting outside of the Council's permission. But, the Council seemed to be a defunct network of leaders now, so the threat seemed minimal.

"That's how we came to the edge of the sphinx city, just before the Ragnarok came," Victoria finished.

"How did you make that tornado?" Anna asked. "I've never seen anything like it."

Victoria shrugged. "I don't really know. I just wanted to keep the Ragnarok out. They seemed very intent on getting in."

"Which they did." Ambrosia added. "Not that I blame you. Your tornado offered me a chance to get out."

No one spoke for a moment. All the adults just stared at Victoria like she had Zeus' lightning bolt in one hand and Thor's hammer in the other. "I know you all think I'm some kind of legend."

"You don't?" Worthmere asked. "After a story like that, how can you think you're not?"

"The dreamwalker is to blame for much of that." Victoria looked at Anna then Foley. "I know I am. I am the Lost Painter."

Trina smiled. Anna paled. Worthmere turned and started pacing. Foley put his hand on her shoulder and gave her an encouraging squeeze.

"What do I do now?" Victoria asked.

Worthmere stopped pacing. "Now we fight. Now we make the legend of the Lost Painter a reality. Now we take back the dignity of the Mage Society."

TINT'S SONG

"How much farther?" Tucker asked for the fifth time that day.

"For you?" Stoneman, the guard riding next to him pulled a knife from a sheath on his belt and held it in a tight fist. "You don't have to suffer another minute. Ask again and your journey is over."

Tucker sighed, completely unimpressed with the threat. He knew that Martina, their long-lost aunt, had given specific orders that none of them be killed. She had said nothing about injuring them, however, and Tucker sported a swollen black eye. It was delivered on the quick knuckles of Stoneman, who quickly tired of Tucker's constant badgering.

Just then, a hawk's screeching call surprised them all when it swooped above their heads. The lead guard, or at least the bossiest and most short-tempered of the group, held out his arm and the bird landed.

What do you suppose? Tucker asked Bobby.

A message.

Sure enough, the guard plucked a small piece of paper from

a strap on the bird's leg. After reading it, he pulled off the top of his ring and pressed it onto the paper, leaving an imprint of a small seal. After the paper was rolled and securely tucked into the pocket on the bird's leg, he released the hawk.

For a moment, the guard watched the bird, then turned toward the group. "We go north."

Adjusting their direction, they continued on the new course.

They don't even know where we are going, Bobby realized.

Great. Just great, Tucker said.

The horses walked slowly and the group again settled into a quiet stupor. Tucker was concerned about Collette. She hadn't uttered a word since their capture two days before. She wasn't crying or raising a fuss or even giving the guards a difficult time. She simply looked ahead and rode. It wasn't as if there was much choice to do otherwise. With their hands tied behind their backs, the horses they rode were guided by Martina's men. They had stopped for water and food earlier that afternoon. The ropes binding their hands behind their backs were taken off, but quickly tied again in front of them so they could feed themselves. Tucker tried to make eye contact with her, to speak with her the way he spoke with Bobby, but nothing worked.

Late in the afternoon, Collette started to hum. It was soft and beautiful. The melody was sweet and her voice was pure. After a few moments, one of the guards, Smithy, a grubby man who seemed to sweat oil, glanced her way with a look of surprise on his face. Collette paid him no attention.

"I haven't heard that song in years," the youngest guard said. The other guards called him Tint, obviously a nickname, but how he came by it they hadn't a clue. Tint was the one who had shot many of the rabbit-dogs that had attacked, but he said little and contributed less to keep their prisoners under guard. He was the guard that would ride ahead and scout out the area. The fact that he spoke at all surprised his companions.

Collette looked at him. "I didn't take you for the type to know this song."

His cheeks flushed angrily. "You know nothing of me."

"I don't have to know anything," she looked back in the direction they were riding. "Your choice of friends tells me all I need to know."

She calmed her nerves with a deep breath, then continued her humming. The tune had Irish undertones with a lilting, bittersweet melody.

"What song is it?" Bobby asked.

"It's a prayer," Tint said. He glanced at Collette, then at Stoneman.

"It's a myth," Stoneman said, then spat sloppily on the ground. "A myth for fools who reduce themselves to the whims of a so-called Creator."

Collette stopped humming. "You don't believe in the Creator?"

All the guards except Tint laughed. "Have you ever seen the Creator?" Stoneman said. His face was smiling, but his eyes and the way he leaned his forehead toward Collette meant the question was a challenge.

"Our gifts are from the Creator," she said. "How else would you explain these abilities?"

"Human evolution. It was simply the process of human growth and the refining of skills."

Collette shook her head sadly and continued humming.

Tint joined her, singing the words to the myth, the song that divided believers from non-believers.

"You are an enclosed garden, my sister, my bride,
an enclosed garden, a fountain sealed.
You are a park that puts forth pomegranates,
with all choice fruits;

Nard and saffron, calamus and cinnamon,
with all kinds of incense;
Myrrh and alves,
with all the finest spices.
You are a garden fountain, a well of water
flowing fresh from Lebanon.
Arise, north wind! Come, south wind!
blow upon my garden
that its perfumes may spread abroad."

The song ended. Collette stopped humming when Tint stopped singing.

"That's all I remember," he said.

Smiling, Collette nodded.

Bobby and Tucker exchanged a look. *What do you think?* Bobby asked.

He doesn't have a great singing voice.

No, idiot! Bobby tried to keep his face free of expression. *The words. The myth. That's scripture. Song of Songs. It's from the Bible.*

Really? What's the Bible doing here?

Bobby looked at the guards. *I suppose it came here the same way we did. Or perhaps God exists in all the terraces.*

That would be good. Tucker looked directly at his brother. *We could really use a miracle right now.*

Post Script to the Reader,

This story is unfinished. Yes, there will be a third installment and as time goes by, more of the characters are reaching out to me in my daydreams and telling me their stories. To receive updates on *The Elemental Chronicles*, sign-up for an email notice on my website www.BooksByJessica.com

Peace,

JESSICA SCHAUB

Jessica Schaub

Book III of The Elemental Chronicles:

CRIMSON

ARROWS

PROLOGUE

Worse than the cold nights and the soaking drizzle that oozed through the thin tarp and dripped on his head were the looks of disappointment from his wife. It hadn't been his fault, he told himself again. His wife never uttered a word about "fault" but he knew she blamed him. What could she possible know? Any savvy business man would have done the same. Any man who hoped for a richer future would not have thought twice about it.

He remembered back to the night of the murder, when the men came through Woodland Hills searching for an escaped prisoner, he had kept the bag he'd taken from Sophia safe. The bag with the scrolls had to be worth a fortune if those men were willing to kill for it. With it safely tucked under the floor boards of their pantry, he and his wife had claimed innocence. Actually, his wife had been truthful. She knew nothing about it. And a good thing, too. She shook so badly from fear that night, she would have handed over anything the men asked for. Even when those men tore apart their little house, tossing blankets and cushions, searching drawers and even dumping the flour on the floor (as though the scrolls would have fit in that basin!) he kept his mouth shut. While his wife counted the destruction as a great financial loss, he saw the ability to replace it all—ten-fold—within his reach. Those weren't just papers in that bag, they were a ransom for silver. Possibly gold.

He even hid the bag from Sophia's niece when she came looking. He knew that woman was a mage. The way her eyes were different colors and the confidence with which she walked and talked. Those mages with their high and mighty ways. He didn't know exactly what a mage could do, but he knew they had abilities that no human should have. It just put others at risk. His wife scolded him and reminded him that they had never had any trouble from the mages or the sphinx. They all just kept to themselves and were always very civil. She was a fool, he shook his head sadly at her poor, misguided thinking.

A drip of cold water plopped on his bald head and ran down his back. The tarp was only slowing down how quickly the water reached his skin.

"We need more dry kindling," his wife said. Between them, a small and smoky fire struggled to remain alive. The little warmth it provided was worth the smoke that burned his nose.

"I don't think there's a dry piece of wood in a hundred miles." He looked at his wife. She was thinner now, but still a sizable woman. It would have been easy for him to feel sorry for her if she wasn't scowling so darkly at him. They had eaten their last meal yesterday. His stomach growled noisily at the memory of the thick, stale bread and last few drops of wine from the flask. They had refilled the wine flask with water, which now tasted sour with the tinge of fermented grapes tainting the iron flavor of the ground water.

He looked around at their tarp shelter. This hadn't been the plan. They weren't supposed to be here in the rain, starving, but living in Delphi in style. It had all started well. With the wagon and the two mules, they dressed in their best and rode grandly through the gates of Delphi. He sauntered into several stores, treating his wife to a new wool scarf, and demonstrated how successful he was with purchases of rich meats and cheeses from the vendors that lined the main road. He spoiled her with the baked pastries that dripped with honey. They stayed in a beautiful inn where, with a flash of silver coin, they were given a very good room.

He took the scrolls to the Magistrate's Office, bragging to his wife that he would sell it to them for a price. The Magistrate's assistant asked to see what was in the bag, but the Mayor refused. "The Magistrate will know the value. I don't trust anyone else."

And so he waited another day. The Magistrate's schedule was busy, but tomorrow, the assistant said, he would have five minutes.

After another night in the inn, there was less money clinking in his pocket.

Another day of enjoying the sites of Delphi. More silver left his pocket, but now his wife knew what a man of influence he was. Not just in their little hamlet of Woodland Hills, but here in Delphi, too, people were eager to please him.

Not the Magistrate, however.

The Magistrate of Delphi was a slight man with thinning hair and a pointed nose, who was not easily won over. The Mayor was not impressed with the Magistrate either, for that matter. He set the bag heavily on the Magistrate's desk and opened it for him. "What have we here?" the little man asked, thoroughly unimpressed.

The Mayor knew this technique; drive down the price by claiming that the item for sale isn't worth much, if anything. But he knew. A glint of surprise had flashed behind the Magistrate's eyes. He knew these were valuable.

"Ancient scrolls." Taking one out of the bag, the Mayor unrolled it for the Magistrate to see. "Valuable pieces of history."

"Hmm." The Magistrate studied the writing on the scroll. "How did you come to have these?"

He was prepared for this. "They are pieces of my family's ancestry."

"You are willing to part with these for a price, I assume?" the Magistrate narrowed his eyes.

"They are extremely valuable."

Standing, the Magistrate took the scroll, studied it for another moment as he held it right under his nose with his eyes squinted, then shook his head. "I sometimes purchase old scrolls to scrape clean and re-use. I'll give you seven."

"Gold?"

"Goodness no!" The Magistrate laughed. "Coppers."

"These are valuable pieces of history. Can't no one scrape this off!" The Mayor nearly shouted.

The Magistrate held up his aged hand, "It can be scraped off, my greedy friend. You are simply disputing whether it should be."

"These are valuable!"

"Yes, so you said," the Magistrate said, he walked around his desk and opened the door, indicating that the Mayor's five minutes were over. "I wish you the best of luck in finding someone who understands the value of old scrolls."

"Ancient scrolls," the Mayor corrected.

"Good day," the Magistrate bowed his head slightly and the meeting was over.

That afternoon they checked out of the Inn and carried their baggage a few streets over to a smaller Inn with smaller rooms, darker walls, and creaking stairs. His wife appreciated the room and told her husband it was wise of him to not waste their money on such finery. This room was clean and tidy, she said, and she would be very happy here until they could sell the scrolls.

While she settled into the room, the Mayor went to the stables to sell his wagon. He traded it for enough to live in the Inn for another week. He knew he could buy it back, so he didn't worry about the loss. It was all temporary. An investment in appearances until the right buyer could be found.

His wife sneezed and more rain ran down his back. "We need some dry kindling for the fire." He sighed. She wasn't going to stop until he built up the fire.

He scratched at the bites from the gnat swarm that had scoured the city that afternoon. It was, without a doubt, the strangest thing he and his wife had ever witnessed. As they walked toward the scholar's quarters, screams and the rumbling thunder of scrambling people stormed toward them. They stopped for a moment, trying to figure out the cause, when the street suddenly burst with panic. People ran, flailing their arms, swatting at a dark cloud that rolled down the street. At first it looked like a dark fog, but the blackness clung to the buildings and the people. Millions of gnats settled on anything and everything, crawling over their clothes, into their hair and down their necks. Screams and scratching and disgust infected the city. The Mayor and his wife joined the mass of people running out of the city. Their mules were nowhere to be found and his wagon had been destroyed when the horses in the stable, in absolute fright, tried to escape the swarming infestation. As they ran from the city, he grabbed any food he could stuff into the bag with the scrolls.

He had a purse filled with coins from selling the wagon, but everywhere they went, people turned them away, money or no. Illnesses, infestations, and fear ruled the world and no amount of money could inspire people to help them.

Dreams of vast fortunes were dashed as they walked toward Woodland Hills. His wife was silent about the discomfort, but she voiced all shades of disapproval with her expressions.

The fire sputtered and hissed as a stream of rain spilled off the tarp and onto the red coals. The Mayor sighed sadly and unlatched the bag. His wife had been comfortable at home. She was an honest woman who deserved to have a warm fire to fight off the cold rain. He pulled out a scroll and fed it to the flames. A burst of heat filled their damp tent, lighting the space with warm light. He looked across the flames to his wife, he saw her smile. She was a good woman. This was all his fault.

1

ROCK OF REFUGE

The smoke from the sphinx city filtered through the forest, choked its way around the trees, over the moss-covered ground, and replaced the fresh woodland air with a sick scent of burned books. A day had passed since the mad escape when the Ragnarok burned the sphinx right out of their ancestral homes and toward the subterranean holes that housed the sphinx in ancient times.

The caves were not stone outcroppings in a mountain or dark caverns. When Victoria first followed Ambrosia into the cave, she walked down an earthy ramp, which followed the outside of an oval underground room. The walls had been reinforced with stone, and the floor was smooth slate, the ceiling was cave-like with a few stalactites forming from years of neglect. Overall, it was a comfortable space in the sense that it was dry, but a few cushions would go a long way for true comfort, something Victoria believed she would never experience again.

The scent of the fires singed into every nostril, and soot stained their fur or clothing. More than half of the mage and sphinx refugees were in need of burn treatments. All they had for first aid was water.

Hushed voices and sobs, stifled by fists or paws, broke free from inconsolable souls. Desperation clung to every expression. "What now?" "What will happen?" were whispered here and there, answered by those only slightly injured who asked, "Why didn't I do more?"

The sudden appearance of blood and fire defiling their precious lawns and buildings traumatized their minds. Sphinx and mages alike whispered Elder Parnassus' name in complete shock at his death, a death earned in defending the city when so many other sphinx had run in utter fear. Centuries had swept by the sphinx city without a battle being fought on their soil.

Unlike the sphinx who spent the first day searching the caves for family and loved ones, Victoria was one of the few to celebrate a reunion. Anna and Worthmere doted over her, checked her for injuries, asked her again and again if she was okay and what had happened, but did not give her a moment's breath to answer. Bobby and Tucker were not there. Only God knew where they were.

"I'm sorry about your father," Victoria leaned on Ambrosia's shoulder.

Ambrosia tipped her head down to meet Victoria's and they hugged. "My father was not the only casualty. Frigg, too, fell."

Victoria's eyes widened. "No!" she could only whisper. Pressing her face into Ambrosia's fur, she tried to picture Frigg the last time she had seen her, sleeping in that barn a terrace away. "I'm so sorry."

"I know, little one," Ambrosia straightened and Victoria wiped her face on her sleeve. "I see you've returned to your denim slacks," Ambrosia teased.

"Jeans," Victoria reminded her. "I'm afraid the clothes you gave me were ruined."

"I don't have replacements for you this time," Ambrosia said as she looked around the inside of the cave.

"This cave is well stocked," Foley commented. "Who had the brains to prepare?"

"Elder Amberson, my father, and I have prepared of the caves for just such a turn of event," Ambrosia said.

Worthmere pointed upwards, toward the noise of defeat from the sphinx still wandering around outside. "Shouldn't we help the others?"

Ambrosia looked down and shook her head. "There is too much pain right now for us to do much good. I have bandages, but that's not the right kind of healing they need."

"If you have food," Anna started, but Ambrosia continued.

"If the others would stop and look, each cave has a supply. But, being blinded by their pride, they might not notice until later." She turned to face Anna. "Let them sort it out for themselves for a while. I've had enough for one day."

Anna and Trina found the food Ambrosia had stocked in her cave and they ate in silence. Like the bomb shelters in the Fourth Terrace during the 1950's this cave was well-stocked and ready for months of living away from home. From outside, arguments were rabid as sphinx tried to claim possession of the caves that were in better repair than others. Disagreements fueled by hunger and fear left more than one sphinx bleeding. Without the Elder's Circle, the government system to resolve disputes, conflicts escalated quickly.

Ambrosia had welcomed Abner, Anna, Worthmere, Victoria and Foley to her cave. It hadn't been designed for two sphinx and four people, but with two blankets strung over small alcoves, they had a men's room and a woman's wing which afforded them some privacy.

"Father thought of everything," Ambrosia smiled as she found a half dozen sleeping mats. Anna placed her hand on Ambrosia's shoulder.

As the sun set closing the first day after the attack, the enormity of the situation fell on Victoria suddenly and her heart nearly stopped when she took a moment to think about all that had happened and how little had been accomplished. Where was her mother? Her friends? What had happened during Elder Parnassus' last moments? Why was Ona fighting so fiercely for the Grandfather's Weapon? Was there more she could have done to stop it all?

Victoria pressed her face with her hands, trying to stop the tears that refused to dry out. Sobs were stifled at first, but gained as she could not hold back any longer. Memories of events from the moment she slipped through the painting in the art room blasted through her mind. Fear, pain, and loss were real horrors. But it was the loneliness that extended her despair. If only she could see her mom. If only Bobby and Tucker were here. She felt like she could do anything if she could only have them here, safe and huggable.

She feared sleep. Several times when the dreams haunted her rest, she jerked awake. The last time she woke, it was because Foley shook her from a nightmare. Not a dream-walk, but a true nightmare in which she had tried to protect her mother from Ona, and called the lightning to do her bidding. Everyone was burning in her dream when Foley finally woke her.

"You were crying," he said.

She couldn't stop. At some point, she knew she would have to stop, but it wouldn't be tonight.

"So much," she sobbed, but couldn't find the words to explain it fully.

So much loss. Pain unlike anything she had imagined. Fear haunted her sleep, tormented her waking hours with exhaustion. There were so many needs that would possibly never be met. What would happen if she never saw her mother again? There were thousands of people out there who had lost both of their parents, who had suffered unimaginable terrors. Victoria never thought she would be one of them. She never understood why she had a single mother and never dreamed that her father had been a part of an elaborate scheme to take down the entire world. Or worlds.

"I know," Foley said. He held her as a father would. As her father's friend, he did what her father had never had the opportunity to do. He consoled an inconsolable young woman. He allowed her to cry without trying to calm her fears with false promises. Foley didn't try to make the situation less desperate. He simply cried with her.

In his arms and feeling the tears fall from his eyes onto her head, she knew that her emotions were acceptable. Now she wasn't alone. For the first time in weeks, she could share the burden with another. It was permissible to cry, to feel so much grief.

A long time later, when the sobs had stopped wracking her breath, Victoria was finally able to ask the question that started it all. "What will we do?"

Foley lifted her chin so they were eye-to-eye. "We will do the next right thing. Always."

Books by Jessica Schaub:

Gateways, Book I of The Elemental Chronicles
The Elder's Circle, Book II of The Elemental Chronicles
Crimson Arrows, Book III of The Elemental Chronicles

Gravity: A Short Story

Unforgettable Roads

Coming soon:

Lies in the Shadows
Circle of Pride

Visit: www.JessicaSchaub.com to follow Jessica on Facebook, Twitter, and Instagram, and to learn about her new books.

www.ingramcontent.com/pod-product-compliance
Lightning Source LLC
Chambersburg PA
CBHW022139170626

46807CB00005B/2001